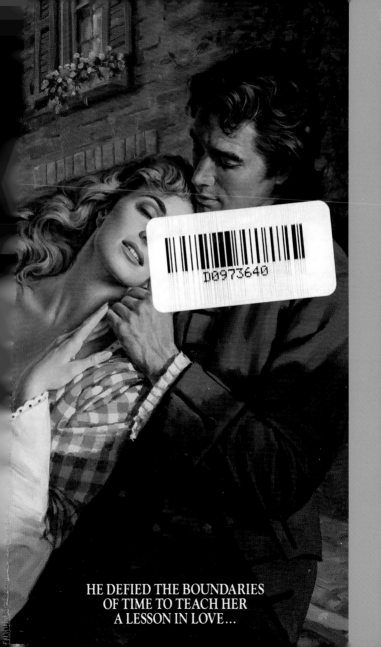

HE DEFIED THE BOUNDARIES
OF TIME TO TEACH HER
A LESSON IN LOVE...

"WHAT DO YOU THINK YOU'RE DOING?"

"I'm going to give you a bath."

"The devil you are!" Before she could finish, he'd un-buttoned all twenty-seven of the little buttons on her dress and pulled it off her shoulders.

Outraged, she just stared at him. The man was good, she'd give him that!

"It seems you're determined to stand in this stream all day complaining, but I have other commitments," he said.

After stripping the dress over her head, he calmly tossed the fabric aside. It floated away and lodged against a nearby rock.

Aaron's mouth suddenly went dry . . . his gaze moved upward over the inviting sight, traveling slowly up from her pink bra to the lush curve of her lips. For the briefest of moments he was tempted to take her, swiftly and with no mercy.

"You can forget it." Her eyes warned him to perish the thought.

With the barest hint of a smile, he let his gaze travel over the gentle flare of her hips, coming to rest on the scrap of cloth she'd called bikini panties. His body stirred, reminding him of how long it had been since he had had such a woman. . . .

FOREVER, ASHLEY

Also by Lori Copeland

LORI COPELAND

Forever, Ashley

A DELL BOOK

Published by
Dell Publishing
a division of
Bantam Doubleday Dell Publishing Group, Inc.
666 Fifth Avenue
New York, New York 10103

The trademark Dell® is registered in the U.S. Patent and Trademark Office.

ISBN: 0-440-20807-6

Printed in the United States of America

Published simultaneously in Canada

July 1992

10 9 8 7 6 5 4 3 2 1

OPM

To Emily Reichert, Leslie Schnur,
and Carole Baron—

with my deepest respect and gratitude

Prologue

A soft chime sounded throughout the Great Hall of Apocalypse. Daniel stood up quickly, taking one final glance through the well-worn folder he carried.

Trying to quell the prick of anticipation he felt, he closed the Record Book that he used to keep track of his earthly charges. Well, Daniel old man, you'll just have to do the best you can, he told himself.

At the end of the hallway, palatial doors swung open, and an older man, clad in a long, flowing, butterscotch-colored robe, appeared. "Daniel?"

"Yes, sir?"

"Gerrbria will see you now."

"Thank you." Drawing a deep breath, Daniel followed the old man through the doorway. No matter how many times Daniel met with Gerrbria, Most High Exalted Clergyman of Women, he got nervous.

Upon entering the Great Hall, Daniel was, as usual, overwhelmed by its magnificence. The room was lit by a million candles, all glowing in ethereal beauty.

Daniel's soft slippers glided across the floor of glistening pearl. He was most eager to dispense with his unpleasant task as quickly and efficiently as possible.

The angelic voices drifting through the air gave Daniel

pause that morning. The voices sounded as though they came from a great distance, yet were very near. Their melodic strains bathed his frayed nerves and soothed his soul. No matter how often he heard the music, he was filled with delight each time he entered the Great Hall.

And today was certainly no different.

"Come, come." Daniel quickened his pace obediently as he heard Gerrbria urging him closer. "I understand you wish to speak to me?" Gerrbria had found Daniel's request to see him quite odd. Matters of this nature were usually handled through lower channels, but the message Daniel had sent seemed urgent.

"Ye-yes, sir," Daniel stammered, embarrassed that Gerrbria had caught him dawdling again. Time meant nothing here, but on earth it was of the essence. Especially today.

Gerrbria motioned for Daniel to approach his desk. "There is something troubling you, Daniel?"

"Yes, sir."

"You may speak."

"Well, sir . . . *she's* done it again!" Daniel blurted out impatiently.

Gerrbria scowled, knowing at once of whom Daniel spoke. "Surely not."

"Yes, sir, I'm afraid she has."

Gerrbria shot to his feet, heat suffusing his round cheeks. *"Bubbleshocks!"*

The sound of Gerrbria's beefy fist angrily smacking the desk echoed throughout the Great Hall. The music suddenly faltered, the voices pausing expectantly.

Daniel waited patiently, having fully anticipated Gerrbria's reaction. It was a rare case that could reduce the High Exalted Clergyman of Women to use such vulgar language, but then Daniel knew that Ashley Wheeler *was* a rare woman.

"Well? What's she done this time?" Gerrbria demanded.

"She's left the ring on his desk—but with a note this time," Daniel conceded.

"*Bubbleshocks!*" Gerrbria smacked the desktop again, clearly at the end of his wits.

After marching to the fratmore machine, Gerrbria couldn't keep his hand from trembling as he poured himself a brimming cupful. He tipped his head back and took a long swallow, letting the soothing, delectable liquid trickle down his throat.

When he finally lowered the cup, Daniel was relieved to see that Gerrbria had regained his wits. "You must forgive the outburst, Daniel, but the woman is giving me rotworst," Gerrbria said repentantly.

"I understand, sir." And Daniel did understand. Ashley Wheeler would give anyone a *roaring* case of rotworst.

"Well, she simply cannot be permitted to continue in this vein," Gerrbria conceded. He took another long drink from his cup, then, suddenly recalling his manners, he smiled. "I'm sorry, Daniel, would you like a cup of fratmore? It's quite tasty this morning."

"Thank you, sir." Daniel relaxed a little. To be invited to share a cup of fratmore with Gerrbria was quite an honor. Now he would have something to brag about to the others later.

"Limpid?"

"Uh, no, I take it with a little mosby, if you don't mind."

"Certainly, certainly."

When Gerrbria handed Daniel the cup, he sipped from

it, his eyes closing with ecstasy as the delicious juice trickled down his gullet. Lowering the cup, he smiled. "Excellent, sir. Truly excellent."

Gerrbria nodded. "Now, to the matter of Ashley Wheeler. Do you have any specific recommendations, Daniel?"

"I have tried to think of a proper recourse, sir, but I'm afraid I haven't been able to come up with a thing. I mean, after all, she has been given ample opportunities to find her true love." Daniel set his cup on the corner of the desk and opened his thick folder, his eyes scanning the long columns on each page. "She was scheduled to be married by the time she was twenty-one. It's all right here in her book. See? Twenty-one. But she's nearing thirty, and she eventually finds something she doesn't like about every man we send her."

"Yes, I know." Gerrbria sat down behind his desk, philosophically stroking his bushy brows. His job as head overseer of women wasn't easy—not easy at all. "Let's see . . . we have provided her with commendable candidates—the cream of the crop?"

"Yes, sir—the very best we have to offer."

"Mmm—yes, there was Jon and Eddie . . ."

"Yes, sir. And Lon, the senatorial candidate?"

Gerrbria frowned. "Oh, yes. Whatever did she find wrong with Lon?"

"He wanted to move to California, sir."

"Oh." Gerrbria knew he wasn't supposed to have any opinion concerning one earthly place or the other—but California . . . well, the girl had a point.

Gerrbria remembered only too well how he'd met his death in Los Angeles in the middle 1950s. During an earthquake, trapped on the top floor of a thirty-story building—screaming like a deranged billetworst!

It had been pure snoptz. Not to mention highly embarrassing. He had endured a merciless amount of teasing about it for months upon arriving here.

". . . and now she's just dumped Joel, her fourth," Daniel was saying. He paused, releasing a sigh. "We simply can't permit her to go on this way. We've already logged in well over three hundred hours just trying to get her settled."

Ashley was the only one of Daniel's charges behind schedule, and she was *ruining* what until now had been a sterling record. "We have a future to run here," Daniel reminded.

It was Gerrbria who sighed this time. "Well, perhaps it is time for extraordinary measures."

Daniel nodded gravely. "I thought perhaps you might have an idea."

"Shock tactics," Gerrbria proclaimed gravely.

Daniel sat up straighter. "Shock tactics, sir?"

"Shock tactics. It's time Ashley Wheeler was taught a lesson."

"Yes, sir!" Daniel couldn't agree more. He couldn't keep sending Ashley perfectly good men who would each make her an excellent husband and have her keep casting them aside. No, sir. After all, she wasn't the *only* single woman on earth looking for a husband! There were at least twenty other women under Daniel's protection whom he had to consider. Twenty other women who weren't so picky.

Leaning back in his chair, Daniel enjoyed another sip of fratmore. It was time for Gerrbria's wisdom of women

—something Gerrbria was known to have an extraordinary amount of.

"Well," Gerrbria said, his features assuming his most solemn, wise expression. "It is not our policy to administer punishment but rather to provide guidance for our subjects. But we are now forced to make Ashley understand that after not one but *four* opportunities for lasting love, she must be willing to accept it."

Daniel nodded. "I agree."

"Now," Gerrbria mused, "we must come up with an effective way to administer the lesson."

"I suppose a gentle reprimand is in order?" Daniel knew that was how Gerrbria handled most matters.

"Not necessarily. Apparently it's going to take more drastic action to gain Ashley's attention," Gerrbria conceded.

Silence fell upon the two men as they racked their brains to come up with the perfect way to teach Ashley Wheeler a long-overdue lesson. She was a sweet young woman, but a bit stubborn at times.

"She works as a legal secretary by day and as a tour guide in a Boston museum by night, is that correct?"

"Yes, sir."

"Her life is good, isn't it?"

"Excellent."

"Mmmmm." They thought some more. "Broke up with the surgeon, did she?"

"A few minutes ago. Just left his ring and a note on his desk." Daniel shook his head, still finding it hard to believe that she'd do such a thing.

"What doesn't she like about him?"

"She likes him—in fact, she could love him if she would permit herself, but she doesn't know that."

"Mmmmm."

They thought some more.

"Well, obviously we're going to need an unusual man to make her realize that true love doesn't come along every-day," Gerrbria mused.

"Yes, sir. Most unusual."

They went back to thinking.

"Likes history, does she?"

"No, sir, she hates it, particularly the eighteenth century. She only accepted the job at the museum to supplement her income."

"Oh?"

Daniel nodded.

"She works in an eighteenth-century museum and she *hates* history?"

"You've never met Ashley, have you, sir?"

"No."

Daniel sighed nostalgically. Oh, to be so favored. "No, she doesn't like history. Claims she'd never be able to exist in such crude conditions—you know . . . she can't give up her mousse and Red perfume."

"Uh-huh." Having been High Exalted Clergyman of Women for many years now, Gerrbria knew all about those perfumes and mousses his flock admired so much.

"Too bad we can't send her back to the eighteenth century," Daniel said. "Show her how good she has it—"

"Oh! Oh!" Gerrbria exclaimed, interrupting Daniel's musings. His cheeks filled with color, and there was a naughty twinkle in his eye.

Daniel started. "Yes, sir?" He grinned. This was going to be great! He could just feel it.

"I know just the thing and just the man!" Gerrbria

leaned forward and began to whisper gleefully into Daniel's ear.

Daniel's face lit up, his grin widening as he listened to the slightly unorthodox but completely suitable plan Gerrbria was concocting. "Yes . . . perfect! Perfect! That'll make her think twice about dumping another man! Oh, sir, I can hardly wait to set the plan in motion. But we'll need a storm—a big one. Perhaps even this afternoon?"

"Consider it done." Gerrbria sat back, smiling with satisfaction. For a moment there, he'd thought that Wheeler woman had him stumped. "I'll arrange for a storm—a real doozy! It shall take place around four."

"Wonderful!"

They lifted their cups of fratmore, saluting each other's wily ingenuity.

After draining the last of his cup, Daniel stood, hurriedly gathering his folder. There was work to be done.

Gerrbria sighed. All these problems. Today's American women were just *never* content with what he gave them. No matter what he did, Gerrbria couldn't keep them satisfied.

"You know something, Daniel?" he said thoughtfully.

"No, sir. What?"

"I think that earthly talk show host—what's his name? Monahue? Sponahue?"

"Donahue, isn't it, sir?"

"Yes, yes, Donahue." Gerrbria sighed again. "I think he's hit the nail squarely on the head."

"About what, sir?"

"America's going to snoptz in a handbasket."

1

"... and so, ladies and gentlemen, the Revolutionary War did not begin in 1775, as most people assume. It began several years before. As early as 1763, the first important incident of the war was instigated by the British decision to keep a standing army in North America without consulting the colonists. That was followed by the Navigation Acts, which included the Quartering and Stamp acts of 1765, which further angered the colonists."

Ashley Wheeler paused to draw a deep breath. The museum was unusually hot and stuffy tonight. She glanced at the darkening windows, frowning. It was going to rain again, she just *knew* it.

"The Townshend Acts of 1767, which placed duties on tea, paper, lead, and paint imported into the colonies, further fed the colonists' anger. They began a boycott, refusing to buy British goods, thereby forcing Parliament to repeal the duties in 1770—with the exception of the tax on tea. Britain steadfastly retained the tax to prove it claimed the right to levy taxes for revenue. The British sent troops to garrison Boston, and a fatal clash between the redcoats and the townspeople occurred on the night of March 5, 1770, which was later called the Boston Massacre. In 1772 Samuel Adams and James Otis persuaded

Boston to appoint a Committee of Correspondence. This committee was formed to explain to other towns and to the world the rights of the colonies and to show how Britain had violated these rights."

Ashley paused a second time to wiggle her toes inside the pair of satin, embroidered, buckled slippers. A mother of a blister was already forming on her big toe, and the whalebone corset she wore, along with the steel collar with long needles stuck upright to keep her head erect, were nothing short of murder.

Drawing a deep breath, she eased the slipper off her foot and tried to mask a grateful sigh. "Marie Antoinette should have been beheaded a year earlier for introducing her latest 'vogue' in women's gowns," she muttered.

Ashley's friends would attest to what a lovely young woman she was, with only one minor character flaw: speaking before she thought. Over the years she had worked on correcting the problem, but at times she experienced minor failures—but only minor ones.

"Speak up," someone in the crowd shouted. "We can't hear you!"

Straightening, Ashley jerked her collar off, then tugged back into place the wide farthingale that encased her hips. Forcing a smile, she wedged her swollen foot back into the shoe and continued. "Then came the famous Tea Act of 1773. On December 16 of that year a band of colonists disguised as Indians raided British ships anchored in Boston Harbor and threw the tea overboard.

"In 1774 the Intolerable Acts were passed by the British government to close Boston Harbor to commerce until the city showed 'repentance' for its 'tea party.'

"As a result, the colonists met in the First Continental Congress in Philadelphia in September 1774 to defend

American rights, and they decided not to export anything to the British Isles or the West Indies until abuses were corrected.

"It was during this time that Patrick Henry sounded the rallying cry: 'I know not what course others may take; but as for me, give me liberty, or give me death!'

"So by the year 1775, the quarrel between the American colonies and England had reached a point where it seemed impossible to avoid war. A forbidding array of tall-masted British warships sat in Boston Harbor. Occupation troops dressed in scarlet coats marched in the streets, scoffing at the resentment they stirred. The British believed themselves to be far superior in courage and fighting ability to the Americans, whom they considered to be a ragtag, disorganized force of small consequence."

The air seemed closer. Not a breeze stirred in the small museum. The form-fitting gown with its tight corset, high waistline, and Empire bust clung to Ashley's body like epoxy. She winced as she heard the first roll of thunder rumbling in the distance. Wouldn't you know it? Another spring storm, and every window on her car was rolled down.

Occasional flashes of light illuminated the windows now as Ashley moved the group from room to room.

The petite tour guide couldn't be called uncommonly pretty. Slender, but not fashionably gaunt, she had nice cornfield-blue eyes, an unruly mane of copper-colored hair, and more freckles than she'd ever wanted.

In school, Ashley had been the class tomboy, but at twenty-nine, she prided herself on being more together, except when it came to men. A frown marred her features as she thought about Joel. She had come so close this time . . . so darn close.

Moving to the Washington Room, Ashley continued to point out various items of interest, deliberately pushing Joel from her mind. It was over, and that was that.

The tourists moved about, murmuring *oohs* and *ahhs* as they snapped pictures of heirlooms once belonging to George and Martha Washington.

Ashley found her ears tuned to the storm as it grew closer. Did she dare cut short the tour and roll up the windows on her car?

Hold off twenty minutes, she implored silently as another crack of thunder shook the museum. Twenty minutes, and she would be spared the agony of sitting on a wet front seat again.

But hope grew dimmer as a searing bolt of electricity sliced across the sky, followed by another thunderous boom.

Shoving her heavy wig, adorned with flowers, lace, feathers, pomatum, and powder, farther back on her head, Ashley sighed. *Wet seat, here I come.*

She waited at a set of double doors until the small group had once again collected before her.

"Ladies and gentlemen, we are about to enter the 'bedroom' of the museum, where you'll find authentic costumes of the Revolutionary period on open display. Please remain behind the roped areas, and, for the comfort of others, please refrain from smoking, eating, or drinking. Thank you."

After swinging open the heavy wooden doors, Ashley leveled herself against the wall, stifling a groan as she felt both her feet being trampled by the zealous group surging through the doorway.

Tears stung her eyes as she molded herself against the door frame in an attempt to escape the onslaught.

Dear God, now she was maimed for life!

Snapping open her fan, she closed her eyes and fanned herself rapidly, praying she wouldn't keel over in a dead faint.

"Are you all right?"

Ashley opened her eyes to see a fellow tour guide, Sue Martingale, peering anxiously at her.

"No, I'm crippled for life," she predicted.

Overhead, rain began falling on the window skylight, lightly at first, then more heavily, until it sounded torrential.

"Darn it!" Ashley snapped the fan shut irritably.

"Your car windows rolled down again?" Sue guessed.

"Yes. Sue, I hate to ask, but can you take over for me? I'd hoped to get to the health club right after work, and I don't want to sit in a puddle of water!"

Sue straightened her mobcap bravely. She was a little eccentric but was known around the museum as a real trooper. Her fellow workers knew that Sue could be counted on in a crisis. "Say no more. Martingale to the rescue!"

Ashley wilted with relief. "Thanks, I'll give you my firstborn." Last time it rained, it seemed as if she'd walked around with a damp backside for days.

Sue started forward, then suddenly turned, lowering her voice apprehensively. "The weirdo isn't in the group, is he?"

"No, no sign of the pincher," Ashley whispered, grateful she'd at least been spared that.

Sue's face grew solemn as she studied Ashley for a moment. "You sure you're okay?"

"I'm fine, except I think I'm getting another cold." Ash-

ley avoided Sue's probing gaze and turned back to look at
the milling group.

"Did you see Joel?"

Ashley appeared not to hear the question.

"Ash?"

"Yes?"

"Did you see Joel?"

"Yes."

"And?"

Ashley's cheeks colored. "I took the coward's way out."

"Oh, great."

"I know, but he was busy with an emergency appen-
dectomy. . . ." Ashley knew she sounded more defensive
than was necessary. After all, whose life was it?

"And you couldn't have waited until he was through to
let him know that you were ditching him?"

Ashley's chin firmed. "I didn't 'ditch' him. I just bowed
out . . . quietly." At Sue's look of disbelief, she hastened
to add, "It just wasn't right, Sue. I was always waiting
around for Joel."

That was the problem. She'd spent their entire *court-
ship* waiting. Joel was always in surgery, making rounds,
or with a patient. Granted, some people might think she
was being petty, even selfish, but she was tired of hanging
around a doctor's lounge until all hours of the night in
order to spend a few, brief moments with the man she
was engaged to marry. After all, wasn't an engagement
period a time when the two participants got to know one
another better? That was how it was supposed to work,
wasn't it? But in the three months she and Joel had been
engaged, she could count on one hand the times they had
been able to share an evening alone without the phone or
the beeper interrupting.

"So now what have you done?" Sue said hopelessly.

"I left him a note . . . with the ring inside the envelope."

Sue looked aghast. "Oh, Ashley. Not again. Every time you get near an altar you back out!"

"That's not fair. I don't 'back out,' I just change my mind." Well, yes, she did *back* out—maybe more like run out—but marriage to one man seemed so . . . *permanent*.

"Ash, you've had more marriage prospects than most women dream about, yet you continue to cast men aside like dust balls. Are you nuts? You love Joel. This time it was the real thing!"

"Maybe . . ." Ashley swallowed the lump in her throat. Joel was different; Sue didn't have to remind her of that.

"First there was Jon—"

"Jon was a two-timer. I caught him with another woman, and he had the nerve to say she was a secretarial prospect."

"Didn't he hire her?"

"Well, yes, but—"

"And Eddie? What about Eddie?"

"Eddie wasn't ready to make a commitment."

"He asked you to *marry* him, didn't he?"

"Well, yes, but I don't think he meant it."

"What about Lon? Lon was a prime husband candidate if I ever saw one."

"Maybe, but he wanted to move to California and I don't—besides, being married to a senator and living separate lives . . . well, that isn't what I want either."

"And then there was Joel." Sue shook her head sadly. "Honestly, Ash, Joel's perfect for you, and now you've let him go. How many chances do you think you'll have to find true happiness?"

Ashley didn't feel good about what she'd done, and wasn't at all sure it was the right thing—but it was done, and she couldn't undo it. By now Joel had found her note and the ring. Besides, another man would come along in a few months, and she would think she was in love with him too. It always worked that way.

"I'll admit that maybe I should have given this engagement a little more time—but my mind's made up. I never see Joel. And once we're married, it's not going to get any better." She shrugged lamely. "I've had to cancel so many parties that most of my friends believe Joel's a figment of my imagination."

"Ashley . . . he's a *doctor,* and he just happens to be everything you want in a man. You've got cold feet again, tell the truth."

Ashley's chin firmed. Joel *was* almost everything she wanted in a man—except that he was already married. To his profession. Call her selfish, call her shallow and unreasonable. Was it wrong to want to be called Mrs. Joel Harrison and have a man to back up the claim?

Another clap of thunder shook the building as Ashley looked anxiously to the windows again.

"You're a fool, Ashley Wheeler. Men like Joel aren't shooting out of the ground like mushrooms," Sue warned, glancing at the crowd that was wandering about restlessly now.

"Well, mushrooms have a tendency to give me the hives," Ashley returned lightly.

"Sheesh." Sue straightened her mobcap again. "You're hopeless."

"I have to go," Ashley murmured. "My car is probably floating down Huntington Avenue by now."

"So go—big chicken."

The two exchanged forgiving grins.

Turning, Sue addressed the group once more. "Ladies and gentlemen, my name is Sue and I will be continuing the tour with you. To your left, you will find an original gown worn by Betsy Grisom Ross. There are records indicating that Betsy was employed making ships' colors, et cetera, but there is no real evidence to support the story that Betsy Ross made the first American flag. The legend was started in 1870 by her grandson, William Canby, in a speech to the Historical Society of Pennsylvania. . . ."

Ashley hurried toward the entrance, pausing long enough to grab her large catchall bag—the bag Sue called Ashley's "trunk" because she carried everything she owned in it and never went anywhere without—and rummaged for her keys. If she was lucky, she could pull the car closer to the entrance and avoid another drenching when she got off at nine.

The buckled slippers weren't going to allow her a graceful retreat, Ashley realized, as she made her way to the front door. Heads turned and eyes narrowed with disapproval as the heels clattered noisily against the wooden floor.

The curator of the museum stepped out of his office, his brows knitting together portentously at the sound of all the ruckus. His forefinger shot to his lips as he scowled at her.

Nodding apologetically, Ashley slowed her steps, tiptoeing the rest of the way across the room.

Pushing through the swinging doors into the foyer, she spotted an umbrella and quickly commandeered it.

Rain was falling in a deluge as she pushed through the front glass doors. Though it was only four, rush-hour traffic was already backing up.

Watery pellets stung her face as she popped the umbrella open, then started down the long flight of stairs to the street.

Concentrating on holding the hem of her dress out of the water, balancing her bag and the umbrella, she made her way down the row of stairs, mentally cursing the blasted buckle slippers. Belatedly it occurred to her that she should have changed into her street shoes, but it was foolish to go back now.

Halfway down, she felt her foot slip on the wet concrete. Pausing, she steadied herself. All she needed was a broken leg.

Continuing more slowly, she caught her breath as the umbrella suddenly turned inside out, propelling a wall of rain back in her face.

She jerked the umbrella upright, which caused her to lose her balance again. Her foot gave way, pitching her forward in a clatter of buckle shoes, flying bag, and flyaway umbrella.

She found herself tumbling end over end, praying she wouldn't break every bone in her body. Panic seized her as unsympathetic concrete rose up to slam painfully against her ribs.

Joel's image flashed before her as she tumbled out of control, her head smacking against the step. Dear Lord, she was about to die. Didn't a person's life flash before her when she was about to die?

She grabbed for a railing and missed. The wig flew off, flowers going one way, birds and feathers the other. The buckled shoes went next, soaring through the air like a kite on a windy March day.

Dying in a broken heap in a rainstorm was her punishment for breaking up with Joel, she realized too late. She shouldn't have left him a note the way she did—she should have invited him to some nice little Italian restaurant and—no, he wouldn't have shown up! Someone with an infected gallbladder would have taken priority, and she would have been left to finish off the basket of breadsticks all alone.

She tumbled over and over, the agony of her sins haunting her. Maybe she *should* have given the relationship a little more time—been more patient with him. The doctor's lounge wasn't so bad. She'd met a lot of weird but interesting people there.

Maybe Joel hadn't found the note yet. Hope sprang anew in her. *Yes,* he would still be in surgery! It would be hours before he discovered what she'd done. If she lived, she would still have time to remedy her mistake.

Please God, don't let there be anyone watching. Her skirt went over her head as her bottom up-ended again. *Thirty-five—thirty-six—thirty-seven—thirty-eight* . . .

Spilling onto the sidewalk, she finally landed in a tangled heap.

Groaning, she rolled onto her back and lay prostrate as she tried to orient herself. She couldn't move. There wasn't a single place on her that wasn't throbbing like an abscessed tooth.

Lying with her eyes closed, she tried to summon up enough strength to move. She was only vaguely aware that the wind and the thunder had suddenly died away, and it was cool and strangely quiet now.

She could feel curious eyes fixed on her. And why

wouldn't they be? It wasn't often that Bostonians were met with the sight of a woman dressed in a Revolutionary War costume lying spread-eagle in the middle of the sidewalk. How embarrassing! She could imagine the spectacle she had just made of herself. Arms and legs flailing about wildly as she pitched headlong down the flight of stairs. She groaned again. And her bag . . . all of her personal toiletries were scattered in the middle of the sidewalk!

"I'm all right," she murmured in a modest attempt to soothe the onlookers' curiosity. She attempted to push herself upright, trying to still her spinning head.

The strained silence was suddenly shattered by the frenzied sound of chairs scraping against stone and knocked to the floor in haste.

"My *word!* We have been set upon from above!" a man's voice exclaimed.

"Stab my vitals! What manner of wench have we here!" A second voice sputtered.

Ashley's eyes flew open, growing wider as she stared into the astounded countenances of six very strange-looking men. The men, all dressed in beautifully authentic commoner eighteenth-century costumes, stared back at her.

She stared blankly at the three-cornered, cocked black hats, the full peri-wigs, the sleeveless waistcoats, breeches, and gaiters.

"A damn Tory spy," one man spat out disgustedly. "Have the British completely lost their minds?"

"Excuse me?" Ashley murmured, for the men appeared to be expecting some sort of an answer from her.

"'Tis the truth," another agreed. "*Damn* their miserable hides!"

The men tilted their heads upward, peering at the large

hole in the ceiling as Ashley struggled to sit up. Her head spun, and she was feeling slightly nauseated from her fall. "Please . . . could one of you gentlemen give me a hand?" she asked feebly.

Pushing herself up on her elbow, she waited.

And waited.

The men stood, hands on hips, staring contemptuously at the gaping hole in the ceiling.

Ashley's eyes followed the men's gaze, her eyes widening again as she became aware of her surroundings.

An audible gasp escaped her as the six men turned, focusing their attention on her again. She was lying on the middle of a table, surrounded by clumps of dirt, pieces of thatched grass, and rotten timber.

She looked about in disbelief. Why, she wasn't in the middle of the sidewalk, but in a small, low-ceilinged, dimly lit room where particles of light struggled to work their way through a narrow window.

She grew even more confused when she saw that chairs were overturned and pieces of a checker game were scattered on the floor. A beer stein dangled limply from one man's hand, while the others stared at her as if she were a bug-eyed alien who had just popped in for a visit.

She swallowed, searching for her voice. "Excuse me . . . I . . . where am I?"

"Better the question of *who* are you?" A man's voice, deep and resonant, sounded from the shadows.

Ashley strained to discern the man's features in the dim lighting. He was tall with a menacing presence that made a shiver slide down her back. There was a cold, dangerous edge about him that made Ashley draw back protectively.

The man stepped out from the shadows, his eyes flickering with contempt. "Who are you?" he demanded.

Ashley stared into steel-gray eyes that were totally lacking in warmth.

When she failed to find her voice, one of the men standing next to her chuckled mirthlessly. "Shall we toss a coin to see who shall have the privilege of returning her to Gage and permitting him to see what a fool he has employed?"

Who *are* these men? she wondered frantically. Especially that one with the cold eyes? And what was he doing in such a costume? Was he part of a reenactment group hired by the museum? The man's lawn shirt was unadorned, and his waistcoat and coat were a matching tobacco brown marked by silver buttons. He was breathtakingly handsome, but something wasn't right. If this was a reenactment group, why were they angry with her? After all, she was the one who had taken a hard fall.

"Look, I don't understand what is going on here." Ashley slid off the table, sending dirt flying in all directions as she shook out her skirts.

"She plays the innocent," one of the men scoffed.

Ashley reached to collect her shoes. "I don't know what you're talking about," she snapped.

"Explain yourself," the man with the cold eyes demanded.

Ashley answered guardedly. "Why should I have to explain anything? You are the ones who have some explaining to do. And I demand—"

"You are in no position to demand anything. What is your intent here?"

Ashley whirled to face the man who spoke. "Intent? The windows on my car are open and—"

"What is *your* name?"

"My name is Ashley Wheeler."

The men exchanged looks. "Wheeler? We know of no such name in Boston."

"She is English, no doubt."

"Mayhap. The Tories are well versed in the art of disguise," the tall one conceded, "though this is somewhat ambitious, even for them." His gaze swept ruthlessly over Ashley as he bent to catch the hem of her skirt and jerk it down over her exposed calf.

"If she is not a spy, then what was she doing on the roof?"

"I think we can safely assume that she is a spy."

"What!" Fighting back a wave of dizziness, Ashley gripped the table for support.

A hand on her shoulder shook her fiercely. "*What* is your true name?" the tall man asked.

"Ashley Wheeler," she repeated, then a sharp pain in her eye caused her to blink rapidly. Darn! Something was in her contact lens, and it hurt like blue blazes!

"Perhaps a time in the jail would help you regain your senses," one of the men suggested.

Jail? The word sent fear racing through her. Ashley wasn't sure what was happening to her, but the idea of spending time in a cold, dark prison was sobering, even in the best of circumstances.

Ashley blinked rapidly again, her heart pounding. Maybe this was just a dream. That's it. She was *dreaming!* She would wake up anytime now and be in her own bed.

"These are desperate times," the tall man soberly reminded her. "You have placed yourself in a dangerous situation. I only hope the lobsterbacks are paying you enough."

Lobsterbacks! Ashley struggled to remind herself this was only a dream. That's all it was. A crazy dream!

Blinking furiously, she dabbed at the tears rolling from the corners of her eyes. A crazy dream.

"The woman is mad! Completely mad!" one of the other men observed.

Ashley purposefully blocked out the men's voices. If it was only a dream, what they said or threatened didn't matter. She would wake up any minute now.

Moving away from the table, she sent clots of dirt scattering across the floor as she spied the catchall that doubled as her purse. She leaned over to scoop up the spilled contents, dismayed to see that her small bottle of perfume had broken. After dumping onto the table an assortment of lipsticks, loose change, compact, mascara, billfold, sunglasses, car keys, aspirin, cold and cough medicines, and old tissues, she rummaged through the pile, searching for the small bottle of saline solution for her contacts.

A lipstick rolled across the table, and she snatched it up before it fell off the table.

The men watched, completely speechless now.

A tampon fell to the floor, and Ashley grabbed for it, her face flooding with color.

The tall man lunged forward, snatching the long white cylinder from her hand. Balancing it in the palm of his hand, he motioned for the others to gather around to inspect it.

"Careful, men. The wench plans to do away with herself," one of the men warned.

With a tampon? Rolling her eyes, Ashley turned back to the table, picking up the small vial of saline solution. Weirdest dream she'd ever had. She tilted her head backward, dropped three drops into her eye, and blinked hard.

"Here now!" Three of the men bolted forward. "She's putting her eyes out!"

Ashley squealed as her arms were captured and brought swiftly behind her back. "I'm only wetting my contacts!"

The men gasped. "God's teeth!" *Wetting on* her contacts? The woman was clearly daft!

The tall man grabbed the bottle of saline solution from her fingers and lifted it to the light.

"What manner of evil does she use?" another asked.

"Wetting solution," he read.

The men exchanged meaningless looks.

"For contacts," he added.

The men's jaws firmed.

"Who is your contact, young woman? Give us a name and you may avoid a hanging!"

Ashley's eyes widened. *"Hanging?* Okay. Wake up! Wake up, Ashley. Nightmare's over!"

"Now who is she talking to?" one of the men demanded.

"She is addlebrained," another reminded.

"Or pretending to be," the third conceded.

Ashley blinked rapidly, trying to clear her eyes.

"See how she rolls her eyes."

" 'Tis only a ploy."

"Wake up, Ashley, time to wake up," Ashley chanted. She jerked free of the man's grasp, still chanting. "Wake up, wake up, wake up . . ."

"Let her be," the tall man ordered as the others scurried to capture her arm again. "She cannot escape."

Shooting her captors a smug smile, Ashley calmly reached up, pulled at her eyelid, and popped her contact lens out into her palm.

"God's teeth!" someone murmured. "The wench has dislodged her eye!"

"What has been wished upon us? She speaks of contacts, obviously Loyalist, but denies being a spy. Is she a fool, or merely a poor, demented soul?"

"She's clever, would be my guess," the tall one returned softly.

Ashley squinted in his direction. She was so nearsighted that without her contacts anyone or anything more than five feet away was reduced to a blur. "Now that we know who I am, a daft, poor, demented spy, *who* are you?" she challenged, getting a little tired of the men's chauvinist attitudes.

The men exchanged pained looks.

"Be not fooled. She knows our names, would be my guess," one in the group observed, disgruntled. "She must be disposed of immediately."

"Gentlemen, gentlemen. Where are your manners?" the tall one chided. Ashley eyed him warily as he approached. "The young woman has inquired of our names." He bowed mockingly. "Aaron Kenneman, physician, at your service."

"So very nice to meet you, Dr. Kenneman." Ashley calmly squeezed a few drops of the saline solution into the palm of her hand. She was going to have a good laugh about this dream in the morning.

When the contact was thoroughly rinsed, she caught it on the tip of her finger and popped it back into her eye. After blinking three or four times, she relaxed. Wonderful. She could see again.

"Now, Dr. Kenneman." Her smile was decidedly cool. "If you would be so kind as to tell me what is going on?"

Dreams have an odd way of leaving a person at a disadvantage at times.

His smile was as cold as his eyes. "Going on? Why, my

dear, you're in the Green Dragon Tavern. You didn't know?"

Ashley frowned. "In Boston?"

"In Boston," he verified dryly.

Ashley's eyes moved around the room curiously. "What is the date?"

"Date?"

"Yes, tell me the date."

"April 15, 1775."

"The Green Dragon Tavern. April 15. *Income tax day.*" And she still had her tax forms lying in the front seat of the car. The rest of what he'd said suddenly penetrated her mind. "Seventeen seventy-five." Ashley hesitated. Seventeen seventy-five? Three days before Paul Revere's famous ride. Oh, this was cute. The dream had taken her back to Paul Revere's day! "And I suppose this 'meeting' I've disrupted is to decide what to do about the British?" She grinned. *Sure* it was.

"Aha! I *told* you she was a spy!" one of the men exclaimed. "How else could she know about our meetings, Aaron?"

Oh, this was *rich!* Ashley stared at the man who had just spoken, and it suddenly dawned on her who he was. Paul Revere. It was *Paul Revere!*

Well, sure, why not? Ashley leaned forward to get a closer look at the men now seated at the table staring at her. The dream was remarkable. These men looked even better than the pictures of the American Patriots in the history books.

"Paul Revere?" she said aloud, pointing to the portly, fortyish-looking man.

He had been momentarily distracted by her tangled

wig, which lay amid the rubble on the table, but he glanced up when she said his name. "Yes?"

"It's really you? Paul Revere?"

Paul looked at the other men disarmingly.

Ashley grinned as she looked slowly around the table. Yes . . . yes, the dream was exceptional, all right. She remembered seeing all these men in the history books—except Aaron Kenneman.

She pointed to the man sitting next to Revere. "John Hancock, first signer of the Declaration of Independence."

"It is assured. She is daft," Hancock grumbled.

Her finger moved about the room randomly. "And . . . you are John Adams and you are . . . Church . . . Dr. Benjamin Church."

Each man nodded solemnly. The wench was amazingly well informed.

Ashley smiled, enthralled by the dream's authenticity. "And you're Dr. Joseph Warren?" Ashley's gaze focused on the man in his mid-thirties sitting to her right. "From Lexington."

Warren nodded gravely.

Dream or no dream, this was *amazing!* " 'Dr. Joseph Warren, the greatest incendiary in all America,' " she quoted. "You're a member of the Massachusetts Committee of Safety, and temporary president of the Provincial Congress, *and* the man who sent William Dawes and Paul Revere to Lexington to warn Hancock and Samuel Adams of British plans to arrest them."

Warren paled. "Gentlemen, the woman is ruinous. She must be disposed of with no further delay."

Ashley sprang to her feet. "No!" she exclaimed. "No, I'm *not* a spy."

"Then pray tell, lovely lady, who *are* you?" Aaron Kenneman demanded.

"I'm . . . I'm . . ." Ashley shrugged helplessly. Turning her palms up, she smiled at the men. "Dreaming?"

2

"Dreaming?" Eyes of cold gray steel challenged Ashley. "I think not, wench. State your name!"

"We can delay no longer, Aaron," Warren warned. "The woman must be done away with."

Ashley tensed, vividly recalling the methods of punishment handed out in 1775. Visions of ducking stools and the pillory mixed with branding, mutilation, and hanging haunted her.

"Lashes would loosen her tongue, I assure you," Warren threatened.

Names that had meant nothing to her when she'd studied history suddenly sprang to Ashley's mind. *John Morris found guilty of sheep-stealing and receiving a brand in the middle of his hand, Daniel Martin receiving fifteen lashes for stealing a wooden horse. Good heavens. What would they do to a spy! What if they paraded her up and down the street, or put her in the stocks?*

"You can't do that" she whispered, frantically grabbing the tall man's shirt. "I'm *not* a spy."

Aaron coldly peeled her arm from his sleeve. "One must be prepared to pay for one's actions."

"But I've done nothing! Nothing!"

Church lost his patience. "God's teeth, cease her babbling, Kenneman. We must choose our course of action!"

"Babbling! Can't you see I'm not a spy? Do I look like a spy?"

The men studied her costume. " 'Tis a fine garment," Revere conceded. He reached out and felt the material of her sleeve, rubbing it between his fingers thoughtfully. "Excellent cloth."

After a moment's hesitation Church did the same, his face flushed with anger now. " 'Tis only further proof."

"What proof!" Ashley exclaimed.

"Proof you are not a patriot," Warren accused.

"You judge me guilty by the dress I wear!"

"And a wretched spy you are," Church jeered. "Patriots have sworn not to purchase English goods. The colonists are sworn to wearing only their hand-woven cotton and wool. The cloth you wear is too fine not to have been imported from England. Do you deny this?"

"Yes, I can and do," Ashley said emphatically. "This is a simple polished cotton blend, so the costumes won't wrinkle when they're washed. And this lace is plain old polyester . . ." She faltered when she saw her words were falling on deaf ears.

"Babble," Church muttered beneath his breath.

"It's not! It's the truth!"

"I say we take her to the jail and be done with it," John Hancock interjected. "We have wasted enough time."

"No!" Ashley clutched Dr. Kenneman's arm again. "Don't let them do this to me!" This was *crazy!* Was she actually going to have to endure a hanging before she woke up?

"My dear young woman, we are indeed serious," John Adams assured her gravely. "We are in the midst of a struggle that will change our lives. Our mission cannot be endangered from any quarter. Most especially not by the prattlings and rantings of a demented young woman, whether that guise be a ploy to gain information or the true ravings of a depraved mind. Be you a witch? Or be you a spy?"

Visions of burning at a flaming stake flashed through Ashley's mind. "No, I'm not a witch! I don't know what's happening to me, but you've got to help me!" She looked beseechingly at Aaron Kenneman.

"One should more seriously consider the consequences before becoming a spy for George."

"George?" Ashley asked vacantly.

Kenneman's look was disdainful, and Ashley's back stiffened in resentment. Obviously the man meant King George of England, but this whole thing was so absurd. . . .

"She knows something of what we're about," Revere conceded. "Mayhap she could be persuaded to share her information, or its source?"

The men's eyes focused on Ashley.

"I don't know anything about what you're doing," she vowed, although that wasn't quite true. In college, she had elected to major in history with an emphasis on the Colonial American period. But five weeks into the course she had dropped out, realizing that she really didn't like history all that much. Yet six months ago an unexpected five-hundred-dollar car repair bill had forced her to accept the part-time job at the museum. One of the job requirements was that she memorize large segments relating to the Revolutionary War period, and be able to answer questions concerning that period intelligently.

"If you're reenacting the Revolutionary War, through—"

The men visibly tensed again. "War? Explain your words."

"Could she have intercepted one of our messages?" Warren murmured.

"If she has, we'll soon know of it." Aaron grasped Ashley's arm and turned her around to face him. "You are a Tory spy!"

"I am not!"

"Then you claim to be a patriot?"

Ashley drew a deep breath, trying to think. If she wasn't a spy then there was little choice but to be a patriot. "Of course I'm a patriot."

But the men did not believe her.

"Utter nonsense she speaks," Revere muttered. "We should be done with it before more precious time escapes us."

"Join or Die," Ashley suddenly murmured.

Hancock whirled. "What say you?"

"I said 'Join or Die.' Isn't that one of your mottoes?" She was sure she had read that somewhere.

Revere glanced at Aaron. "But how . . . ?"

"I read it in a book," Ashley explained patiently.

The men stiffened.

"Gentlemen, a word in private," Revere requested.

Ashley tried to collect her thoughts as Aaron drew five of the men to the opposite side of the room. She was aware that they were discussing her fate, but she now felt oddly detached from their quandary. It was only a dream, and dreams eventually ended no matter how scary they became.

Heads pressed tightly together, the men spoke in

hushed tones, glancing up occasionally to stare in her direction.

When this was over, she and Sue would have a big laugh, Ashley decided. Here she was, dreaming of Paul Revere, John Hancock, Joseph Warren, John Adams, and Dr. Benjamin Church. Men—vitally important men who had formed the colonial resistance against England. She couldn't place Aaron Kenneman, though he did seem to be a strong part of this farce. But why dream of the Revolutionary War? She'd obviously been working too many hours at the museum. She needed a vacation.

Ashley glanced back to the men as they conferred among themselves. She smiled. The dream was quite exciting, actually. Naturally the men would be concerned about whether she was a spy for the British if the dream was indeed reality and not fantasy. But if, by some broad stroke of fate, it was reality and not just a dream, and if the men were convinced she was a spy, they would very likely order her death.

Whether she liked it or not, she had to consider that possibility. If she wasn't dreaming, then where was she? Had she fallen into a time warp?

Ridiculous. Time warps existed only in movies and comic books, didn't they?

While the men continued to converse among themselves, Ashley struggled to remember all she could about the era in which she found herself. They'd said it was April 15, 1775. That meant that the Revolution had actually begun fifteen years earlier, in October 1760, when a pop-eyed, twenty-two-year-old in England became King George III. Though young, King George had been certain that kings never made mistakes, which was, in Ashley's opinion, at the crux of the problem.

The Americans were loyal to King George and were under the mistaken impression that Parliament, not the king, was responsible for England's poor policy in dealing with them. England's war with France had been expensive. The English found themselves deeply in debt, and British taxes were exceedingly high. Lord Grenville, who became prime minister in 1763, was a notorious pennypincher, and he suggested that England raise taxes in the colonies. He thought the Americans should support the army sent to protect them from the Indians.

Grenville began trying to enforce some old laws called the Acts of Trade and Navigation. This included taxes payable to Great Britain on imports shipped into colonial harbors. The law also restricted the places where American ships carrying produce could go to sell their cargoes. The law affected virtually everyone's ability to earn a living.

Ashley brushed at her skirt, glancing at the men again. If I can get the facts straight in my mind, she thought, I can convince them that I'm not crazy and I'm not a spy. I don't know what I am . . . but I'm not here to interfere with history. She frowned. This was incredible. Ashley Wheeler, American patriot.

She began to pace, struggling to arrange her thoughts in the proper sequence of events.

The men turned, their conversation dying away as they watched her talking aloud to herself as she paced.

"Grenville's next plan was to tax a variety of papers: legal documents, newspapers, marriage licenses, college diplomas, ships' papers, and a good many other things. All such papers were required to carry a large blue paper seal called a 'revenue stamp' as proof that a tax had been paid.

"The mandate created two major problems: The tax denied Americans the right to fix their own 'internal' taxes, and it was very expensive. Americans began to hate the stamp. The rallying cry became 'No taxation without representation.' " Ashley ticked off the points on her fingers as she paced back and forth across the room. "The confrontation was now between the American assemblies elected in each colony by the people against the English Parliament.

"In July 1765 Lord Rockingham succeeded Grenville as prime minister. Rockingham recognized that the Stamp Act was costing more than it brought in. He began to talk with British merchants and persuaded them to complain to Parliament. As a result, in 1766 Parliament repealed the Stamp Act, which overjoyed the colonists. But a new law surfaced: the Declaratory Act, another unfair law that Parliament passed at the same time it repealed the Stamp Act. If anything, the Declaratory Act was worse. It stated that Parliament had the power to write laws for the colonies 'in all cases whatsoever,' which meant they could write *all* tax laws."

"Mistress Wheeler?" Paul Revere prompted from the sidelines.

Ashley continued pacing, deeply absorbed in her thoughts now. "England still wasn't satisfied with its money situation, so King George changed prime ministers, but he made a poor choice. William Pitt was a sick man and spent little time at his job. Younger cabinet ministers took over, namely, Charles Townsend, who was chancellor of the exchequer, or head of treasury."

"Mistress Wheeler . . ." Revere prompted again.

Ashley paused, meeting the men's stupefied expressions expectantly. "Yes?"

"Ur . . . mayhap you should sit down. The fall seems to have left you a bit . . . addlepated."

"Thank you, but I'm fine. Please." She dismissed his concern absently. "Go on with your meeting."

The men exchanged alarmed looks as she resumed pacing. "In 1767, on Townsend's suggestion, Parliament passed a new set of taxes for Americans to pay: import duties on shipments of paper, paint, glass, lead, and tea from England coming into American ports. Parliament also ordered suspension of the New York Assembly, which had rejected the order to pay the costs of keeping a few British soldiers in New York City. The colonists hadn't minded the fact they were there, but they didn't want to be 'ordered' to do it."

"Mistress Wheeler!"

Having concentrated so deeply on recalling historical events, Ashley was startled once more by the sound of Revere's thundering reprimand.

"Yes?" Paul didn't look much like Ashley thought he would. The little silversmith was short and rather portly. Certainly nothing like a man destined to father *sixteen* children.

"How do you *know* these things of which you speak?"

"I told you. It's in the history books."

Paul exchanged a grim look with Aaron.

Church spoke up again. "She shall be taken to authorities immediately. They will deal with her promptly."

"No!" Ashley burst out.

"We cannot do otherwise," Warren said firmly. "We cannot allow ourselves the folly of believing her denials. Even the knowledge that we have met together will be enough to put us under suspicion. We must protect ourselves at all cost."

"Warren speaks the truth," Revere agreed.

"Now wait just a minute!" These men truly intended to report her as a British spy!

"We can wait no longer." Church seized her arm painfully.

Kicking and screaming, Ashley could do nothing to prevent Church from dragging her across the room. Clearly he intended to deliver her to the proper authorities. Church. Church! What was it about the man that bothered her more than the others?

"Gentlemen, mayhap we are being hasty."

Ashley went weak with relief when she heard Kenneman's deep voice. But when she looked at him, it was obvious that he felt no sympathy for her predicament.

"Perhaps we should contemplate this further," he said quietly.

"What thinking is there to do?" Church demanded. "She is obviously not a patriot. And if she is not demented, then she is a spy. Either way, we must rid ourselves of her. And immediately."

"But in what manner?" Aaron asked calmly. "Are we to drag her through the tavern, drawing attention to ourselves? Are we to take her out and publicly stone her? There will be questions, gentlemen. She is not likely to remain silent of all she has witnessed." His gaze swept over Ashley indifferently. "If we take her before the authorities, what will she respond when questioned? That she 'fell' in among a strange meeting? She will name names," he warned.

"Yes . . . 'twould be risky," Revere conceded, stroking his chin as he thought. "We are in a critical situation. Mayhap we should allow time to consider this matter more thoroughly."

"Don't be a fool!" Church snapped. "She should be dealt with immediately!"

Ashley glared at him as she drew closer to Kenneman's side. There was definitely something about the man she didn't like.

"If only we had a place to restrain her until we knew her purpose for intruding," Revere mused.

"Intruding!" Ashley cried. "I *fell* in here by accident. Believe me, it wasn't something I planned!"

"*Cease* your useless grievances, wench!" Aaron said shortly. "Your intent was to listen and observe, then carry back to whoever has employed you the information you gleaned. Falling through the roof was, I agree, unplanned, but it in no way alters your intent."

"I didn't hear anything!"

"Your protests are meaningless," Church dismissed impatiently.

"What are you going to do?" Ashley asked softly, ignoring Church and meeting Aaron's eyes now.

"Drowning you like a cur pup comes to mind. 'Twould be the simplest and most effective."

Anger firmed Ashley's lips, but she bit back the sharp retort that came to mind. He was an arrogant son of a . . . "You wouldn't dare!"

His eyes grew colder. "We have dared much already."

Ashley swallowed nervously.

"We must rid ourselves of her immediately," Church urged. "I will take her to the magistrate." He reached for Ashley's arm again. "Silencing this spy is of the utmost importance if we are to maintain our secrecy."

"I agree, but I repeat, exposing her may expose us as well," Aaron repeated.

"Then what do you suggest?" Revere prompted.

Aaron studied Ashley for a long moment. Finally he spoke, regret evident in his tone. "I will assume guardianship of her for the next few days, until we are more clear on what the British are planning."

Yes! Ashley thought jubilantly. At least for now she would be spared a terrible fate, though Kenneman looked as if he'd rather have seen her hanged.

"You are certain you want to assume this unpleasant task?" Revere inquired.

Ashley chanced a glance at Church, who seemed none too pleased about the turn of events.

"It does not please me," Aaron admitted, "but it is the only recourse at the moment if we are to avoid jeopardizing ourselves and our goal."

"It is decided then," Revere said. Ashley could almost see him dusting his hands of her. "Dr. Kenneman will take charge of Mistress Wheeler."

"Until you ride to warn the minutemen," Ashley quickly added. Once that happened, even in a dream, the men would be too busy to worry about her.

"*God's eyes,* but she is unnerving!" Warren sputtered.

"You needn't worry," Ashley said. "I can't do anything to keep you from warning the people that the British are coming."

"You *know* they're coming?" Revere blustered. The men were so easily unnerved by proclamations that she was tempted to tell them all she knew, but she didn't dare risk any more of their anger.

"Then mayhap you might be so kind as to tell us *when* and *how* they shall come?" Aaron said calmly.

"Well," Ashley began modestly, then stopped. If she told them how the British were coming, she would only confirm their suspicions that she was a Tory spy, and they would hang her. By her heels. At dawn.

"Well . . . no, I can't tell you *how* they're coming." If she told them, it might alter history, and who knew what the ramifications of that might be? If something went wrong, it wasn't going to be her fault!

Exasperated by the wench's refusal to cooperate, Paul spotted her key chain lying on the table. He pondered it for a moment, then said, "What manner of trinket be this?"

Of course being a silversmith he would be interested in the key chain, Ashley realized. The sterling silver initial had been a birthday gift from Joel.

"It's a key chain."

"Interesting." Paul's fingers caressed the metal thoughtfully. "Remarkable workmanship."

"And what be this?" Adams asked, picking up a small zippered bag.

"A makeup bag."

He looked up blankly.

"Cosmetic bag . . . a bag to carry blusher, lipsticks, collagen creme for my face?"

Adam sent Aaron a mute apology. Pity the poor man who had been elected to care for this demented soul.

"And what manner of device be this?" Hancock's slim fingers toyed inquisitively with the zipper.

"A zipper. Here, it works like this." The men leaned forward expectantly as she ran the zipper open and closed two or three times.

"By God's eyes," Revere breathed. "Amazing implement."

"Yes . . . most amazing," Adams agreed.

"And these other trifles?" Warren prompted, poking around inside the cosmetic bag.

Ashley removed her compact, then eyeliner, mascara, blush, and lipstick. Many of the objects were familiar to the men but the packaging had them stumped.

"Here. You want to know who I am? Here's my driver's license and credit cards." She shoved the plastic-coated driver's license into John Hancock's hand.

Revere's gasp caught her attention. " 'Tis a most incredible miniature," he breathed. "The workmanship is superb!"

Ashley glanced up to find him staring at her photo on the driver's license. "No, that's a photograph."

The men looked at her blankly. "Photograph?"

"A picture, taken by a camera." Now they were completely lost. "You know . . . you look through a box with film in it and snap it, then take it to a store and have the picture developed?"

"Nay, we know nothing of this," Warren admitted warily. The men took a protective step back as if she had something catching.

The door suddenly opened and the men whirled to find a young man entering the room. He closed the door quickly behind him.

"Is there trouble?" Aaron immediately broke from the group to stride across the room to confront the boy.

"The Tories are moving." The boy glanced questioningly at Ashley.

"Choose your words carefully," Revere warned. Taking the boy aside, Paul conversed with the boy in hushed tones. A moment later he returned, his features grave.

"It is as we fear, gentlemen."

"The storm clouds are gathering," Warren murmured. "I feel the crackle of lightning in the air."

Glancing at his pocket watch, Hancock said, "We must disperse least we invite unwelcome comment."

"It is imperative that we maintain our scheduled time of arrival and departure if we are to continue our pretense of a weekly game of five and forty," Warren agreed.

"Aaron, you and Mistress Wheeler take your leave first, while the tavern is heavy with patronage," Hancock directed.

"What shall we do about the hole in the roof?" Warren asked, gazing upward at the large opening.

Picking up his tricornered hat, Aaron viewed Ashley coolly. "Say nothing. I shall explain it."

Her pulse jumped as his eyes skimmed her impersonally. He was damned handsome, she'd give him that. And it wasn't hard to see that he found his assignment to escort her heartily disagreeable. Yet Ashley knew that a man like Aaron Kenneman would do what he must. "You will go with me quietly," he said. "Not one word, or I shall hand you to the first authority I see."

The threat in his eyes was unmistakable. Ashley would do as he said, or she would be cast to the wolves. Her choice was obvious. Dream or no dream, she would cooperate.

Because she knew history, she knew there was a certain desperation in these men. A quiet desperation that led men like Aaron Kenneman to perform extraordinary acts.

Drawing herself up straighter, Ashley met Dr. Aaron Kenneman's autocratic gaze respectfully. "I'll do as you say."

Aaron nodded gravely.

Well. The British *were* coming. What choice did she have?

3

⫷⫸⫷⫸⫷⫸

The smell of cooking fat and scorched meat mixed with pipe tobacco and the odor of unwashed bodies made Ashley's stomach roll as Aaron steered her through the small tavern.

The air was filled with the babble and boisterous laughter of men sitting at small tables swilling rum from tall mugs.

Two buxom serving girls carried pots of hot mulled ale to a group of men settled in front of the large fireplace. Smoke whirled and circled in the air as it drifted from the long-stemmed clay pipes that Ashley remembered were called, ironically, church-wardens.

As they made their way across the room, a few men raised their hands to Aaron, calling his name in amiable greeting.

A man well into his cups suddenly lurched toward Ashley. Aaron calmly pulled her in front of himself as he continued to guide her through the crowd.

"Who's the wench, Kenneman?" a well-dressed man in frock coat and breeches called out laughingly.

"She refuses to say!" Aaron called back good-naturedly. Ashley stiffened resentfully as Aaron's grip tightened around her arm.

A slovenly looking chap at a nearby table removed a chewed stick of snuff from his pocket and used it to massage his gums thoroughly as he joined in the ribald laughter.

"What a terrible thing to say," Ashley accused. He was making it sound as if she were a prostitute!

"You are to remain *quiet*, wench."

"Stop calling me *wench*."

He ignored her, hurrying her through the crowded room.

"I refuse to be treated this way," she protested as she struggled to keep pace with his long-legged stride.

"Hold your tongue," he warned softly. "And keep moving. The gentleman to your right seems to have developed an eye for you."

Ashley quickly darted between two tables to avoid contact with the burly seaman who was clearly ogling her.

A stooped, white-haired man with a stained apron encasing his slim hips straightened from a table where he had been talking with two others. "Aye, Doctor! A trophy from th' game?" he called out.

"Aye, and a fine one," Aaron called back. "Oh, Loyal? I'd do something about that hole in your roof. It looks like falling weather."

The innkeeper frowned, scratching his head. "Hole in me roof?"

"Yes, and a rather large one," Aaron reminded. "Should be repaired immediately."

"A *hole* in me roof?" Loyal was still scratching his head as the good doctor and his bunter slipped out the front door.

A large, ornately dressed man was just about to enter the tavern as Ashley and Aaron emerged. The man paused, tipping his hat to Ashley as she hurriedly sidled around him and down the steps. Drawing a deep breath of fresh air, she tried to rid her nostrils of the tavern's stench.

Moving her along briskly to a dark bay tied at the hitching rail, Aaron said quietly, "Not a word as we ride through town. Understand?"

"Perfectly."

Did he think she was daft—well, yes, he did, but she wasn't.

"Where are we going?"

"That needn't concern you."

Ashley viewed the horse anxiously. She'd never ridden a horse before and wasn't especially eager to start. "I don't ride."

"You do now." After swinging easily into the saddle, he extended his hand to her. Ashley placed her foot into the stirrup and groaned as he pulled her up awkwardly behind him.

Grasping his waist, she gasped as the horse lurched forward. "Slow down! I've never even been on a horse!"

"This is not a pleasure ride. Try to bear that in mind."

The horse galloped off, and all Ashley could do was hang on, praying that she would wake up and be done with this ghastly dream!

Boston in 1775 was an awesome spectacle. The gathering twilight bathed the bustling town in a mellow coral glow as the horse galloped through narrow, winding dirt streets. The odor of fish hung heavily in the air, and Ashley could hear the muffled throb of ships laying at anchor in the harbor.

Gazing about her in bewilderment, she found the skyline flat, not the Boston she knew. The flurry of activity was far removed from the midtown traffic to which she was accustomed. She could see candles being lit inside quaint brick homes, and men carrying lanterns strode alongside the road.

To the right lay the harbor where she saw a tubby British vessel with a hornlike head projecting from its bow. A smaller American craft, built mainly for fishing and coastal trade, bobbed beside it in the water. Ashley noticed the American ship had fewer square sails and more of the handy fore-and-aft sails, which hung parallel to the keel.

Shouts suddenly drew her attention. Two ruffians were engaged in a fistfight where a crowd was gathering. Street vendors ignored the rowdy cutpurses as they went about crying their wares.

Ashley turned, gaping over her shoulder at what appeared to be a pickled pirate's head perched upon a pole for exhibition. As she grasped Aaron tighter about the waist, she felt him urge the horse to a faster gait.

Curiosity mixed with wonder, astonishment, and apprehension made her head swivel like a top as she took in the sights and sounds of eighteenth-century Boston.

Ships were being unloaded at the docks and freight wagons rumbled past, carrying what few goods were allowed to the merchants. Recalling history again, Ashley knew the ships contained everything from turtles to chandeliers. In 1775 the port of Boston had been closed to all commerce since June 1 of the year before, until the city paid for the tea that the colonists had dumped into the harbor. The tea had been worth thousands of dollars. The boycott had been a great sacrifice for the colonists, for it meant that they had to do without a great many things they'd thought necessary for living.

Ashley suddenly wondered if Aaron Kenneman had been involved in the Boston Tea Party.

She sat up straighter, about to ask him, then didn't. Paul Revere and the others had accused her of being Gage's spy, and the question would only arouse more suspicion. General Thomas Gage, she remembered, was the new governor and commander-in-chief of the British forces in North America, and he was assigned the task of enforcing the Boston Port Act.

Aaron was most likely one of the colonists who formed a provincial congress at Concord to govern Massachusetts. That congress, she knew, would force Gage's raid on colonial military supplies in Lexington and Concord within a few days.

She closed her eyes. This was absolutely the most absurd dream she'd ever had. Why couldn't she be dreaming that Kevin Costner and Mel Gibson were fighting over her, and, out of desperation, Mel Gibson kidnapped her, then rushed her off to the Hawaiian Islands for a life of paradise?

Instead she found herself riding on the back of a horse behind an American patriot in the eighteenth century, only days before Paul Revere's famous ride to warn the colonists that the British were about to attack.

They emerged from the harbor area and entered the main part of town. The air was putrid there. Gutters ran the lengths of the street, forming open sewers. Slops and human filth had been tossed out the windows into the gutter, and droves of wild hogs wallowed in the muck and fed on garbage left to rot in the passageways between houses.

Ashley gasped as a man almost ran into the horse, another man close behind him.

"Thief! Thief!" the second man shouted.

The horse darted around the man, forcing Ashley to grab hold of Aaron's coattail to avoid being dumped into the slimy muck.

"Cutpurse," Aaron murmured more to himself than to her. He deftly maneuvered the horse through the milling crowd. "Since the embargo has lengthened, more and more people grow desperate."

The horse galloped on as Ashley turned and watched the thief being overtaken and thrown to the ground.

The horse continued through the town, up winding alleys and down dark passageways. A church bell rang, signaling twilight. Ashley gazed up at the unadorned meetinghouse. The frame building was painted a dull white, but the belfry on the roof was lovely with its moldings and tall spires. The classic columns in front were severely plain, yet they added a note of dignity to the structure.

The horse rounded a corner, and Ashley slipped sideways in the saddle. Aaron reached back to steady her, and she held on to him tighter, trying to hitch herself up more solidly on the rump of the horse.

"How much farther?" she shouted. Her bottom was numb already.

"Until we get there," he called over his shoulder.

Turning down another alley, Aaron slowed the horse. Ashley's gaze quickly took in the painted signs of various size and ornateness, marking the mercantile, a bank, a boardinghouse, and—she shivered—the bared narrow openings in a wall housing the jail. As they rounded a second corner, her eyes caught the sign on the silversmith shop and she squealed. *"The Silversmith Shop:* P. Revere, Prop."

Paul Revere's silver shop! Ashley remembered Revere's business was barely surviving in 1775 because of the worsening situation with England. But then Paul was a busy man. He was not only the leader of the Sons of Liberty, a group that had found varied ways to oppose the English, but he was Massachusetts' number-one express rider between Boston and Philadelphia.

Tugging at Aaron's coatsleeve, she pointed to the shop excitedly. "Look! It's Paul Revere's silversmith shop! I wonder if Rachel's there!" Ashley hoped the dream would allow her to meet a woman of the 1700s. There were so many things she wanted to ask!

Aaron stiffened, glancing over his shoulder at her. "You know Rachel?"

"Well, not personally, of course. But I've read—"

She saw the muscle in his left jaw working tightly. "You've read what?"

It was more of a statement than a question, reminding Ashley that women didn't read anything of substance in 1775. It was not thought proper. But women's roles had changed drastically since Aaron Kenneman's day, and Ashley wasn't going to lie to him.

"I've read that Paul took over his father's silversmith business when he was only fifteen."

"And?"

"And awhile later he married his first wife, Sara Orne. Paul and Sara had six children—plus two who died at birth."

Aaron swore impatiently. *God's teeth*, the wench was unnerving!

But Ashley went on with her alarming recitations as if she were in no danger of being throttled. "The surviving children's names were Deborah, Paul Jr., Sara, Mary . . .

and Francine . . . no, it was Frankie . . . no, maybe it was Faith, no—"

"Frances!" Aaron snapped.

"Yes! That's it, Frances, and Elizabeth."

"Your memory serves you well," Aaron said shortly. The woman was a *witch*. First she babbled about things that made no sense; now she was babbling about things that were true. Yet she claimed she was not a spy. "You know much about a man you profess to have never met," he accused.

Aaron scowled as he thought about her wealth of knowledge. Was it possible Paul knew this woman? Could he be romantically linked with her? Of course not. Aaron dismissed the thought as worthless. He'd never known Paul to be a womanizer. Paul didn't have the time.

"I only know what I've read," Ashley repeated stoically, knowing it was a waste of time to argue with a dream.

"Perhaps you only have visions," Aaron suggested, and none too kindly.

"Visions?" She laughed softly. "No, I don't have visions. I must have eaten pepperoni before I went to bed."

Yes, that would explain it. She had eaten pepperoni again. Pepperoni invariably caused her to have nightmares.

Aaron turned slightly in the saddle to glance at her. She was talking gibberish again.

Ashley sighed. "Never mind. You wouldn't understand, even if I could explain."

His eyes returned to the road, but she noticed he chose his words more carefully this time. "Those who have a strange turn of mind often see things others cannot."

A beautiful woman with a demented mind was a waste,

in his estimation. And he didn't deny Ashley Wheeler was lovely, though she did babble incessant nonsense.

"You think I'm crazy."

"Mayhap not mentally deranged, but there are those individuals who brew spells and potions and often profess to see things others don't."

"Oh, you think I'm a *witch.*"

"You deny that you're not?"

"Would it do any good if I did?"

A witch with an irreverent mouth, he thought irritably. "Tell me more of what you have 'read,'" he mocked.

They were riding down an open road now. The horse's gait slowed as they wound along what was little more than a dirt path. The woman's knowledge both fascinated and annoyed Aaron, but he found himself powerless to cease his questioning.

"You and the colonists think King George is quite a nice fellow, but he isn't," she complied, grinning as she felt him grow tense again. "Everyone's blaming Parliament for the mess the country's in when it's really King George and the head of the English treasury demanding more and more of your money."

"*You* have 'read' this," he scoffed.

"I read it," she verified happily. Oh, he was a handsome rascal, but his lack of respect for her knowledge annoyed her. "Dr. Kenneman, in spite of the general opinion that women are made only for the delight and pleasure of a man, we do have brains. A woman of the nineties no longer has merely to parrot a man's views," she took pleasure in informing him.

"The nineties? Fifteen years from now?" he scoffed again, wondering why he even listened to such prattle.

"No, *two* hundred and fifteen years from now."

He turned to look at her again.

She grinned. "You don't believe me?"

"There is nothing worse than a sharp-tongued woman with a higher opinion of herself than can be substantiated."

She pinched his ribs. "Listen, buddy. If this wasn't a dream, you would be talking an octave higher right about now for that kind of chauvinist remark."

Wincing, he shook his head in wonder. "What manner of wench are you?"

She was tempted to tell him, but even in a dream, it would be a little impertinent on her part. But one more macho remark like that one, and he was asking for it.

"You feel that women are inferior to men?" she challenged.

"Women have their place," he conceded. He didn't personally harbor the common belief that women had no right to education or personal opinion, but he had no objection to men who did. Besides, he didn't know why he was trying to carry on an intelligent conversation with this woman. His only duty was to see that she did not escape until plans could be made to get rid of her.

"And where might that place be, good doctor?" Ashley goaded.

"Women should take care of the home, raise the children, read their Bible, perhaps a cookbook if they're not naturally talented."

She laughed.

"You find my observations amusing?"

"I find *you* amusing."

They rode in silence for a spell. Ashley realized that she was exhausted. A dull headache throbbed at the base of her temple, and she longed for the bumpy ride to be over.

The sun had gone behind a low bank of clouds, and the air had an uncomfortable chill to it now.

"You spoke of Paul." Aaron's voice suddenly broke into her scattered thoughts. "What more do you know of him?"

"Well, he's been working since he was a child. Learning the silversmith business from his father, ringing church bells, whatever, to earn money. He took over the business when he was either fifteen or nineteen, depending on whose opinion you read, and made beads, rings, lockets, buttons, pitchers, teapots, which was a fine business considering the tea party episode. Once he even made a silver collar for a man's pet squirrel.

"History says that when his first wife died, Paul became involved with the Sons of Liberty. He eventually hired Rachel Walker to keep house and care for the children. Apparently the children liked her so much that Paul asked Rachel to marry him. Eventually Paul had sixteen children. No *wonder* he had a hard time making ends meet. Anyway, when English ships sailed into Boston Harbor to try to sell their tea, the Sons of Liberty demanded the ships leave by December 16 or they'd throw the tea in the harbor. When they ignored the ultimatum, the elder Revere and his son Paul joined 150 others who dressed as Indians to dump the tea—all 114 chests of East India that was aboard the *Dartmouth* and two other ships that were tied up at Griffin's Wharf that day—the *Eleanor* and the *Beaver*. It was raining—and cold. But by nine o'clock, more than ninety thousand pounds of tea were floating in the harbor. All they needed was a big slice of lemon."

Aaron turned to look at her again.

Ashley smiled, pleased that she could distress him so easily. "Isn't that the way it went?"

"*God's teeth! Who* told you that Paul and his son were involved?"

"I read it—"

"In a book," he finished wearily. "What kind of book might this be?"

"History. All kinds of history. Columbus. Napoleon. All of it. From the beginning to the twentieth century."

"You are to be complimented. You are well versed in events."

"Well, I thought I hated history, but I've had to memorize so many facts for my job."

He frowned. "A job as what?"

"My job as a tour guide at the museum. And I know about the Boston massacre too."

Aaron's features paled, but he remained silent. Curse his luck! He should have made John Hancock take her home with *him*.

Ashley crawled wearily off the back of the horse thirty minutes later. She was just thankful Aaron Kenneman would never be behind the wheel of a car. He rode like a maniac!

She turned, eyeing the disreputable-looking tavern that they'd stop before apprehensively. "What is this?"

"The Black Goat." Aaron busied himself tethering the horse to a broken rail.

"What's a 'Black Goat'?"

"An inn."

"We were at an inn," she reminded sharply.

"But this is where we shall spend the night."

Ashley recoiled at the thought of spending a night in such an establishment. Though it was dark now, she still had no trouble seeing that this inn was as carelessly kept as the other. "I thought you were taking me to your house."

Her words were met with a cold pewter gaze. "I changed my mind."

"Thanks for telling me."

Aaron ignored her. Taking the wench home with him would be ill advised, he had realized. The Black Goat was a noisy place with a bad reputation. If she got it in her mind to try an escape and he was bid to tie and gag her, her screams would cause no question from the clientele who frequented the establishment.

Ashley sighed as she stared at the dilapidated inn. If this wasn't her luck: a grade-B dream on a low budget.

Her opinion of the Black Goat worsened when they stepped inside. The air reeked with the odor of unwashed bodies. "Now, honestly, we're not going to stay here, are we?" Ashley complained. "In my day the board of health would close this place in an instant."

"The beds are adequate and the food filling." Aaron nudged her toward a vacant table toward the back.

"Jeez," Ashley grumbled.

When they were seated, Aaron signaled for the serving girl. "Not a word," he warned as the barmaid started toward them.

"Have I been talking too much?" Ashley goaded innocently.

"Yes."

"What'll it be, matey?" The voluptuous girl approached the table, her limpid blue eyes sliding over Aaron appreciatively.

Ashley noticed the girl's hand lingered on Aaron's shoulder longer than necessary as she reached to scoop up two dirty mugs from the table with the other hand.

"Two ciders and two meat pies." The way he returned the barmaid's smile was entirely too cordial. Ashley suspected that Aaron Kenneman was not exactly a stranger to the Black Goat.

The girl turned her back to Ashley, but Ashley still caught the invitation in her voice. "Anything else to suit your fancy, handsome?"

"Not today." Aaron and the young woman exchanged what Ashley considered meaningful looks.

He jumped as Ashley gave him a firm kick beneath the table.

Stunned, he looked at her.

"You're here on business," she snapped. *The randy buck.*

"Don't do that again," he warned tightly. His patience was wearing thin with this wench! Demented or not, the woman was not going to kick him in the shins and expect to get away with it.

They glared at one another, each drawing an invisible line the other wasn't to cross.

"Haven't seen you here for a while, Doctor."

Aaron glanced up to find the little rotund owner of the inn standing beside the table. The man's bulging stomach was covered by a stained apron with an adequate display of the week's menu splattered across the front.

"It has been awhile, Medrian. My work keeps me busy."

"Aye, so I hear." Medrian Frolonzo smiled knowingly at Ashley. "It be a fine day we're having, mistress?"

"No," Ashley said. "It's a perfectly rotten one."

Medrian stared at her vacantly.

Aaron nudged Ashley warningly with the tip of his boot beneath the table. "You must excuse her, Medrian. The lady grows weary." He nudged her again, urging her to confirm his observation.

She looked at him. "What?"

"The *lady*," he enunciated, "grows weary," he said again.

"Oh . . ." Ashley yawned obediently.

"Ah . . . yes." Medrian smiled.

"We'll need a room for the night," Aaron requested in a low tone.

Ashley booted his shins hard again.

Sucking in his breath, he gave her a black look.

"We'll need two rooms," Ashley corrected nicely.

"*One* room," Aaron repeated, booting her back.

She booted him again.

He booted her back.

The little proprietor eyed the table anxiously as it jiggled merrily.

Whack!

Crack!

She gasped. "Darn it! That hurt!" *He* was the most uncivilized apparition of fantasy that anyone could have the misfortune of being stuck with!

Aaron smiled pleasantly at Medrian. "The young lady is only being modest. One room."

Medrian stepped back, giving the couple plenty of room. "'Tis no concern . . . your regular room is waiting." The look in his eye assured Ashley that she had played right into Aaron's hands. The innkeeper thought what Aaron intended for him to think; she was nuttier than a fruitcake.

Flipping the innkeeper a coin, Aaron looked at Ashley. "You must eat, darling." He smiled indulgently. "You'll need your strength."

Her tone dripped disdain. "*Regular* room?"

"I travel often."

"I'll bet."

The serving girl returned, carrying a tray laden with food. After balancing the tray on her hip, she placed a large meat pie, a hunk of bread, and a mug of ale in front of Ashley.

Ashley sat up straighter, her eyes scanning the meat pie anxiously. What did people eat in the eighteenth century? She tried to remember. Birds? Rodents? Insects?

"Something displeases her highness?" Aaron asked.

Ashley glanced at him weakly. "What's . . . in this?"

He looked at the pie, then back at her. "If you are hungry enough, you will eat whatever it is." He forked a succulent piece of meat from the pie and calmly chewed it, his eyes locked with hers stubbornly.

It was the vague *whatever* that bothered her. She sighed, glancing toward the dirty back room wistfully. "I suppose there's no hope of getting an order of nachos, is there?"

Aaron took a second bite of his meat pie. "What are 'nachos'?"

"They're these crisp little tortilla chips with hot peppers and cheese."

"Of course." He continued eating.

"They're great with Pepsi or Coke."

"Of course." He went on eating as if he weren't dining with a halfwit.

Ashley brought the fork hesitantly to her mouth, taking a tiny exploratory taste of the pie.

Aaron watched from the corner of his eye as she lowered her fork and nibbled the fare experimentally. Deciding that it was edible, she cut another slice, sighing as she chewed it.

As she ate, her gaze swept the room filled mostly with men who were either eating or playing cards. All of them were drinking beer from fat little steins.

A wide fireplace dominated one end of the room. An iron crane jutted out from the back and a large, black pot was suspended from it.

The serving girls regularly moved to the pot to swing the back pole out and dip stew from the kettle into large bowls. A spit with half a skewered cow hung over the fire. Ashley focused on a small boy who sat to one side, chin in hand, turning the spit with a wooden handle.

"What's the boy doing?" she asked.

Aaron glanced up, his gaze following the direction she was pointing. "The spit-turning boy?"

She frowned. "Spit-turning boy? That's his job? To sit there and turn the meat?"

Aaron shrugged, his attention drawn back to the meal. " 'Tis honorable work for the lad."

"Does the job pay well?"

Absently tearing off another hunk of bread, he studied her. She had an innocence about her that disconcerted him. One moment he was sure she was daft, then, in the next instant, she appeared to be quite sane. "Frequently a turnspit boy is working out a debt, either his father's or his own," he said.

He resumed eating, and it wasn't hard for Ashley to see that he was more interested in his meal than in conversation with her.

Ashley sat back to observe the boy, mentally comparing the youth of today with the small lad patiently cranking the spit. Would a youngster of the 1990s accept such a subservient job to repay his parents' debt? she wondered.

"Do all inns employ such young children?"

"Some inns have jacks."

"Jacks? What are they?"

"Dogs that are trained to walk on a treadmill to turn the spit. A few of the larger establishments use them."

Ashley was amazed. "Dogs?"

"You would do well to cease your prattle and eat," he warned.

Ashley picked up her fork again. "You would do well to bug off."

He glanced up again. "Bug off?"

"Bug off."

He nodded graciously. "As you say."

Ashley ate what she could of the meal. The pie crust was thick, the potatoes overcooked, and the meat tough as shoe leather, but it eased the hollow pang in her stomach. "What do you plan to do with me?"

"It has not been decided."

"When will it be decided?"

"When it is decided."

"Dr. Kenneman!" A man staggered toward the table, his leering gaze sweeping Ashley disrespectfully "I don't believe I've had the pleasure of seeing this lovely little doxy before." He lurched again, obviously in his cups. "She is most fair of face."

His fetid breath made Ashley draw back defensively. She glanced anxiously at Aaron for help. Though she didn't particularly like the doctor, she realized that, for the time being, she was dependent on him.

"She is not a Bostonian," Aaron said quietly.

"I am too!"

"She isn't," he said again matter-of-factly.

"Aye," the man conceded. "One could see that. Her dress is very fine. She is obviously"—the man grinned—"well paid for her wares." He reached out to finger the ruffle adorning the neckline of her dress, then trailed downward to feel the texture of a strand of hair that had escaped the chignon into which Ashley had rolled her hair before putting on the wig that evening.

The wig!

Her hand flew to her head. She'd lost it! She groaned. The museum would insist she pay for a replacement.

Swaying closer, the man boldly let his finger trail lower, brushing the front of her bodice.

Ashley sprang to her feet. The sound of her hand cracking against the bare flesh of his cheek echoed throughout the room.

"Now see here," Aaron warned, shooting Ashley a don't-cause-a-scene look. The last thing he needed was for her to draw attention to herself.

The noise in the room died away as eyes swung toward the table.

"Keep your hands *to yourself*," Ashley told the man coldly.

The drunken man rocked back, his hand coming up to cover his reddened cheek. "Why, *no* woman slaps Jack Milletson!" he blustered.

"She darn well will if Jack Milletson doesn't keep his hands off her!"

"Now see here," Aaron warned again.

Jack reared back to knock Ashley senseless, but she slapped him again first. The sound of flesh meeting flesh ricocheted around the room.

After flinging a bench aside, Jack and Ashley went after each other as the room burst into cheers.

"*Now, see here!*" Aaron roared for the last time.

Fists and scratching nails obediently froze in midair as his thunderous order bounced around the room.

After getting slowly to his feet, Aaron calmly stepped between Jack and Ashley. "The lady is with me, Jack."

Rubbing his glowing cheek, Jack stared at Ashley with hate. " 'Tis a stroke of luck in her behalf, to be sure."

Aaron surveyed Ashley aloofly. "That it is."

Ashley reached out and started to slap Aaron's face, but he caught her arm, smiling. "Here now!" he said loudly. "We'll have none of that, my pretty! Save that lusty spirit for the bed."

Ashley's eyes narrowed. "You—" Her other hand shot up to belt him a good one. She hadn't been raised with four brothers and not learned a thing or two about defending herself.

Aaron caught her up, swinging her over his shoulder as if she were nothing more than a sack of grain. "Ah, yes, my lovely. I think it's time we retired too!" He winked at the other men. "Excuse us, gentlemen, she pleads exhaustion."

"Put me down!" Ashley demanded through gritted teeth as he turned and strode toward the stairway.

Throwing back his head, Aaron laughed merrily as if she had just said something delightfully witty. "Ah—eager, my love? Of course I can walk faster!"

"Pig!" She whacked him across the back, hard.

"Worrisome *wench!*" he muttered, whacking her back.

"Help!" she shouted, thinking surely one of the drunken goons sitting around watching this outrage would come to a woman's rescue. "Someone help me!"

But the men only laughed uproariously as Aaron began to take the stairs two at a time with the doxy screaming in protest.

The men's eyes lit with envy. They *loved* a woman with that kind of pluck!

"Aye, ride her for me," one shouted.

"Tame the cat, Kenneman," called another.

Ashley's cheeks flamed. He was deliberately making those louts think that she was his prostitute, bought for a night's pleasure.

Well, he'd see how much "pleasure" he got tonight, she vowed as he reached the top of the landing and turned to stride down the dimly lit hallway.

Before the night was over, Ashley Wheeler would make Aaron Kenneman think he had died and gone *straight* to hell.

4

Ashley remained calm as Aaron hauled her through the narrow hallway. Let him think I'm a helpless little ninny, she thought, seething. He'd find out different. She ducked, barely avoiding hitting her head on a wooden beam as he turned the corner, carrying her over his shoulder like a prize turkey.

Without breaking stride Aaron kicked open the door of a room where he unceremoniously deposited her onto the sagging bed.

Ashley caught herself before she rolled off the other side. "You *jerk!*"

"Must I bind your mouth shut?" Aaron kicked the door shut, then slipped the lock.

"You just try it, mister!"

By the look he sent her, she knew that he didn't feel the least bit threatened.

After lighting the betty lamp, he strode to the narrow window and pulled the dirty curtain aside to assess the darkened street below.

Everything appeared to be in order. No one lingered outside; no one was leaving the tavern in haste. Perhaps the ruse had worked. The men believed the woman was a punk hired for his pleasure. Relieved, he let the curtain drop back into place. He would keep the wench here until morning, then send word to Revere where he was. By then, a decision would have been made on what to do with the woman. Since time was of the essence, she would have to be disposed of before Gage realized she had been discovered.

"Everyone down there thinks I'm a prostitute," Ashley accused as she rolled to the side of the bed and sat up. She felt as if she had been dragged through a knothole.

"Precisely as I intended." Turning from the window, Aaron surveyed the room disdainfully. "And if you have any sense about you, you'll not bother to inform them otherwise."

Closing her eyes, Ashley grabbed a piece of flesh on her arm and squeezed it tightly.

Aaron watched as she repeatedly pinched herself.

"What are you doing?" he asked calmly.

"Pinching myself."

"I can see that. Dare I ask why?" he returned pleasantly.

"Because I want to wake up!" Meeting his eyes determinedly, she pinched herself again, hard.

Leaving her to amuse herself in her eccentric manner, he crossed the room and sat down on the side of the bed to remove his boots.

Dropping back onto the lumpy pillow, Ashley stared at the ceiling bleakly. "I want to go home."

She hadn't realized she'd spoken aloud until Aaron answered quietly. "I cannot release you."

She sat up, pulling the pins from her hair. Aaron frowned, finding himself disturbed by the sight of the crimson cloud that invited a man's distraction. "If I could only wake up," she murmured, more to herself than him.

Aaron's gaze suddenly softened. The wench was lovely —stupid, perhaps, but lovely. "You waste time with such prattle. It would serve you better if you told me who has sent you."

"I wish I knew."

"You insist you are caught up in a dream?" he asked.

"I know I am . . . or a time warp."

He sighed. She was speaking nonsense again. "Would that we both were dreaming, but it is not so."

Drawing a deep breath, Ashley slid off the bed. She winced when she caught sight of herself in the small looking glass hanging above the washbowl. Her hair was standing on end, her makeup was smeared, and dirt smudged her face and hands. Why, she looked worse than the wench who had served them earlier.

She sighed. Listen to her. *Wench.* Now she was even beginning to *think* like him.

"Are you worried someone has followed us?" she asked when she noticed he had returned to the window.

"The thought has crossed my mind."

"They haven't."

He looked up. "You know this?"

"Well, I nearly know it." If this was three nights before Paul Revere was to make his famous ride, then she knew history confirmed that all had gone well. Of course, she'd read nothing about a doctor standing guard over a woman from the twentieth century, but then historians couldn't know everything that happened that night . . . if this really was happening and was not a dream.

"You nearly know it." He went back to looking out the window. "Why does that fail to comfort me?"

"I don't know. It should. What happens now?"

"We wait."

"Wait for what?"

"Morning."

Ashley frowned. "Just . . . morning?"

"You ask too many questions, Mistress Wheeler."

"I hope you're a good doctor because your bedside manner could do with some improvement," she complained as she turned back to the mirror. She surveyed her dress in disgust. The museum director would kill her for doing this to one of their costumes.

"We are not here to talk."

"What are we here for?"

The look on Aaron's face was clear. He wasn't there to answer her questions, that was plain to see. "I am going to rest. I was up all night with a patient, and I grow increasingly weary."

Ashley watched as he shrugged off his coat and tossed it across the foot of the bed. A moment later he stretched out on the bed, heaving a deep sigh.

"Don't think of attempting an escape," he warned. "Without my protection, you will be in even worse danger."

Ashley shuddered as she recalled the motley group of men gathered below, and how their hungry eyes had raked over her. If she tried to escape, it wouldn't be through the tavern. She went to the window and gazed at the thirty-foot drop. It was too high to climb down, even if she had a place to go. Think, Ashley, think. This has to be a dream. But if it isn't, what should I do? If, by some wild stretch of the imagination, this is real, then what should be my next step?

She glanced at Aaron, who seemed to have dropped off to sleep. She studied him for a long moment. He appeared to have more than looks. He was a man fully dedi-

cated to a cause. Though he was a doctor, sworn to pre-
serving life, there was no doubt in her mind that his only
reason for saving her from being branded a spy and perhaps killed was to prevent exposing the others. If keeping
her alive threatened him or his group, Dr. Aaron Kenneman would not hesitate to do away with her, she was
certain.

A shiver of apprehension rippled down her spine. He
might be handsome, but she had the sense to realize that
he could also be very dangerous.

She walked to the washstand. The pitcher was full of
clean water. Glancing toward the bed, she assured herself
again that he was sleeping soundly now.

After pouring water into the bowl, she unbuttoned the
front of her bodice and removed the scrap of lace that
acted as a modesty piece. She tossed the fabric onto the
dresser, loosened the lacings, and drew the first comfortable breath she'd had all day.

Glancing toward the bed again, she quickly gathered
her skirt around her waist, untied her petticoats, and let
them drop to the floor. She caught the rim with her toe
and tossed it onto the chair. Much better, she decided,
pushing up her sleeves. Now for the farthingale.

She hitched up her skirt again, then twisted around
until she could find the fastening. It was knotted by now,
and she had to pick at it blindly to get it to release. When
it finally gave, she jerked the nuisance off and tossed it on
top of the hoops. Then she stepped out of the skirt and
shook it free of the remaining dirt and debris.

Aaron watched her measures through slitted eyelids.
He was prepared for her to attempt an escape. If she
tried, it would settle the question of whether she was a
Tory or patriot. Instead, she had decided to remove all of

her clothing. What was she going to do? Stand there stark naked? It didn't matter that she thought him asleep, this woman had no modesty! The scraps of underclothing she wore covered nothing.

His eyes cracked open a bit more. *Nothing.* He could feel his body responding to the sight of her bare, slender legs, and he quickly rolled onto his side.

After dampening a rough square cloth, Ashley began to scrub at the smudges on her face and arms. She dipped the cloth into the bowl again, then leaned forward, peering into the looking glass to pat the soft swell of her breasts.

God's eyes, she was beautiful, Aaron thought in agony. Sweat broke out on his forehead as he continued to feign sleep. If she was a spy, it would take a strong man to resist her charms; that was precisely why she has been chosen to infiltrate the group, he realized. Gage was a sly fox.

Despite his attempt to control his response, he felt the pain in his groin grow even tighter as she reached up to free the snap on her bra.

Ashley suddenly tensed as she saw Aaron move out of the corner of her eye. "You're not sleeping," she accused.

"Nay, I sleep very soundly," he lied.

Ashley's cheeks flamed. "You've been watching me!"

His eyes opened slowly, allowing his gaze to meander over her with tantalizing care.

Following the direction of his gaze, Ashley looked down. Her pale-pink bikini panties and demi-cup bra seemed to be holding him spellbound.

"What manner of . . . device is that?" he asked. Whatever it was, he hoped it caught on.

"A . . . bra and panties," she snapped, snatching up her skirts and holding them in front of her. "Much more comfortable than pantaloons or whatever contraptions your women wear."

"What is their purpose?" he asked.

"Purpose? Well . . ." Was he serious? "Well, to . . . cover . . ."

"Then its purpose is not achieved," he commented dryly, his eyes focused on the looking glass behind her.

Suddenly Ashley realized that though she was covering the front of herself with the skirt, her backside was clearly visible in the looking glass.

After stepping hurriedly back into the skirt, she snatched up the bodice of her costume and shoved her arms into the sleeves.

"You could have looked the other way," she snapped.

"It is my duty to watch you," he reminded.

She turned her back to him, pretending to study herself in the mirror. Her cheeks resembled strawberry Pop Tarts as he continued to gaze at her in the muted candlelight. Ashley was appalled to find herself responding to his disconcerting pewter-gray eyes traveling over her. She wasn't sure what this man was willing to do to protect his country, and she wasn't sure she wanted to know.

She quickly restored her top to decency, determined to ignore his penetrating gaze.

But his interest had been piqued. "Are you accustomed to baring yourself in front of a man?" Aaron found the thought that she was frequently in a state of undress in the company of a man annoying. What were these eighteenth-century women coming to?

"I thought you were asleep."

"That was not the question."

"No, I'm not accustomed to 'baring' myself in front of men."

Returning to the mirror, Ashley studied her reflection, suddenly wishing that she were prettier. It would take a woman of considerable beauty to attract a man, an obvious rake, like Aaron Kenneman. Oh, she would be considered passable, but she didn't come close to being beautiful. A wave of homesickness washed over her as she thought about Joel and how he had always contended that she was pretty, though she knew she really wasn't.

"Come now," Aaron chided. "A woman with your beauty . . . mayhap there is someone you have favored?"

"Well . . . only one man, Joel Harrison, my fiancé," she admitted.

"You have undressed in front of this man before marriage?"

She turned, staring at him. "Well, yes . . . we were engaged."

"And being 'engaged' in the—what century do you claim to be from?"

"The twentieth century."

"Women in the twentieth century—they allow men such liberties?"

"Well . . . sometimes I guess so."

"When will you marry?" His gaze moved over her slowly.

"We won't now," she confessed, determined to ignore the heat that was suddenly building inside her at his intimate and softly provocative words. "I broke the engagement. Just before I . . . landed on your table."

Her wide-eyed, innocent expression was so sincere, so straightforward that for the briefest moment Aaron was tempted to be swayed by her performance. Was it possible she actually believed this absurd story that she told?

No, Gage had chosen well. The wench was not only clever, she was convincing.

"Is this man a Tory also?"

"Joel? Of course not!"

"Why did you break the engagement?"

"None of your business why."

" 'Tis a pity," he said softly.

"That I broke the engagement?"

"No, that twentieth-century women allow men such freedom." His eyes moved over her very slowly again. "If I were the second man, I would feel defrauded."

Ashley finished buttoning her bodice and tucked it back into the skirt of her costume. "Well, things are different now than they were in your day."

After rolling out of bed, Aaron walked to the window to look out again.

"You might as well relax," Ashley told him. "We're safe for the time being."

Stooping down, Ashley gathered up the discarded petticoats and farthingale from the chair, then laid them across the dresser.

It was a long time before Aaron finally moved from the window. She glanced at him, her behavior softening when she realized that he was truly exhausted.

After emptying her wash pan into the slop jar, she poured fresh water into the bowl. "You may wash now."

He unbuttoned the top three buttons of his lawn shirt as he sank to the edge of the bed. It was hard as the wench's heart, but there would be little rest tonight anyway. After pulling off his boots, he let them drop to the floor with a thud, then wearily stretched out on the bed.

Ashley watched his actions from the corner of her eye. His lean body was stretched diagonally from corner to corner, and she had to smile. The bulky knitted socks encasing his large feet were such a contrast to the expensive silk hosiery Joel wore.

She turned away, trying to ignore him, but she could still see his image in the looking glass. His shirt gaped open to reveal his broad, tanned chest, well muscled with a thick coating of light-brown hair. He wore his hair long and tied at the nape of his neck in a fashionable queue. Sinfully long, dark lashes made crescent shadows against his lean cheeks. His mouth was finely carved, and his chin was, if possible, even more stubbornly decisive than Joel's.

"Where am I supposed to sleep?" She wrung out the cloth and laid it across the washbowl while her eyes surveyed the small bed. It wasn't large enough to accommodate two.

Aaron opened his eyes and gazed at her calmly. Was she hinting at joining him? While his body was willing, he wasn't that big a fool.

"The chair appears to be available."

Ashley's eyes narrowed. "You expect me to sleep in a chair?"

"I expect you to be *quiet* while I sleep. Where you plan to carry it out is none of my concern."

Ashley's hands shot to her hips impatiently. "If you think—" she began, but Aaron interrupted.

"Mistress Wheeler, you seem to believe that you have some say in what happens to you. Believe me, you don't. You forfeited that right when you fell through the roof of the tavern tonight. So *muzzle* yourself!"

"Muzzle myself!"

"Muzzle yourself."

"I have little choice but to accept your deplorable behavior, do I?"

"That does appear to be the situation," he conceded. That *damn* Revere! *He* was going to have to deal with this chit tomorrow night!

"Very well." She walked to the chair and seated herself, wrapping her cloak of martyrdom about her.

"A word of warning: I will be watching you, even though my eyes are closed. Don't attempt to escape."

"I wouldn't dream of it."

The noise from the tavern below drifted up to them as silence fell over the room. Aaron forced from his mind the image of the young woman in the chair. He wasn't going to spend what little dozing time he had thinking about the wench's bare shoulders or her full rounded breasts that the open bodice of her gown revealed. And her shapely bottom didn't bother him any either.

He dozed for a moment, then bolted partway up as he heard her dragging her chair to the window.

Her eyes met his obstinately. "Oh, are you trying to sleep?"

"What would you guess?"

"I'd guess I'm annoying you."

"Then you'd guess right."

She settled back against the hard rocker, staring out the window.

It was pitch dark outside; only a few lanterns in windows broke the blackness. Drawing a deep breath, she reached over and cracked open the window for a breath of fresh air.

She was so tired. If she could just snap her fingers and be back home, she would never again complain about anything or anyone.

Resting her head against the back of the chair, she stared into the darkness. What could have happened to whisk her to this place? She remembered the thunderstorm and rushing out to her car. Then she'd fallen . . . Lifting her arms, she examined her elbows. The bruises and scrapes were there.

Then . . . she remembered nothing until she'd fallen through the roof of the Green Dragon Tavern onto a table.

The whole thing was absurd! She'd read about this kind of thing happening but always thought it was pure fantasy. Could she have fallen into a time warp of some sort? Was that possible? If she had, could she ever convince her captors that she wasn't a spy? And supposing she was able to do that, could she then convince Aaron to help her somehow find her way back home?

Her gaze traveled back to the bed, and she wondered why she felt so darn safe with him. Though he wasn't at all like Joel, except that they were both doctors, there was still something very . . . familiar about him. It was crazy. He was holding her captive, yet she felt no real sense of fear.

Her mind refused to release the certainty that she was only dreaming. But if she was dreaming, why couldn't she wake up? More important, would she *ever* wake up? The new, even more disturbing thought frightened her. Really frightened her. Maybe she'd never awaken, and maybe she'd never get back home. Oh, dear Lord. What if she was permanently caught in the eighteenth century?

It was so frustrating! Tears stung her eyes as she balled her fists and screamed.

Frantically scrambling to a sitting position, Aaron stared back at her, his eyes wide-eyed and glassy. "What . . . ?"

"Sorry," she murmured, realizing that she had screamed aloud. She was going to *have* to act in a more rational manner, or she would never convince him to help her.

"This wench is—" Tacking on something Ashley felt certain wasn't exactly a compliment, he dropped back onto the pillow, still mumbling beneath his breath.

Well, she supposed plotting against the British could be demanding, but he didn't have to be so ill-mannered and testy about it.

Leaning back in her chair, she resumed her fretting. Considering the present circumstances, she supposed, dream, time warp, or whatever, she was in danger.

If it was indeed April of 1775, then she had better curb her tongue and smother the urge to say whatever popped into her mind. Women of the 1700s were second-class citizens as far as men were concerned, and if she hoped to survive and not be accused of being a witch or worse, she'd better think twice before blurting out her opinions.

Her breath caught when something moved on the street, but she relaxed when she saw it was only a dog.

The whole thing was so eerie. The Boston she'd seen today from the back of Aaron's horse was not much different from the one she'd talked about while escorting visitors around the museum. From what she'd learned it was considered the most politically and culturally advanced city in the colonies, boasting some forty streets, nearly as many lanes, half that many alleys, and a thousand brick houses.

A dog barked in the distance, and Ashley grinned, remembering that at one time the city of Boston had had so many dogs that a law had been passed prohibiting people from having dogs more than ten inches high. Since it had been difficult to keep pets from growing taller than that, and it had been equally difficult for people to part with dogs that had defied the law and grown larger, everyone had paid little attention to the statute.

While she was riding with Aaron through the common that afternoon, she remembered that the public area had originally been set aside as a training field and a place to feed cattle. Recalling the Frog Pond that the Puritans had used to duck persons who'd disobeyed the Sabbath laws, she shivered. Would Aaron allow her to be subjected to such public humiliation? Did they still do such things?

Though Aaron may have attempted to confuse her, Ashley thought she knew approximately in what part of town she was. She tried to visualize the maps she'd studied. If Boston Common was in the heart of the old city, then Beacon Hill was north of that. The Market District was near Dock Square where the famous Faneuil Hall was located. The ground floor of that old building had been a market area where Bostonians went to shop, if she remembered correctly.

Considering that they'd been near the harbor, and then wound down into town and past the common, then back again . . . then the Black Goat must be in the oldest section of the town, perhaps even on the peninsula that extended into Boston Harbor, which was the innermost part of the bay. No wonder this place was tacky and run-down and the caliber of men was somewhat less than that of the men she'd seen at the Green Dragon.

From out in the hallway, Ashley thought she heard a woman's throaty laugh, and the tramp of heavy boots on the stairway. She tensed, glancing toward the bed anxiously. Should she wake the chauvinist pig and warn him?

"Remain quiet, and you'll be in no danger." Aaron said in a low voice, though his eyes were still closed.

The footsteps approached their door, then continued on. Ashley breathed a sigh of relief as they faded down the hallway.

The woman's breathless giggles and the man's lewd comment made Ashley painfully aware of what kind of establishment she'd been brought to. The women downstairs were prostitutes, and the sounds of coming and going up and down the hallway were nothing more than five o'clock rush-hour traffic.

Tears stung her eyes again as she huddled in the chair. Her eyes turned resentfully toward the bed. Maybe she should try to slip out of the room, down the stairs, and make a break for freedom. How much more danger could she be in if she hid in a park or behind a bush rather than waiting for her fate to be decided by six men who were convinced that she was either a witch or a spy or both?

Her eyes moved back to the door speculatively. The tavern was almost quiet now. Perhaps everyone had finally gone home. Leaning forward, she debated her next move. If she—

"Don't even consider it."

Ashley started at the sound of Aaron's voice. How could he have read her mind! "I thought you were sleeping."

"You thought wrong again."

She dropped back against the chair in defeat.

Well, let him think he had the upper hand. She'd eventually catch him off guard, then she would open the door, step out, and close it so silently that he'd never know she was gone until he awoke the next morning.

Yes, that's what she'd do.

But where would she go? The Boston she knew didn't

exist yet. And she couldn't bear getting on that horse again, even if she'd known how to ride it. Aaron Kenneman wasn't the most congenial companion, but at least she was safe with him. For the moment.

Ashley closed her eyes, resigned to suffer more discreetly. She couldn't afford to have him leave her in this rat-infested hole.

A smile shadowed the corners of Aaron's mouth as he heard her sigh. He'd watched her struggle with whatever was on her mind for the past hour, wondering if she would be foolish enough to try an escape. He watched the play of emotions cross her face, first anger, then wistfulness, then resigned acceptance.

Each time she'd turned to study him, he'd sensed turmoil in her, a weighing of decisions. He had to give her credit. She was smart. She knew she was safer with him than alone, and she'd chosen to act wisely.

Her sigh a moment ago had been one of quiet desperation, but he knew she wouldn't attempt an escape, not tonight.

Settling deeper against his pillow, Aaron grinned. Yes, the wench had spirit.

An optimistic sliver of sunlight trying to force its way through the dirty windowpane awoke Ashley the next morning.

She stirred, lifting her hand to shield her eyes from the cheerful little ray. She groaned, every joint in her body stiff as she moved.

A brisk rap sounded at the door, and Aaron was instantly on his feet.

Ashley held her breath as he strode across the room and cracked the door open. "What is it?"

"Aaron Kenneman?"

Aaron viewed the elderly, stoop-shouldered man uncertainly. "Yes."

"Medrian said you were a doctor?" Aaron could see the man was breathing heavily, as if he'd taken the stairs faster than a man his age should. "It's me wife . . . she's sick."

"Where is she?"

The little man wrung his hands anxiously. "You'll have to come with me—she's home."

Aaron reached for his boots as the man turned and fled back down the stairway. Glancing at Ashley, he grimaced. What was he supposed to do with the wench? He couldn't leave her alone.

Ashley eyed the bed enviously. The chair was so uncomfortable that she'd barely slept a wink all night. While Aaron was taking care of the sick woman, she'd take a little nap. She was heading toward the bed when a hand came out to stop her.

"You're coming with me."

She groaned. "Cripes! I hate this!" She had spent half her time with Joel, sitting in the car, twiddling her thumbs, while he checked on one or another of his patients at the hospital. "You go, and I'll stay here and—"

But by this time Aaron was propelling her toward the open doorway. "You're coming with me."

"No! Why do I have to go? I'm not the doctor."

"No, you're the prisoner," he explained in a tone any kindergartner would recognize. "And since I *am* the doctor, and the doctor can't leave you alone, I guess that means you and I are inseparable for the time being." He smiled. "Well, 'cripes,' " he mocked her, "have I made myself clear?"

She stiffened at his condescending tone. "Perfectly."

"Then let's go."

She jerked free of his grasp, giving him a dirty look. "At least let me comb my hair."

"Forget about your hair. It looks fine."

Just like a man. She started straightening the bodice of her gown, then began a search with her toes for her shoes. After grabbing a handful of her hair, she wound it into a knot and stuck a hairpin through it as he called for her to follow him.

"All right, all right. I'm coming!" She hadn't even had her first cup of coffee!

Grabbing her purse, she followed him down the stairs, trying to keep her balance. Maybe it was the sauerkraut she'd had at lunch that had made her have this strange dream!

"Wait! Wait a minute!" she cried as she almost lost her balance. The pin in her hair had come loose and she knew she couldn't afford to lose it. She had a feeling there wasn't a K mart within fifty miles. Hurrying to keep up, she yelled, "Slow down!"

When they reached the bottom of the stairs, Aaron grabbed her hand to pull her along. Ashley tried to jerk out of his hold but he only tightened his grip and sailed her across the empty tavern more determinedly.

"Quiet down," he ordered.

"You miserable . . ." She halted, trying to control her straggling hair. "I've never spent a more miserable night, with a more infuriating man in my whole life! You are a selfish, egotistical, unfeeling—"

Ashley glanced up then to see Medrian behind the counter, grinning. It wasn't hard to see what the inn-keeper was thinking, and her cheeks reddened.

Lifting her skirts higher, she raised her head proudly and marched straight past the innkeeper and out the front door. Let the fool think what he wanted. Aaron *knew* what she meant.

Giving Medrian a man-to-man wink, Aaron grinned at the innkeeper.

"Morn', gov'nor. I trust you had a pleasurable night?"

"Most pleasant, Medrian, thank you!"

A young boy was holding the reins of Aaron's horse as they came out of the tavern. Dawn streaked the sky a pastel pink, and the noise from the harbor heralded a new day. Catching sight of the doctor, the elderly man mounted his horse, motioning for Aaron to follow.

Ashley's stomach growled as Aaron hoisted her up on the horse. She wasn't too crazy about having his hands on her bottom, but since it was impossible for her to mount otherwise, she kept quiet. "Watch it—I'm sore." She winced.

Settling herself, she looked down at him. "I'd kill for an Egg McMuffin and a cup of hot coffee."

"That does sound tasty," Aaron agreed in a tone of someone accustomed to dealing with the insane.

After mounting behind her, he wheeled the horse, and they galloped off.

A short time later the elderly man's small house came into view. The whitewash on the old cottage was stained and the door sagged on its hinges. The house wasn't exactly a picturesque setting out of a history book. Ashley saw two small children crouched upon a tiny hearth feeding a small fire with sticks of kindling as she entered the front room.

Ashley had to squint to make out the furnishings. She

was blind as a bat without her contacts, and she'd taken them out the night before. Reaching into her purse, she withdrew her glasses and put them on.

After moving toward the fire, she warmed the tips of her fingers as she looked at the furnishings in the sparse room. Other than a table and three chairs, there was only a scarred lowboy, a small cabinet that held a few dishes, and a dry sink. The curtains at the narrow windows had faded to a nondescript blue years ago. The family obviously was very poor.

A tired-looking woman appeared from the back room, carrying a pan of water and a cloth.

"How is Rebecca?" the old man asked anxiously.

"She is not good," the woman said, shaking her head sadly.

Aaron shrugged out of his jacket, handing it to Ashley as he followed the woman and man into the bedroom.

Glancing over his shoulder, he motioned for Ashley to follow.

"No!" she mouthed silently.

"Yes!" he mouthed back. "Now." He looked at her glasses and frowned. The frames were most unusual.

Ashley followed him unwillingly.

The room was small, the darkness broken only by a small candle burning beside the bed. The woman on the bed was so pale she appeared waxen.

Stepping back into the shadows, Ashley watched as Aaron began to examine the woman. As he worked, he spoke reassuringly, trying to calm the woman's fears.

Ashley had a feeling he was an excellent physician, though she knew his knowledge was pitifully limited. She thought about all the things people had learned about the science of medicine since Aaron Kenneman's day, and she suddenly had an overwhelming urge to share with him the exciting news about polio, diphtheria, whooping cough, heart disease, cholesterol, oat bran, X rays, CAT scans, and penicillin. But she dismissed the idea. He wouldn't believe her. Not in a million years.

"Been painin' most of the night, Doctor. Don't know what it could be," Rebecca complained. " 'Fraid a pox has been sent on me."

"When did the pain begin?"

" 'Bout an hour after I ate."

"What did you eat?"

The woman sent a suffering look toward her husband.

"Cabbage, rutabagas, and beans, Doctor. Nothin' else," the man assured him.

Ashley puffed her cheeks out. *Gas*, she thought.

Aaron smiled, patting the woman's shoulder reassuringly. "Well, we'll see if we can't make you—"

Beebeepp. Beebeeppp. Beebeeppp. Beebeeppp.

The woman drew back warily. "What . . . is it, Doctor?"

Ashley froze as the alarm on her watch began to play a perfunctory seven o'clock wake-up call. The watch had been a gift from her sister, who found it amusing that the alarm played an old World War I tune, *"I hate to get up, I hate to get up, I hate to get up in the morning!"*

She glanced up to find four pairs of stunned eyes transfixed upon her.

Aaron shot her an I-don't-know-what-it-is-but-stop-it-look. *Now.* " 'Tis nothing to concern you, Rebecca."

Smiling lamely, Ashley nonchalantly slapped at the alarm, trying to silence it. She could see the noise was upsetting the old man and woman.

"It's nothing . . . just my watch." She pointed at her wrist apologetically.

Rebecca drew back on her pillow, her eyes growing very large. " 'Tis a witch, Hubert . . . 'tis a *witch!*" she breathed fearfully.

The exact same *witch* who'd most likely sent a pox upon her!

"See here, Doctor! You had no call to bring a witch into our home!" Hubert accused.

Ashley slapped the watch more forcefully, mumbling under her breath. "*Shut off*, you stupid thing."

Rebecca began to weep and wail, thrashing wildly about upon the bed in an effort to escape the evil power.

The tired-looking woman sprang bravely forward to try to knock the watch off Ashley's wrist while Hubert bolted toward the bed to throw himself protectively over his wife's body.

Swearing softly, Aaron stepped between the bed and Ashley and took her firmly by the arm.

"What? . . . Oh, for heaven's sake, it's only a *watch*," she explained as he proceeded to drag her from the room.

Aaron didn't know what it was that this strange woman was wearing strapped to her wrist, but *it* was leaving.

"This is stupid . . . I can explain . . . let go of my arm!" she demanded as he hauled her out the doorway, past the two round-eyed children sitting on the hearth, and out the front door.

Her indignant shrieks shattered the serenity of the quiet countryside as Aaron dragged her out the back door of the cottage and calmly propelled her across a side yard toward a small lean-to. She had to run to keep from falling on her face in the blasted cloth slippers!

"Where are you taking me?"

"I'll tell you where I'd *like* to take you," he snapped.

"And I'll tell you where you can *go*," she shot back. "You're not my keeper!"

He jerked the door and pushed her into a small shed that was dark and smelled of . . . *cow!* Before she knew what he was about to do, Aaron had found a length of twine and bound her hands like a Christmas goose. "Now *stay* here, and be quiet!" he ordered.

"You jerk!"

He strode out of the shed and slammed the door without so much as a backward glance.

"Ooohhhhh!" She was mad enough to spit. How *dare* he tie her up in a smelly old shed and leave her there!

She sat for a moment, trying to figure out what to do.

Moooooo.

She lifted her gaze to find a cow placidly chewing on a mouthful of hay, staring at her.

"He thinks he can get away with this," she seethed.

Moooooo. The cow contentedly munched on hay, apparently agreeing.

Ten minutes later Ashley had managed to loosen with her teeth the twine tied around her wrists. In the process she'd lost a hairpin, the cow had trampled it into a pile of manure, and she'd caught her skirt on a nail and it now had a jagged three-corner tear in the front. But it didn't matter. She was free, and she'd love to see the look on the schmuck's face when he came back and discovered that she had outsmarted him.

Ashley snatched up her canvas bag and crept out of the shed. Luck was finally with her. A narrow lane ran behind the shed, and all she had to do was follow it back to town.

After kicking off the tight slippers, she started off down the road at a brisk pace. It was still early, and few people were stirring. She had no idea where she was going, but she would not permit a man to treat her with such disrespect.

She walked for over a mile before she dared to lessen her pace. The sun was up now, and the day promised to be a muggy one.

Slogging along, head down, dejected, weary, and just plain exhausted, she swore to give up sauerkraut and pepperoni for the rest of her life.

A man's voice suddenly came to her from behind.

"Well, well. And who might this be?"

"A pretty young maid," a second man's voice answered.

Ashley whirled, her heart slamming against her ribs as she discovered the source of the masculine voices.

The first voice belonged to the incredibly handsome dragoon leading the mounted infantry; the second belonged to one of the fourteen British soldiers riding with him.

5

Ashley's heart dropped five stories. British soldiers. Fifteen of them. Dressed in the uniform of the English ordinary soldier, they stared back at her, but it was the captain leading the mounted infantrymen who commanded her rapt attention.

The man sat upon his horse with a jaunty air that fairly shouted his importance. He wore a bright-red frock coat, the skirt rakishly held back by the hilt of his sword, and knee britches. His black boots had been shined carefully, and the white gloves he held in his right hand were immaculate. He was quite a magnificent sight, this masculine specimen of over two hundred years ago.

"Good morning, mistress," he said with a slight nod. "I am Captain Benjamin Browning. Where might a maid such as yourself be going so early in the morning?" he asked.

"I'm . . . " Ashley's mind raced feverishly for a reason he would find plausible, "taking a walk," she said, summoning up her most winning smile for him. " 'Tis a splendid morning, isn't it?"

Captain Browning leaned easily on the pommel of his saddle. "It is rather early in the day for one so fair to be taking a walk, is it not?"

"Well . . . I didn't plan to walk this far." Ashley turned, gazing about her with innocent confusion. "I don't seem to know where I've wandered, kind sir."

His brow lifted with concern. "Mayhap you are lost?"

She lifted her hand to her temple, pretending to be hopelessly mixed up. "Oh, dear, mayhap I am."

The men shifted in their saddles, exchanging amused looks. The untidy doxy was clearly from one of the local nunneries. A couple of the men chuckled as they viewed her dirt-smudged face, flyaway hair, and tattered dress. Though winsome, this lovely one obviously commanded little coin for her skills.

Thinking to tease her a bit, the captain leaned forward again, smiling. "Or mayhap you are a spy, and you are walking the back lanes to carry messages?" His eyes sparkled devilishly as his experienced eye measured her from head to toe.

Ashley shook her head mutely.

"No? Mayhap you've gained some bit of information from a British dragoon well into his cups?" the captain needled.

Oh, Lord, he *knew*, Ashley thought hopelessly. She might as well be honest and just pray that she could gain his sympathy. "Well, no, I'm not a spy, but listen, I'll be honest with you. I'm . . . I'm not just taking a walk, I'm trying to escape from someone," she admitted.

If she was in the protection of fifteen British soldiers, Aaron Kenneman wouldn't dream of trying to recapture her.

The captain's smile faded slightly. "Oh?"

"Yes, a—a doctor. Please." She stepped forward, holding her hand out to him imploringly. "You must help me."

"You are trying to escape from a doctor?" he inquired pleasantly.

"Yes, and he's an arrogant ass!" she snapped, shifting the strap of her bag higher on her shoulder.

Fifteen sets of brows rose simultaneously this time.

"An . . . ass?" the captain repeated.

"You wouldn't believe what an ass—but we don't have so much time that we can stand here wasting it." She glanced down the road anxiously. It was imperative that she remain calm and not say anything that would alert the soldiers to the fact that in some circles she was thought to be crazy, although she knew that it did sound strange that she was attempting to escape a doctor. Maybe she shouldn't have told them that. "Uh . . . the man will be coming after me any minute now. We'll have to hurry."

"This . . . doctor is holding you against your will?" the captain asked, trying to make sense of what she was saying.

"Listen." Ashley thought that the captain looked like an understanding type. "I know I can't explain this sensibly, but there was this little misunderstanding about my watch —the one my sister gave me for my birthday? It plays this silly little World War I song: *'I hate to get up, I hate to get up, I hate to get up in the morning . . .'?*"

The captain nodded as if he'd heard the song.

"Oh, you *have* heard it?"

He glanced over his shoulder, flashing his men a wry smile. Turning back to Ashley, he nodded. "Of course. Please, go on."

Encouraged by his amazingly astute perception of her situation, Ashley continued. "Well, Rebecca really lost it. She started screaming and carrying on, accusing me of being a witch, and so . . . the doctor"—Ashley carefully refrained from revealing Aaron's name, realizing the soldier could still decide to hand her back to him—"he *drags* me out to this stinking shed, *ties* me up, and leaves me with a cow! Can you believe it?"

The captain shook his head sympathetically. "You are Rebecca?"

"No, my name is Ashley Wheeler. Rebecca is *Hubert's* wife."

The captain nodded again as if he understood perfectly.

"Can you just please call me a cab?" Ashley finished wearily.

The captain turned to look at his men again.

The men shrugged, then nodded charitably.

The captain turned back to Ashley. After clearing his throat, he complied gruffly. "You are a . . . cab."

"What?"

"You are a . . . cab."

"Oh . . . no, I mean . . ." Ashley froze, realizing the serious slip of tongue she'd made. She wasn't in twentieth-century Boston, she was in eighteenth-century Boston, and these men had never heard of a cab!

"I . . . meant to say, could you call me a . . . horse," she amended quickly, knowing that sounded even more stupid, but she had to have some form of transportation to escape.

The captain turned to look at his men again. This time their faces clearly indicated that this is where they drew the line. Daft or not, they were *not* going to call any woman a horse.

"I'm afraid I am unable to assist you," the captain said at last.

"Then could you just take me with you, and drop me off at the first town we come to?" At least she would be safe from Kenneman, and would have more time to decide what to do.

"Of course," said the captain. "I'll have one of my men take you wherever you wish to go."

"Oh, thank you!" So he *didn't* think she was crazy after all.

"Bennett, there is a jail nearby," the captain said quietly. "See to the young lady's comfort while she is escorted there."

"Yes, sir!"

The captain lifted his hand, and the line of troops began moving forward.

"Jail? No, wait a minute!" Ashley shouted to the captain's retreating back. *Why* had she asked him to call her a cab? Where was her mind? Of course he would think she was crazy!

"You're a danger to yourself, my lovely, wandering about, babbling like a demented magpie," he called laughingly.

"No, listen to me, please!" she cried. "I'm telling you the truth! I'm having this crazy dream . . . you *have* to help me!"

"The guards will find someone to assume responsibility for you," he promised.

Stunned, Ashley felt herself being lifted off the ground and placed on a horse behind one of the soldiers. Dear Lord, they were really going to put her in prison until someone came to claim her! And no one would ever come! Aaron would have no idea what had happened to her, and, even if he knew, there wasn't a prayer he would come after her. Not after the trouble she'd caused.

In all too short a time, the small infantry reached the jail. Ashley looked at the solidly built stone building with thick bars on the narrow windows, and she knew she was going to be sick.

Clamping her hand over her mouth, she bolted toward the bushes, and, while the men looked on, she threw up.

The soldiers wrinkled their noses, stoically trying to keep from gagging as they listened to the anguished heaves, strangled gasps, and muttered oaths coming from behind the bushes.

Returning a moment later, Ashley, pale and shaken, marched past the white-faced men, determined to see this thing through.

Captain Browning emerged from the prison a few minutes later followed by a surly-looking fellow who looked and smelled as if he hadn't hadn't been near water in weeks.

"This is the young woman. She says her name is Ashley Wheeler, though we can't be certain. She babbles madness." The captain's eyes swept over Ashley's pale face with regret. " 'Tis a waste of womanhood, to be sure."

"My name is Ashley Wheeler, and I'm not crazy," she insisted. "You can't throw me in jail just because I was walking along a road."

" 'Tis better to hold your tongue, woman!" Captain Browning commanded.

"I will not! You have no jurisdiction over me. I am a United States citizen, not under British powers!"

"Ah-ha! You are a colonial spy!"

"No!" Ashley retorted warily. "I'm not a spy."

"Then what are you?"

"Nuts," she conceded. It was better that they think her crazy than a spy.

"See how she babbles. I will leave her in your command," the captain said to the jailer. "I will notify the authorities in case someone should be looking for her."

" 'Tisn't likely," the jailer conceded. "But she can stay."

His beady eyes studied her from head to foot, and Ashley instinctively drew closer to the captain's side.

"You can't leave me here with this . . . this man," she whispered. "I don't like the way he's looking at me."

"There is nothing more that can be done with you," Captain Browning said, tugging his cocked hat lower on his forehead. "Take her," he directed the jailer.

Ashley struggled to elude the jailer, but he pried her from the Tory's grasp and marched her, screaming, into the prison.

As the burly jailer pulled her inside the dank building, her senses were assaulted by myriad terrible sights, sounds and smells. Her feet slid on the slimy floor, and her stomach rolled.

"I'm going to be sick again," she warned.

Laughing, the jailer snagged a ring of keys off a hook and unlocked a thick wooden door leading to a narrow passageway. After yanking her through the doorway, he dragged her along a small corridor where the darkness was broken by low-burning torches. There was the sound of wings fluttering overhead and tiny feet scurrying across the stone floor.

Ashley's heart was beating wildly as she stumbled along behind the jailer, her eyes growing wide as voices from dark cells called to her.

Poor, tortured souls dragged themselves to their feet to peer through the narrow bars on the doors, their hands extending beseechingly to her.

"Help me . . . help me . . ." the voices pleaded weakly from the bowels of the blackened cells.

At the end of the long row, the jailer unlocked a door and thrust Ashley inside. She cried out as she tumbled onto a pile of damp, dirty straw.

"Oh, please, you can't put me in here," she pleaded.

The jailer laughed, his round belly jiggling merrily. "If there be anything I can do to make you more comfortable, just let me know, my lovely! Thomas Bulfoonery be at your service!"

"No, please!" Ashley raced toward the door as it swung closed with a dull *clang*. Doubling up her fists and sobbing now, she beat on the heavy wood, but her hysteria only made the jailer laugh harder. He turned and walked away, leaving her in the darkness.

A damp cold penetrated her body as she huddled on the straw. She closed her eyes, refusing to accept the fact that she was in an eighteenth-century prison. It couldn't be, it just couldn't be.

Sounds closed in around her. Low moans, wailing, a man's voice babbling gibberish in a nearby cell.

After what seemed like hours, Ashley summoned enough strength to pull herself to a sitting position. She was thirsty. Her eyes located a wooden water bucket with a gourd dipper to one side, and she wondered how long it had been there. A filthy metal pot was set in the opposite side of the cell. Apparently the pot was the only bathroom facility available.

Ashley closed her eyes. Oh, please, she prayed. Just let me wake up. I'll do anything. *Anything.* But when she opened her eyes, the same dismal sights confronted her.

A squeak in the corner made her freeze. Rats, three of them, scampered across the floor, their red eyes watching her warily.

Ashley leapt to her feet, pressing herself against the door. "Help! Help! There are rats in here!"

A burst of laughter came from the cell opposite her. "Rats, you say? Then you'll have meat for supper, my lovely!"

The rats scurried into the cracks, but it was several minutes before Ashley could move. Rats. She shuddered.

Spotting the tiny window, she edged her way around the cell, still pressed to the wall. Standing on tiptoe, she peered between the bars at the small court enclosed by stone walls. Her heart sank when she saw that the court-yard was empty.

Wrapping her hands around the bars, she tried to pull herself up higher, hoping to catch a breath of fresh air. She was so out of shape! With a groan of disgust, she dropped back to the floor, heartsick. She swallowed a cough that persisted in tickling her throat. Great! All she needed now was a case of pneumonia.

She glanced around and spied the water bucket again. After moving closer, she hesitantly peered inside. Three large, black, bloated bugs floated on top of the water.

Ashley winced, vowing she wouldn't drink the water even if it meant she'd die of thirst. Not wanting to worsen the already deplorable conditions, she gingerly lifted the bucket with the tips of her fingers, and carried it to the window. A few seconds later she was drenched, but she had managed to fling most of the water through the bars.

Then she flipped the bucket upside down and climbed on it, welcoming the whisper of fresh air.

Laying her head on the wooden sill, she stared bleakly at the deserted courtyard. She should have stayed with that arrogant American patriot.

At least he smelled better than this wretched place.

* * *

Lunch arrived through the slot in the door. Ashley hurried to catch the bowl, but it fell to the floor with a noisy clatter.

"Woe is me! Guess you'll wait till supper," the jailer quipped, then burst out laughing as he moved to the next cell.

Ashley stared at the mess in disgust. Great. She was trapped in a nightmare with Andrew Dice Clay.

The afternoon seemed unending. Ashley spent most of her time standing on the bucket at the window or sitting on the pile of straw filing her fingernails with the file she'd found in her bag. She tried to imagine the look on Aaron's face when he'd returned to the shed and found her gone. She tried to imagine the look on *her* face when she'd encountered the British soldiers and realized what a fool she'd been for trying to escape.

The evening meal arrived, and Ashley was waiting for it. After she caught the bowl as it shot through the slot in the door, she turned up her nose. The meager fare looked to be even worse than whatever still lay on the floor from lunch.

Studying the thin gruel and thick slice of dark bread, she realized she would have to eat it. If she didn't, she would become too weak to escape if the chance were to present itself—which it probably wouldn't, but she had to be ready just in case.

Holding her nose, she lifted the spoon to her mouth. She wouldn't think about what she was doing. Someone would come to rescue her.

Someone just had to.

* * *

Night fell, shrouding the cell in almost total darkness. Ashley lay huddled on the straw, exhausted, but too scared to close her eyes. She watched as the rats crept out of hiding to feast on the gruel splattered on the floor.

Exhausted, toward dawn she finally covered her face with her hands and sobbed, losing hope now. No one would come. She would die in this nasty little hole, and there would be no one to even claim her body.

As dawn broke, a loud clatter brought Ashley upright. She looked about her, realizing that she must have dozed off. She absently scratched her arm and sniffled.

A ray of pale sunlight filtered through the bars as she got slowly to her feet. She scratched again, glancing down to find something crawling up her arm. Leaning closer to the light, she saw it was some sort of an insect.

Lice.

Jumping up and down, she tried to shake loose the vermin that had taken up residence in her skirt.

Screaming, she jumped harder and faster, realizing that the straw was infested with the tiny bugs.

By now she was making so much racket that the jailer heard her and came to investigate.

"What the bloody 'ell is going on in there!" a voice outside her door demanded harshly.

"*Bugs!* In my *skirt!*" Ashley cried.

"Make her be quiet, gov'nor!" a disgruntled voice whined from a nearby cell. "The wench be a bloody annoyance, she is!"

Ashley didn't care if she was being a nuisance. She wasn't living with lice! She stomped harder, prancing up and down, screaming.

"Be quiet in there!" the jailer ordered.

But Ashley couldn't be quiet. She felt as if there were

thousands of the tiny insects crawling on her. "Don't just stand there, do something," she yelled.

After unlocking the cell door, the jailer stepped inside. "I want it bloody quiet in here, do you understand!"

"I want a bath—a shower! Do *you* understand?"

The jailer left, then returned a moment later with a hand full of cord.

Realizing what he was about to do, Ashley started backing away. "Oh, no you don't. You're not going to tie me up!"

The jailer smiled.

"You'd better not." She pressed herself against the wall, watching warily as he started toward her.

He wouldn't tie her up. He *wouldn't* dare.

Late that afternoon, Ashley managed to struggle to her feet, heavy cord bound tightly around her wrists and ankles. If it wasn't for the rag stuffed in her mouth, she'd scream her head off.

After hopping to the window, she peeked out between the bars again. The courtyard was still empty. She didn't know what she hoped she'd find. The prison wasn't exactly a hub of activity.

She was about to turn away when she suddenly heard voices. Standing on her tiptoes, she saw the jailer and Joseph Warren striding across the courtyard.

Joseph Warren, one of the men at the meeting! Spotting the medical bag he carried, she realized he must be there to attend to one of the prisoners.

Bouncing up and down, Ashley attempted to draw the physician's attention.

"Octor Warorjn! Octor Warorjn!"

Engrossed in conversation with the jailer, the doctor failed to hear her muffled cries.

Look this way! Ashley agonized. "Octor Warorjn! *Octor Warorjn!*"

Oblivious, the doctor stepped through an entryway a moment later and disappeared.

Wilting with disappointment, Ashley tried to think. How was she going to make the doctor aware of her presence? She had to get out of there. Though it would probably mean being back in Aaron Kenneman's care, anything would be an improvement over this rat- and lice-infested cage.

After hopping to the bucket, Ashley began to kick it toward the door of her cell with the tips of her toes. If Warren was here to treat a prisoner, then, with any luck, she might be able to attract his attention.

As she heard the sound of a door being unlocked and men's voices as they came down the corridor, her feet worked faster. *Hurry, hurry! They're coming closer.* Her feet dragged across the dirt floor as fast as the cord tightly binding her ankles would allow. The voices were very near now. The doctor would be approaching her cell any moment.

"*Octor Warorjn!*" Her face turned bright red as she tried to be heard.

She dropped to her knees and worked the bucket upright with her nose.

Then she rolled to her feet, drew a deep breath, and lunged forward in a reckless attempt to hop on the bucket.

With a noisy clatter, the bucket went one way and her bound feet flew the other.

"Ohd shidt!" She rolled to her side, groaning. Just *great.* Now she'd *broken* her arm.

Warren's stride slackened at the sounds of muffled cursing and frenzied thrashing coming from the end cell. He paused, frowning.

The jailer glanced irritably at Ashley's cell. Why did *he,* Thomas Bulfoonery, have to be stuck with the idiots! " 'Tis only the wench," he told the doctor. "No need for alarm."

"Is the poor soul in distress?" Warren asked.

"Nay, only a saucy halfwit."

The two men continued down the corridor.

Warren was getting away! She had to stop him. Groaning, Ashley rolled to the door, banging her feet on the heavy wood, yelling *"Octor Warorjn!"*

Hesitating a second time, the doctor turned to look over his shoulder in the direction of the commotion. "I say, good man, are you certain the wench doesn't need assistance?"

"Nay, only a sound thrashing, gov'nor."

The doctor and jailer proceeded as the pounding grew more persistent.

"Octor Warorjn! Octor Warorjn! Hellhp meee! Pleadse!"

"Now see here!" The jailer lost all patience with the worrisome wench. He whirled on his heel, stalked back to Ashley's cell, shoved the key into the door, and muttered, "The wench is nothing but a bloody nuisance!"

The door swung open, and Ashley nearly fainted with relief when she saw Joseph Warren staring down at her.

Recognizing her as the woman Aaron Kenneman was supposed to be watching, Warren looked aghast. "What is this woman doing here?" he snapped.

"She's daft, Doctor, pay her no heed."

"How long has she been here?"

"Only a spell," the jailer replied, puzzled that the good doctor should inquire.

"Release this woman immediately!"

"Aye?"

"Release her. This woman isn't daft," Warren rebuked, pretending to be shocked by the man's lack of compassion.

"She isn't?"

"No!"

The jailer eyed Ashley suspiciously. "Then what be wrong with her?"

"Putrid fever."

Ashley's eyes widened. *Putrid fever?*

Bulfoonery viewed his ward suspiciously. "She don't look feverish."

"Are you a doctor?" Warren challenged.

"Nay, gov'nor."

"Then I would be well pleased if you would let me make the diagnosis."

As he knelt beside her, Warren removed the rag from Ashley's mouth, then reached into his bag.

"What are you going to do?" she hissed.

"Don't say a word," Warren whispered as he bent closer to peer into her eyes. "Yes . . . ummm . . . definitely putrid fever."

"Ach, we'll have an epidemic!" the jailer exclaimed. He backed into the hallway, his face a mask of horror.

Ashley remembered that spotted fever had been almost epidemic in Boston at one time. She struggled to recall how it was treated, but could not.

"I must purge her," Warren announced. "And I must do it immediately."

Purge? *Purge!* Oh, good Lord! *"No!"* she wailed, but Warren was already rummaging in his bag.

"Remain quiet," he threatened in a low voice, "or I shall leave you here."

"You wouldn't dare . . . I'll scream all I know about you and Kenneman and Revere—!"

Warren clamped his hand over her mouth. He had no doubt that she would. Even though she was considered daft, he could not afford to leave her there. If she babbled about the meeting and those in attendance, her words might strike a chord of truth with the wrong people. He could not permit that to happen.

In a louder voice, the doctor said, "This should do it."

Ashley watched wild-eyed as he poured a vile syrup from a brown bottle into a large tablespoon.

"This should make you feel better," he soothed.

Ashley's stomach turned, and she clamped her mouth shut tightly.

"Take it!" Dr. Warren warned.

Ashley's mind raced. *If I swallow that stuff, I'll be sick as a dog. If I don't . . . I'll still be in jail and sick as a dog.*

She opened her mouth, gagging as the doctor spooned the concoction down her throat. Whatever the medication was, it tasted worse than castor oil, worse than coal oil, worse than . . . She swallowed, wishing she were dead. Shuddering, she struggled to keep it down.

"That should do it," Warren said, tossing the bottle and spoon into his black bag. After helping Ashley to her feet, the doctor smiled as he collected her bag. "I must move her to the pest house so the fever doesn't spread."

Ashley's head spun and her stomach lurched. Pressure to relieve herself of the vile syrup was building in her stomach. She wouldn't have to pretend to be ill by the time Warren escorted her out of the jail. She *was* sick.

The jailer's keys jangled loudly as he snatched them from his belt. "Aye, Doctor. The sooner the better!"

"It would be wise to clear the halls to avoid anyone contracting the fever," Warren advised.

"Aye, gov'nor, to be sure . . . but there be no one in the halls," he said blankly.

"Then stand back, my good man. 'Tis a most infectious and nasty scourge," he confided.

Minutes later the doctor emerged from the jail, escorting a pale-faced Ashley.

Warren hurriedly assisted Ashley into his buggy, then took his seat. He snapped the reins against his horse's rump, and the carriage lurched forward. Ashley's hand shot to her mouth and she glanced at him frantically.

"Try to restrain yourself until we are safely down the road," the doctor cautioned.

But they were only a few yards from the jail when she hung her head over the side and let go.

When the violent seizure finally passed, she struggled to right herself again.

The doctor, looking straight ahead, grinned.

"What was that horrible stuff you gave me?" She groaned weakly.

The doctor's grin widened. "Puke."

"Puke?" Ashley bolted to hang her head over the side again.

" 'Tis only a purge," the doctor said cheerily. "You shall feel ill for a few hours, but I can assure you that you will live."

Ashley leaned back, spent. That's what she was afraid of.

* * *

Lying limply back against the seat, Ashley watched the road roll by. They had been riding for over thirty minutes, but they didn't seem to be getting anywhere.

"Why did you rescue me?" she finally asked.

"Because you are a danger to our plans. What has happened to Kenneman? Why are you not with him?"

"Dr. Kenneman tied me up in a cow shed—stop the buggy!" she suddenly demanded.

Warren pulled to the side of the road, and Ashley scrambled out of the carriage and headed for the bushes again.

Warren called after her. "Be quick about it—"

He broke off as the sound of a horse approaching at a gallop caught their attention.

Aaron rode up, reining his horse to a halt. "Warren, I have been looking for you!"

"And I can well imagine why," Warren returned. "Are you missing something?"

"The woman." Aaron's face colored. "Have you seen her?"

"Mayhap I have."

"Where?"

Warren nodded toward the bushes.

"Damn. Where did you find her?"

"I discovered our comely spy in the jail."

"The jail!"

" 'Tis a lengthy tale that can be explored later. I'm taking her to Church in belief that he will be capable of restraining her until a decision about her fate can be decided."

"He'll need God's speed," Aaron grumbled.

Ashley heard a squeak of leather and the sound of

someone walking through the weeds toward her, but she couldn't have moved if her life depended on it. She lay supine on the grass, staring glassy-eyed at the clear blue sky.

"Ashley?"

She managed to open one eye a narrow slit and found a familiar pair of pewter-gray eyes looking down on her.

"So, we meet again."

"Yeah, how about that." She rolled to her side, holding her stomach.

"Are you ill?"

"I'm dying," she croaked.

"What happened?"

"Ask Dr. Frankenstein."

Aaron frowned. "Who?"

Ashley motioned feebly toward the buggy.

"What's the matter with her?" he called to Warren.

"In order to remove her from the jail, I had to convince the jailer that she had putrid fever. To make it convincing, I gave her a puke."

"You gave her *puke*?" Aaron whistled sympathetically. " 'Tis a powerful purge."

"There was no alternative. It was imperative that she be moved without arousing suspicion."

Ashley opened one eye. Was that a *chuckle* she heard?

"I gave her only a half dose," Warren called again.

Half dose? Thank God he hadn't given her a whole one!

"Are you all right?" Aaron leaned forward, touching her forehead to make sure she wasn't feverish.

"No, I'm *sick!*"

"Can you sit up?"

"No," she whispered, afraid he was going to insist.

"Warren, Church isn't home. I saw him on the road to Lexington early this morning," Aaron called.

Church. Ashley tried to think. Why did that name trouble her?

"Then what shall we do with her?" Warren asked.

After drawing a long breath, Aaron released it slowly. "I'll assume responsibility for her again."

"You tried that once. It didn't work."

"I will be more alert this time."

"You *want* this responsibility?"

Aaron stared at Ashley determinedly. He was *not* going to let a little slip of a wench best him. "Go about your business, Warren. The wench will be safe with me."

"Very well." Warren picked up the reins, eager to have the woman off his hands. The carriage started off, then paused. Ashley's bag suddenly came sailing out the side, and she heard it plop into the grass. "She'll be wanting this," Warren predicted. "I don't know what she has in it, but it weighs more than a plump turkey."

Ashley groaned, rolling back to her side as his buggy headed off down the road.

Aaron Kenneman might be a brute, but at least *he* hadn't poisoned her yet.

"Come on," Aaron urged quietly. "Sit up and sip this."

"What is it?" Ashley asked warily.

"Just water. Try some."

"I can't. I'm dying."

A smile touched the corners of his eyes as he tenderly smoothed back the damp tendrils sticking to the sides of her face. "You're not dying."

She took a small sip, then lay back in the grass with her arm across her eyes.

A moment later she protested as she felt him lifting her upright again. "No . . . please . . ."

"Sit up."

"No, let me die in peace."

"Sit up, Ashley."

She finally managed to open her eyes and found to her surprise that the world wasn't spinning so badly.

"Open your mouth."

She drew back. "Not on your life!"

After grasping her chin, he spooned the liquid into her mouth. "It's only pennyroyal. It will settle your stomach."

"It isn't puke?" she asked gratefully.

"No. You'll feel better in a little while."

For once Ashley believed him; she *couldn't* feel any worse.

6

"Where are we going this time?" Ashley clung tightly to Aaron's coattail as the horse trotted briskly through the countryside. She was sucking the piece of peppermint he'd given her.

When Aaron didn't answer, she sighed. "You're mad, aren't you?"

"No, *you're* mad," he countered, only what he meant wasn't what she meant. "You are fortunate that Warren was called to the prison."

"I know." Ashley realized she had acted rashly by leaving the shed and drawing the attention of the soldiers. She wouldn't do such a thing again; she could promise him that. And she was grateful that Aaron had taken charge of her a second time, even if it was only because Church wasn't available. Though his manner had been kind when she'd told him about the soldiers and how the jailer had thought she'd lost her mind, Ashley knew that Aaron found the task of watching her even more odious than he had the first time.

Well, she had to admit she wasn't the most appealing creature at the moment. Straw was matted in her hair, and she was certain she was crawling with lice. The elaborate costume that she'd worn at the museum was only a tattered rag now, the once-lovely rose color stained with dirt and particles of food.

Ashley sighed, resting her head against the broad expanse of his back as they rode along. She was so exhausted that she didn't want to think anymore. Her skin and hair itched from bug bites, and there was no telling what creatures had made their home in her petticoat.

"You didn't really think I'd stay in that shed with a cow, did you?" she asked in another useless attempt to draw him into conversation. She knew that he was angry at her for running away, but what had he expected? That she would be sitting there, contentedly swapping little moron jokes with the cow when he returned? "Where are you taking me?"

When he refused to answer, she squeezed him between the shoulder blades. "Answer me!"

Stiffening, Aaron forced himself to refrain from throttling her. "You do that one more time, and you'll walk," he threatened.

"*Where* are you taking me?"

"*Only* where I'm forced to take you."

Ashley peered around his shoulder trying to see if she recognized anything. She didn't. Absently scratching her arm, she wondered if she dare ask for a bath. She itched so badly all over she could hardly sit still. She would do almost anything for a bath and clean clothes, but she had been so much trouble already.

She was peering at the latest bite on her arm when Aaron suddenly reined the horse to a sharp halt. When she looked up, she saw they had stopped beside a slow-moving stream.

"Get down," he ordered.

"Get down? Why?"

"I'm going to drown you," he returned without cracking a smile. "Get down."

Ashley flashed him an angry look, but she hurriedly slid off the horse. He wasn't going to *drown* her, that much she knew.

The stream beckoned cool and inviting. Trees and thick undergrowth lined the bank, affording a small measure of privacy should he allow her the luxury of a quick bath.

Kneeling, she leaned over and tested the water with the tips of her fingers. Though the air was warm, the water was icy.

She suddenly felt herself being hoisted quickly to her feet again. "You need a bath." Aaron took her arm and propelled her firmly into the water.

"Wait a minute!" Ashley sputtered, but before she could protest further, he removed her glasses, then unceremoniously dunked her beneath the water.

When she bobbed back to the surface, she was livid. Spewing water like a fountain, she struggled to regain her balance, but he ducked her again.

"Stop it!" she shrieked.

Grinning, he dunked her a third time. "You *stink!*"

Ashley came up out of the water again, her teeth chattering so hard she couldn't speak. "Stop it! I wanted a bath, not a drowning!"

After tossing her a bar of soap over his shoulder, he scrambled for the bank. She grinned, catching the bar of roughly cut lye soap in her hand.

"Coward!" she called.

He pulled off his boots and dumped the water out. "Just use the soap!"

After throwing her matted mass of hair back out of her eyes, she studied the crude bar of soap in her hand. It bore no resemblance to her favorite pink perfumed soap with bath oil, but it was better than nothing.

Trying to control her chattering teeth, she began scrubbing. Again and again, she dunked the bar and rubbed her hands against it, but she couldn't work up a lather.

"We must be off soon," Aaron called from the bank.

Ashley glared at him then turned her back, still trying to create enough lather to wash her face. As she rubbed the bar up her arm, she grimaced at the sight of her nails. It would take weeks to get them back in shape.

"Mistress Wheeler!" Aaron reminded. "I don't intend to sit here all day."

Ashley clenched her teeth. "How do you expect me to bathe in this impossible situation! This soap won't lather, I don't have any shampoo," she complained. "What's wrong with going to an inn and having a real bath?"

Her complaints died away as Aaron waded into the stream again and took a firm grip on her arm.

She frowned. "I'm hurrying—and don't try manhandling me again," she warned when she saw the devilish glint in his eye.

"Be quiet."

"What are you doing?" Ashley tried to break his hold, but he merely turned her around and began to unbutton the front of her dress.

Slapping his hands away, she backed off, her hands coming to her hips. "What do you think you're doing?"

"I'm going to give you a bath."

"The devil you are!" Before she could finish, he'd unbuttoned all twenty-seven of the little buttons and pulled the bodice off her shoulders.

Outraged, she just stared at him. The man was good, she'd give him that!

"It seems you're determined to stand in this water all day complaining, but I have other commitments," he countered at the dark look in her eye.

After stripping the dress over her head, he calmly tossed it aside. The dress floated away and lodged against a nearby rock.

Aaron's mouth suddenly went dry. The pink bra clung to her body, the wet fabric revealing every soft curve of her breasts, which rose and fell with each angry breath.

His gaze moved over the inviting sight, traveling slowly up to the lush curve of her lips. For the briefest of moments he was tempted to take her, swiftly and with no mercy. She had been taunting him from the moment she'd been thrust into his care, and to be thoroughly ravished would serve her right.

"You can forget it." Her eyes warned him to banish the thought.

With the barest hint of a smile, his gaze traveled leisurely over the gentle flare of her hips, coming to rest on the scrap of cloth she'd called bikini panties. A more winsome wench would be hard to find. Though diminutive, her body was well rounded and lush, and before the ravages of spending a night in the jail, her hair had shone with the coppery color of a true Irish beauty. His body stirred, reminding him of how long it had been since he had had such a woman.

"Get your hands off of me," she snapped.

"You will catch your death in this water." He avoided eye contact with her this time, hoping that she wouldn't detect the noticeable change in his anatomy. He began washing her, ignoring her ill-tempered grumbling.

After slapping his hands away again, she finally grabbed the bar of soap. "I can do it!"

"Then see to it!"

"I don't know what good it will do," she complained as she vigorously scrubbed her arms and face. "My deodorant, hair spray, *and* mousse are in my locker at the museum." She could just *imagine* what her hair would look like after washing it with lye soap.

Aaron stepped back, trying to avoid the splatters caused by her energetic splashing. "Moose? Are you hungry?" He assumed that she was still feeling queasy from the purge and that food would be the last thing on her mind.

Ashley paused, then began to snicker. He was looking at her with the oddest expression on his face.

For a moment, she forgot that she didn't like eighteenth-century Aaron Kenneman. After all, he had once again rescued her from harm. She forgave him, if only momentarily, for standing there staring at her as if she had a screw loose. Leaning forward, she impulsively caught his head and drew it closer to hers. "What would you say if I *kissed* you, Aaron Kenneman, American patriot?"

Aaron drew back, meeting her eyes sternly. "You are to wash."

"Huh-uh."

Aaron froze. What did she mean by huh-uh? Was she going to wash? Or would she try to kiss him?

He pushed her back, but she grabbed his head again, laughing. "Coward." Brushing her mouth lightly back and forth across his, she let her tongue probe his mouth invitingly.

"*God's teeth,* you are a bold wench," he murmured, but she felt him relax as he drew her closer. Pressing her tightly against the firm swell in the front of his breeches,

Aaron thought to teach the capricious wench a long-over-due lesson.

But Ashley was far from intimidated. Deciding he needed a lesson in twentieth-century women, she laid her hand lightly on the front of his breeches. She grinned when she heard his sharp intake of breath. He jerked back as if she had stung him.

"Ha, thought you'd scared me, didn't you?" she goaded.

Shooting her a disbelieving look, he glanced over his shoulder at the sound of approaching hoofbeats.

"Oh, look. If it isn't old Paul Revere again," Ashley mocked.

"I say there! Kenneman!" Revere reined his horse to a halt beside the stream.

Aaron casually pulled Ashley in front of him to shield the disturbing effect she was having on him. "Paul," he acknowledged casually.

"I hope I didn't disturb you?" The portly Revere smiled, his gaze enjoying Ashley's state of undress.

"Has something happened?"

Revere leaned forward, his grin widening "I understand you encountered some"—he glanced at Ashley—"trouble?"

"None that I can't handle."

"It was most opportune that one of our men spotted you and Mistress Wheeler heading in this direction," Revere reminded.

"Is there trouble?"

Paul's face sobered. "We have business to attend."

"Is it important?"

Paul nodded. "There is a meeting within the hour."

"Get dressed," Aaron instructed Ashley under his breath.

"But my dress is soaked."

"Do as I say."

Ashley waded out of the stream, retrieving her sodden dress on the way. After disappearing behind a bush, she pulled the dripping garment up over her hips and struggled to redo the long row of tiny buttons.

When she reappeared, Aaron was already mounted on his horse and waiting for her.

"I can't get my buttons fastened," she said meekly.

Dismounting, Aaron turned and refastened the row of buttons.

"You're awfully darn good at buttons," she accused. "You must get practice?"

He merely smiled, extending his hand to help her onto the horse.

Ashley adjusted her skirt over her bare leg primly and bit back the urge to add a *lot* of practice.

The horses galloped side by side as the trio rode back into Boston. Ashley's teeth were chattering by the time they reached the Green Dragon.

Dismounting quickly, Paul drew Aaron aside. "Mistress Wheeler should not be taken through the main entrance," he cautioned. "Her continued presence is sure to arouse suspicion."

Aaron glanced at Ashley, who was pacing now, trying to blow warmth into her frozen fingertips. "She is near exhaustion, Paul. Warren gave her a purge, and she is weak." Ashley saw the quick flicker of concern that crossed Revere's face. "She has eaten nothing, and she is sure to develop a chill. I want to secure a room—"

"No," Paul said shortly. "The wench will be provided with food and dry clothing, but she is to remain with us."

He rested his hand on Aaron's shoulder. "Beware of emotional involvements, my friend. 'Twould be sheer folly. We have a mission."

Aaron's gaze found Ashley again, and he knew Paul spoke the truth. But she was so small, and Warren's purge had made her so damn sick . . .

"There is a window in back," Paul said. "It would be best if you and the girl entered from there."

Nodding, Aaron turned and walked back to Ashley. "Come with me."

Ashley started toward the entrance, but Aaron reached out and pointed her around the side of the building.

"Where are you taking me? I thought we were going inside the tavern."

"We are."

"*This* way?" Jeez, these men were weird.

After pushing aside a row of bushes, Aaron waded through the thick undergrowth, pulling Ashley along behind him.

"Well, honestly!" Ashley gasped as a branch snapped back and hit her in the face. "What's wrong with going in the front door?"

"We cannot enter through the front door."

"Why not?"

"You talk too much."

"And you don't talk enough! Why can't we just walk in through the front door like any other rational human being?"

"Because, my dear, our situation isn't rational!"

The sound of twigs snapping and crunching did little to encourage the quiet entrance that Aaron was seeking. Actually, he was uncomfortable about dragging a woman through a prickly hedge, even if she was a spy. But he agreed with Paul that they should avoid vigilant eyes.

Upon emerging from the brush, Aaron spotted the small window on the far corner of the building. "There it is," he said quietly.

"There *what* is?" Ashley was busy picking twigs and leaves out of her hair. She was thoroughly put out with his caveman tactics. She'd love to get Gloria Steinem alone in a room with Paul Revere and Aaron Kenneman for just *five* minutes.

"There is the way we're going to enter the tavern."

Ashley looked at the window, then back at him. "You're kidding."

But as usual, he wasn't kidding.

Two minutes later Aaron was pushing her through the small window, warning her to remain quiet.

Dr. Warren glanced up from the conversation he was having with Hancock and Revere as Ashley slid through the window and dropped to the floor.

"Guess who's back," she quipped.

The men exchanged pained looks.

Brushing herself off, Ashley stepped aside as Aaron climbed through the window. When she glanced at the ceiling, she realized the tavernkeeper had indeed repaired the roof. She grinned as she imagined the questions he must have had about how the hole had gotten there.

"Ah, Kenneman, my good man. We've been expecting you," Warren greeted. Reaching for a Bible, he motioned for the men to gather around the table. "Gentlemen?"

The men placed their hands on the Bible and prepared to swear the oath that none would reveal the transactions of the meeting to any other than those present, Hancock,

Adams, Dr. Warren, Benjamin Church, and one or two others.

Ashley studied Church intently. What *was* it about that name? It was something important, she was sure, but it kept eluding her.

Warren fixed his gaze sternly on Ashley. "Mistress Wheeler, you will swear with us."

Ashley glanced expectantly at Aaron.

"You are privy to far too much information," he said quietly. "If you value honesty and truth, you will swear a vow on the Bible not to reveal anything of what you hear upon pain of death."

After stepping forward, Ashley placed her hand on the Bible and repeated the oath with the men. She felt like a complete fool, but she did it anyway.

Once the ritual was completed, Ashley moved back to the stove to warm herself as the men sat around the table and began to converse in low tones.

Easing nearer the table, Ashley strained to hear what the men were saying.

"The time grows near," Dr. Warren said gravely. "Boats for moving troops have been seen on the Charles River, and English scouts have been observed on the road to Lexington and Concord."

"You have this on good source?" Church asked.

"Aye. Rumor is spreading fast. A quick-witted stableboy overheard two officers making plans. We must be careful, but watchful too if we are to avoid being caught unaware."

A feeling of sadness came over Ashley as she suddenly remembered what she'd read about Dr. Warren.

Joseph Warren had delivered a Boston Massacre oration in 1772 in the Old South Church after John Adams had declined the invitation. Though his speech inspired no particular fervor, he delivered a second one in March 1775. It hardly seemed fair that he would never live to see his efforts in the revolution realized. History recorded that Dr. Joseph Warren would be killed in June, at the age of thirty-four, in the Battle of Bunker Hill—only a few weeks away.

In spite of their treatment of her, tears suddenly stung her eyes. These men were so fervent, so dedicated, so determined to do what they felt was right. It was sad that so many of them would give their lives for the cause.

Her gaze traveled to Church, and she stiffened, remembering suddenly why his name had bothered her so. Why, he was a—

"Mistress Wheeler."

Ashley glanced up. "Yes?"

Aaron walked toward her, his business concluded for the moment. "Paul has asked that we share the evening meal with his family."

"Oh." Ashley wondered how Rachel Revere would feel about having two unexpected guests at her dinner table. "I suppose we leave by the window?"

A smile played at the corners of Aaron's mouth. "It would seem that is the only way out."

Sighing, Ashley got to her feet. She was learning that keeping company with American patriots wasn't easy.

"Why, gracious me! Who have we here?"

Ashley jerked awake when the horse stopped in Revere's yard and Aaron slid off. Trying to blink the grit out of her eyes, she realized that she must have dozed off.

Yawning, she became aware of a woman not much older than herself coming down the steps. *Rachel Revere.*

Ashley couldn't tear her eyes away from the eighteenth-century woman.

"Sorry to intrude upon you this way, Rachel, but Paul assured me that you wouldn't mind." Aaron swung out of the saddle, then turned to lift Ashley down.

Their eyes met as he slowly lowered her to the ground. Ashley could have sworn she saw the first hint of compassion in the gray depths. His touch warmed her, and she had an inexplicable urge to linger in his arms.

She swayed as he released her, and she reached out to steady herself on his arm. Her knees were weak, and she felt faint with hunger after her ordeal.

"Put another chair at the table, Mother. We have company," Paul called as he handed the reins to one of the young boys who bounded out of the house at the sound of company arriving.

"So I see, dear." Rachel viewed Ashley's weary state with motherly concern. "Good heavens, child, you look exhausted! What have these two peagooses been doing with you?"

Both peagooses had been rude, she wanted to say, but didn't.

"Mistress Wheeler is going to take dinner with us tonight," Paul said as he walked over to steal a welcoming kiss from his wife. The two exchanged a brief, intimate smile before he gave her bottom an affectionate pat and moved on.

A small child clung to Rachel's skirt, and several more were running around in the yard. It looked as if school had let out, with all the yelping and shouting, but Ashley supposed that's the way any household with this many children would look.

"Dinner's on the table," Rachel promised as she turned

and walked back to the house. "I hope you like mutton and journey cakes!"

Taking her by the hand, Aaron led Ashley up the back steps to the Reveres' large kitchen.

As they entered the homey dwelling, the mouth-watering smell of meat roasting over a spit in the fireplace nearly overwhelmed Ashley. After the purge, she thought she'd never be able to eat again, but she found herself looking forward to the meal.

"Paul, I'm sure Mistress Wheeler would enjoy some hot water and a brush," Rachel called as she bustled about the kitchen, swatting youngsters' fingers away from the large bowls of food sitting on the cupboard.

"All right, Mama. Just let me get my boots off."

"Deborah." Rachel motioned to an older girl as she unhooked a large pot from a jiggin iron. "Fetch Mistress Wheeler some water, and be quick about it."

The girl ran off to fetch the water as Rachel called after her. "And bring my brush and comb when you come back!" She turned back to Ashley, smiling. "Sara will show you upstairs where you can tidy up."

Minutes later, Ashley found herself alone in the small bedroom shared by Paul and Rachel. There was hot water in the pitcher, and a coarse white washcloth and soap setting on the washstand.

Young Sara disappeared, then came back a few minutes later to provide a clean dress for Ashley. Overcome with gratitude, Ashley tried to thank the young woman, but Sara had flushed prettily and backed out of the room saying it really was no trouble.

When the door closed behind the young girl, Ashley turned and surveyed herself in the clouded looking glass hanging over the washstand. She winced, deciding that she'd never looked worse. After picking up the bar of soap, she scrubbed every inch of her body, and was relieved to find she was not lice-infested; then she dried herself on the coarse linen cloth that smelled of sunshine and fresh air.

When she went downstairs later, her hair had been brushed to a lustrous sheen, and she was wearing Sara's simple cotton dress. The green and white gingham was a bit loose in the waist and bodice and it tended to gap open if she wasn't careful, but at least it was clean—and free of vermin.

Rachel bustled by, carrying a large platter of mutton and a bowl of carrots. "Oh, my, you are a lovely one."

"Thank you," Ashley murmured, feeling awkward in the situation. By now Paul and Aaron would have explained her presence to Rachel, and Rachel would know that the men suspected her of being a spy.

"Come, supper's waiting," Rachel coaxed.

Aaron and Paul were already seated at the table, deep in conversation. The men seemed oblivious to the state of confusion as the children scrambled for seats.

Smiling, Ashley recalled that with each additional child, Paul simply added another chair around the table. Her smile widened upon seeing the various designs his artistic nature had crafted.

Aaron glanced up as she entered the room, and his features softened when he saw her improved appearance.

Meeting his gaze shyly, Ashley blushed as his eyes skimmed over the bodice. She found herself suddenly wondering if he was involved with a woman, and was startled by the sharp pang of jealousy the disturbing thought brought.

Rachel patted the back of the chair opposite Aaron. "Sit here, Mistress Wheeler."

"Please, call me Ashley," she murmured as she slid into the seat and prepared to look as unobtrusive as possible.

"Ashley? What a lovely name! Were you named after your mother?"

"No, Mom just heard the name in a movie once and liked it."

Rachel's smile wavered ever so slightly. "A movie?"

"Yes, it's . . ." Ashley lowered her gaze to her plate. "It's not important."

Rachel returned to the kitchen for a pan of journey cakes as if it didn't matter to her that Ashley-what-a-lovely-name was a *demented* British spy.

Folding her hands on her lap, Ashley let her gaze roam hungrily over the burdened table. The scent of sizzling mutton roast and boiled potatoes reminded her of how long it had been since she'd had a decent meal. The thick slices of cornbread and freshly churned butter were like ambrosia to her growling stomach.

Rachel took her seat, and Paul motioned for the children to quiet down.

The noise died away, and Paul turned to Aaron and said quietly, "It is good to have friends share our meal. We shall pray."

After joining hands, Paul said the prayer, asking the Lord to watch over them, particularly in the perilous days ahead.

When the prayer was finished, Ashley saw Rachel squeeze Paul's hand lovingly.

Bedlam broke loose as the adults' plates were filled, then the children's, and everyone turned his attention to the business of eating.

Once her initial hunger was satisfied, Ashley began to pay more attention to what was going on around her.

Turning to the small child seated next to her, Ashley smiled. "And what's your name?"

The boy lifted his fork, took careful aim, and let loose. A piece of hominy came sailing through the air and hit Ashley in the middle of the forehead.

"Joshua! Stop playing with your food. Mary, see to your brother," Rachel reprimanded sharply.

"Yes, Mama." Mary reached over and spooned a large gob of potatoes into the boy's mouth.

Discreetly wiping the back of her hand across her forehead, Ashley turned her attention to the friendly bickering going on between Paul and Aaron. Judging by their amicable banter, they had been good friends for a long time.

"Ah, we'll beat these Britishers as quickly as we whipped the French," Paul joked as he buttered his third piece of journey cake.

Rachel shook her head, an indulgent smile playing across her features as she passed the meat platter to Aaron. "Pay no heed to him, Aaron. You know how he prattles."

Aaron laughed, and Ashley decided she liked the sound. It was deep and masculine and sent little shivers fluttering through her. He was so powerfully attractive that she found herself just staring at him.

"But I agree, Rachel. It only took seventy years to send the French back home. We should turn the British back in a good deal less time."

Paul good-naturedly joined in Rachel and Aaron's laughter.

Ashley forked another potato, smiling as she silently

shared their lighthearted banter. The struggle between England and France in the New World had begun in 1690, lasted through four colonial wars, ending with the French and Indian Wars.

"Of course," Paul said. "It ended because they heard I was prepared to join the fray." He laughed heartily, recalling his youthful years. "When news spread that French soldiers along with the Indians were attacking the borders of the colonies, I clapped hat on my head and set off in search of excitement. Being twenty-one, I was prepared to defend Fort William Henry single-handed, if necessary. But alas, I spent the summer sitting around, cleaning my rifle, polishing my sword, and swatting flies! There were *thousands* of flies at Lake George the summer of fifty-six!"

Aaron laughed. "And it still took seven years for the French to realize the danger they were in!"

"Well, think how long the skirmish would have lagged on had I not determined to go!"

The men shared another laugh, and everyone at the table joined in as if something funny indeed had just transpired.

"Ah, 'twas a wonderful time," Paul recalled, his face alight with memories as he reached for the mug of white wine Rachel was pouring. As he lifted the cup to his mouth, his hand suddenly paused as he caught a glimpse of Ashley. "Do you care for basterd?" he inquired politely, though he was aware few women did.

Ashley frowned, wondering why he would ask her something so personal. "No, thanks—but I've dated my share," she confided.

Paul glanced at Aaron blankly, and they exchanged another odd look.

Shrugging, Paul lifted the glass of wine to his mouth as he continued the conversation, and Ashley realized he'd been referring to a crude wine the local people made themselves.

Ashley felt a sense of near envy as she listened to the companionable bantering. For the first time in her life, she saw how nice it would be to have a large, warm family like this one to come home to every night.

By the time the meal was finished, Ashley's head was nodding.

"We must go." Aaron's voice came to her through a drowsy mist. "She grows exceedingly weary."

Laying her hand on Aaron's shoulder, Rachel said softly, "You must treat her kindly, even though you suspect the worse."

"Rachel, have you ever known me not to treat a woman kindly?" Aaron rebuked.

Rachel took an affectionate swat at him. "I have known you to be the worst of scoundrels, Aaron Kenneman. Now see that you treat this lovely creature with respect!"

Aaron turned to gaze at Ashley, whose head by now had nearly fallen to her empty plate.

"I will treat her kindly," he conceded softly.

Stirring, Ashley murmured, "Thank you for the wonderful meal and for lending me a clean dress, Rachel." Ashley thrust her hand blindly into her bag, fumbling for the object she wanted. "I'd like you to have this." She extended her blue Cover Girl compact to Paul's wife.

"Oh, 'tis too much," Rachel cried, her eyes growing wide at the lovely offering.

Lifting her head, Ashley smiled sleepily. "Let me show you how it works." She snapped open the lid, displaying the small mirror and pressed powder. "See? You carry it with you to powder your nose. It isn't much, but you've been so nice . . ."

While Rachel oohed and ahhed, the children's eyes sparkled with delight as they gathered around their mother to view the fancy gift.

"By jove, 'tis a striking trinket!" Paul vowed as he perused the offering that could be found at any twentieth-century discount store for $3.79.

And "by jove," it wasn't *bad* for a spur-of-the-moment gift, Ashley realized when she saw the way Rachel's face gleamed for having received such a wondrous token.

And Ashley was only too happy to be able to give it to Rachel Revere. It was a minuscule, token repayment for a lovely dinner, unflagging kindness, and a gloriously *clean* dress.

7

The ride back to the Black Goat was bone chilling, the night dark and cold with a threat of rain in the air. Ashley's teeth were chattering by the time they reached the inn even though Aaron had stopped halfway back to insist that she wear his coat.

The tavern was filled with the usual rowdies as Aaron and Ashley threaded their way through the smoky room.

"Aye, gov'nor! You've not had your fill of the doxy?" one man jested loudly.

"Back to give 'er a quick flourish, aye, Doc?"

Aaron smiled, waving away the men's ribald comments. He moved Ashley determinedly toward the narrow staircase.

"And what does 'flourish' mean?" Ashley muttered beneath her breath. She was learning that eighteenth-century words didn't mean exactly what they meant in the twentieth.

Aaron rested his hand on the small of her back as they began to climb the steps.

"Well? What's it mean?"

" 'Well,' " he mocked, "you don't care to know."

The room they were sharing was even smaller than Ashley remembered. The bed seemed to dominate the room tonight. The more she was with Kenneman, the more acutely aware she was of what an alluring man he was. If circumstances were different, she might find him extremely desirable.

After closing the door, Aaron tossed the key on the dresser. Ashley walked to the rocker and sat down, her eyes drifting shut with fatigue as he struck a flint to the linen wick laying in the shallow, metal, grease-filled dish. She was so tired her hair hurt. She was desperate for sleep, yet she couldn't bear the thought of spending another night in the chair.

"Has anyone decided what they're going to do with me?" She pulled the clip from her hair, then ran her fingers over her scalp, basking in the relief the motion had provided.

When Aaron didn't answer, she opened her eyes to confront him. "Well?"

He had seated himself on the bed and was beginning to remove his boots. She could see that he planned to ignore the question.

"Are we going to play 'let's not answer Ashley' again?"

After tossing the second boot aside, he reached inside his coat pocket for a smoke. "It has been decided."

She sat up straighter. "It has?" Her pulse quickened. "When?"

"This afternoon."

"At the Green Dragon?"

"Yes."

Ashley wasn't aware that the men had discussed her plight. She thought they had been talking about the British again. Her eyes narrowed. Oh, they were so sneaky. She thought she had heard everything they'd said, but apparently she hadn't.

"What are they going to do with me?"

Her heart was hammering now. Had they decided to hang her? Or worse, were they going to subject her to a ducking stool where passersby could throw objects or insults at her? She glanced at Aaron. No, he wouldn't permit them to do that to her—would he?

"It is nothing for you to be concerned about," he said quietly.

"Nothing for me to be concerned about!" Ashley scrambled to her feet and began pacing. *Nothing for her to be concerned about!* "*What* are you planning to do with me?"

"Wring your troublesome neck like a Sunday chicken." Aaron stood up and moved to the window, trying to cover his amusement. She had been a disreputable-looking sight when Warren had rescued her from the jail. Laughable, actually, if she hadn't been so ill. Dirty, pale from the dose of puke, the spunk had been momentarily taken out of her. But she had quickly regained her spirit. He would have to watch her even more closely or she would be sure to attempt another ill-advised escape.

His features sobered as he stared down on the darkened street. His orders were to return Ashley Wheeler to Gage at first light, in any form he deemed suitable. The muscle in his jaw pulsed as he thought about the responsibility he'd been assigned. He could kill her swiftly—which could prove to be messy and not particularly to his liking—or he could return her to Gage unharmed but knowing she knew more than she should about the colonists' plan to thwart the British. The choice, as well as the consequences of error, would be solely his. He frowned, knowing that he had already made his choice. He would see that no harm came to her.

Ashley suddenly stopped pacing and turned to face him. "I demand to know what you plan to do."

Aaron walked to the table, lifted the betty lamp, and lit his smoke.

"Are you going to . . . kill me?" she asked softly.

His eyes met hers. "You are not to concern yourself with fate. Whatever my plans, you cannot alter them." There it was again, that strange irrepressible urge to protect her when she looked at him with her innocent, wide eyes. *Forget her, Kenneman. The matter is out of your hands.*

Sinking back onto the chair, Ashley swallowed the lump of fear crowding her throat, her mind churning feverishly. If she was to be done away with, it would have to be soon. Paul Revere was fated to make his famous ride the following night.

Seeing her distress, Aaron rested his hand on her shoulder. "Sleep, little one."

Ashley stood and moved woodenly toward the bed. If this was to be her last night, she planned to spend it sleeping in a real bed. After throwing back the coverlet, she peeled out of her dress and crawled wearily between the rough sheets. "You might as well sleep with me," she offered quietly.

Aaron's hand paused on the way to his mouth for another draw off his smoke. He glanced at the dress pooled around his boots, then back to her.

Drawing the pillow over her head, Ashley wondered if she should have phrased the offer differently. She wasn't inviting him to "sleep with her," only to share the bed. There was no reason for both of them to lose another night's sleep. The way it sounded, they would both need their strength come morning.

Viewing her discarded dress, Aaron was annoyed to see his hand begin to shake. Dammit. Was she actually inviting him to her bed? *Dammit.* He couldn't go—he couldn't sleep with a spy.

His eyes moved from the dress, then back to the bed, the memory of her satiny body and those damn things she called "panties" and "bra" floating before his eyes.

He turned to stare out of the window again.

"Are you coming to bed?"

He stiffened as her muffled voice penetrated his thoughts. "Not now."

"You'd better, it's getting very late."

Then again, he thought, who would know if he momentarily succumbed to her charm? Perhaps on the morrow he could take her to the Anglican clergy and entrust her to their safekeeping until he could best decide her fate. Once there, she would be out of the way, properly provided for, and he could be assured that she would not be carrying information back to Gage.

His gaze traveled back to her shapely form lying beneath the blanket. No reasonable man would condemn him for so small and meaningless a lapse of discretion, so why not seize the opportunity to pass the hours until dawn in a most pleasurable diversion?

Half asleep, Ashley felt the straw ticking move a moment later as Aaron eased between the sheets beside her.

"*Don't* take your half out of the middle," she murmured drowsily.

"What?"

"Don't hog the middle of the bed."

Aaron lay back, frowning. Hog the middle of the bed? Was she now implying that he was a swine? She was a puzzling wench!

He settled beneath the blanket, patiently waiting for her to make the first advance. Since she had suggested the romp, he would let her seize the initiative.

When several minutes had passed and the expected overture failed to materialize, his hand arbitrarily crept over to caress her bare thigh.

Ashley's eyes opened slowly as his fingers ambled guilelessly up over her buttocks, pausing here and there to become a little more venturesome.

Lying very still, Ashley waited to see just how far he would go before she knocked his conceited head off.

Aaron smiled as he detected her bewitching attempt to feign shyness. "God's teeth, you are a winsome noodle," he teased as his hand became even bolder.

Pulling himself closer, he let his wandering hand find her breast, and he cradled it. "Your invitation was unexpected, but I concede it will be a most pleasant diversion," he murmured as he nuzzled her neck.

After rolling her onto her back, he covered her mouth with his with an intensity that jolted her. Her first thought was to stop him; her second was more reticent as his tongue met hers. He took her hand and slid it down the front of his body, allowing it to rest on his manhood. "Would you not agree, my lovely?"

Sitting up, she slapped him hard.

Stunned, he moved his hand to his cheek as he sat up and glared back at her. "*What* was that for?"

"I'm trying to sleep."

"But . . . you invited *me* into the bed," he accused.

"To *sleep,* not to fool around!"

"*Fool* around?" Aaron was not acquainted with the strange parlance. "What does this expression, 'fool around,' mean?"

"It means you struck out. Now, if you want to live until morning, keep your hands to yourself." Ashley dropped back onto the pillow and jerked the blanket tightly back in place. "And stay on your own side."

" 'Twould be a *pleasure!*" He snatched the blanket to him as he rolled to his side. 'Twas a rare time Aaron Kenneman "struck out." Whatever the hell that meant.

She yanked the blanket back.

He grabbed it away again.

Exasperated, she hauled it back with a scathing obscenity that made him reconsider repeating that mistake a third time.

The room grew quiet as the two surly inhabitants of the bed tried to sleep. An hour passed, a restless hour spent tossing and turning.

"Aaron?"

Aaron tensed as her voice broke into his semiconscious state. "What?"

"Do you have someone you care about?" Ashley knew a man as attractive as Aaron Kenneman must have someone he cared about, who cared about him. Yet somehow she hoped he wasn't involved. If he said he was, she would feel oddly betrayed somehow, and that she knew was ridiculous. "A girlfriend?"

"Girlfriend?"

Ashley sighed, realizing that communication between them was at a strong disadvantage. "You know, a female friend . . . a regular female companion you see frequently?"

" 'Tis none of your concern." He shifted to his side, his male ego still sorely wounded from her rebuff.

Just as stubborn, Ashley wiggled closer to her side of the bed to keep from touching him. " 'Tis too. If we have to be stuck with each other, what's wrong with knowing something about each other?"

"Why does it matter?"

"It doesn't, but since neither one of us can sleep, what can it hurt? We don't have to discuss anything that would make you uncomfortable."

When he was still silent, she nudged him with her toe. "What about it?"

"What about what?"

"Do you have a lady friend?"

"No."

"Are you sure?"

"Unless someone has given me one and I'm not aware of it, I don't have."

She lay staring into the darkness, wondering if he was telling the truth. There was something in the tone of his voice that made her skeptical. "But you did have."

When he failed to respond, she poked him with her toe again. "Didn't you?"

"Do I have a female companion that I see frequently?"

"Yes?"

"No."

"But *did* you have?" Men had not changed a wit in the last two hundred years. Women still had to drag answers out of them.

"At one time," he finally conceded.

"What happened?"

"We aren't going to discuss anything personal."

"What's so personal about wanting to know just a little about the girl you saw on frequent occasions?"

"We had a disagreement."

Curious now, Ashley rolled onto her back. He was so close she could feel the warmth of his body, and she decided she liked the feeling. After all, he was an extremely attractive man, and she felt wonderfully protected when she was with him, even though she didn't have the slightest idea what morning would bring. "What's she like?" she asked softly.

He was silent for so long Ashley thought he wasn't going to answer again. When he finally broke the silence, it was as if he was speaking to himself. "She's lovely. Like you."

Ashley smiled at the ambiguous compliment. So, his heart belonged to another, she thought, and wondered why the admission would bring about such an ache of longing inside her. Propping up on her elbow, she gazed at him. "How did you meet?"

"We've known each other since we were children," he said quietly.

"And you loved her?"

"We were to be married."

"What happened?"

"My duties kept me away much of the time. As a doctor, it is necessary for me to be available no matter what the day or hour. Quite often my life isn't my own. There were too many times in my work that prevented me from escorting her to various social events she thought important to us both, and she soon despaired that I would ever be available to share in her life."

Ashley flushed, only too aware that she had broken her engagement to Joel for precisely the same reason. It was uncanny the way their lives seemed to parallel.

Aaron's arm bumped hers as he rolled onto his back and laced his fingers behind his head. He gazed into the darkness, surprised that he could talk so easily about Anna now. "There was always a valid reason why I couldn't be with her. My work, loyalty to my country . . . Anna was patient at first, then she . . ." His voice faded. "She was right to break the engagement," he conceded.

Ashley found his hand in the darkness and squeezed it reassuringly. "I'm sure the decision was very painful for her."

"Mayhap. But I should have taken more time with her."

"Is it too late?"

"I don't know . . . this damned war with England seems to be going on and on and on." Frustration was evident in his voice now, and he pushed his fingers through his hair distractedly. "It never stops. As soon as one problem is corrected, there are two more to take its place. We cannot allow England to own us! We are not indentured to the British. We cannot permit ourselves to assume the burden of supporting another nation. We are to conduct our own lives, and conduct them as we see fit. We *will* persevere," he vowed tightly.

Turning onto her side, she rested her hand against his chest. "Don't worry, you *will*," she whispered. "You must continue to fight and you *will* win, in the end."

Compelled by the conviction in her voice, he caught her hand, holding it tightly. "How can you make such predictions when you know nothing of the future?"

"But I do know the future," she returned softly. Their gazes met in the darkness, and though she couldn't see into his eyes, she knew the confusion she would find there.

"*Who* are you?" he whispered.

"Would you believe me if I told you?"

"I'm not sure . . . yet I will try."

"I'm not really crazy, you know."

His lips curved with a wry smile. "I admit that at times that is difficult to believe."

She smiled, aware that she'd done some pretty crazy things since this had all started. As the silence lengthened, Ashley sensed that he was torn by loyalty yet consumed with curiosity. He was a smart man. He knew the things she did and said were peculiar, yet she had caught the look of interest in his eyes each time she had prophesied the future.

"Tell me who you are." He finally yielded.

"All right." Taking a deep breath, Ashley closed her eyes, praying that she would somehow find the words to convince him of who she was. "My name is Ashley Wheeler. I live in Boston—only not the Boston you know." She reached for his hand again, holding it tightly. "Are you with me up to this point?"

"Continue."

"Yesterday—or maybe the day before—I've lost all track of time," she confessed, "but I was working at my second job in an eighteenth-century museum in Boston when it started to rain. The windows on my car were—"

"Car?" He stopped her.

"Yes, car—motor vehicle . . . a piece of mechanized equipment?"

"I do not know of this . . . car."

"No, you wouldn't," she conceded. "But we'll get back to that later. Anyway, I was going out to roll the windows up on my car when I slipped on the stairs and fell. When I reached the bottom of the stairs . . . well, that's when I met you." Her grip tightened. "Are you ready for this?"

His hand returned the pressure lightly. "Continue."

"The day I fell was April 15, 1992."

His grasp suddenly went lax.

"Don't be afraid," she urged. "I know it's impossible to understand, and I can't even begin to explain what's happened, but I'm *not* a spy and I'm *not* crazy. I've thought for the longest time that I was having a dream and I just couldn't wake up, but if that's true, the dream just goes on and on, and now I'm not so sure."

"Nineteen ninety-two," he repeated, stunned. "*Two* hundred and seventeen years into the future?"

"It is incredible," she agreed. "Oh, Aaron, there's so much I could tell you about the future! The marvels in medicine and transportation—we have automobiles with air bags and jet airplanes that fly faster than the speed of sound—"

"*Sound* travels?" he echoed incredulously.

"Yes! Yes, it really does! And we've even put a man on the moon! Right at this minute the American flag is proudly waving on the surface of the moon where Buzz Aldrin put it!"

"The American flag is flying on the *moon?*" he repeated, even more distressed. "Who is Buzz Aldrin?"

"He's an astronaut—oh dear, you don't know what an astronaut is either—but the flag has fifty stars on it now, not thirteen!"

Aaron was trying to comprehend what she was saying, but it was impossible. She spoke unsurpassed nonsense, yet he was sorely tempted to believe her.

"The British?" he interjected.

"Oh, don't worry about the British," she soothed. "Let's see—what is the date today?"

"The seventeenth."

"The British will come by sea tomorrow night," she

promised. "And they will put up a darn good fight, but you'll whip their butts *but* good. When you said no more taxes, you guys meant it!" She grinned, hugging his neck. "I'm so proud of you!"

He grinned, lamely hugging her back but not having the slightest idea of what she was talking about.

"Listen." Her face sobered. "You did a wonderful job, but I'm afraid America is right back in the same shape we were two hundred and seventeen years ago."

"The British are overtaxing you?"

"No, it's our *own* government this time. Isn't *that* ironic?"

Lying back on the pillow, she sighed, relieved to finally have cleared the air. She wasn't sure why, but she felt that he believed what she had told him. At least now he knew that she wasn't a spy, and she could sleep tonight without the fear of impending doom in the morning. Her muscles relaxed, sheer exhaustion overtaking her now. Tomorrow she would wake up and be in her own bed, and she would laugh about all that had happened.

Her hand reached to assure herself that Aaron was still beside her, and she suddenly felt very sad. Tomorrow he would surely be gone.

Aaron settled back beneath the covers, trying to absorb the wonders of which she had spoken. Automobiles, aireo-planes, and an American flag with fifty stars. He shook his head in amazement. Was it possible she was telling the truth? No, 'tis folly! Such a world did not and *could* not exist, he reasoned. And the British arriving by sea on the morrow—they wouldn't dare! Though they threatened, they would not be so bold! No, Ashley Wheeler was lovely, but she knew not of what she spoke.

A moment later Ashley felt his hand creep back to her thigh.

Irritably slapping it aside again, she mumbled something about having a headache and rolled over, dropping off to sleep instantly.

8

The sun was just barely up when Ashley stirred the next morning. She'd hoped that the next time she opened her eyes she'd awaken back in her own bed. Doomsday had arrived right on time, she thought. Aaron was sure to do away with her today.

She opened her eyes slowly and wasn't surprised to find Aaron standing at the window, staring down at the street reflectively.

"What time is it?" she murmured.

"Time for lazy women to be up and about."

Lifting her head, Ashley tried to focus her eyes on the hands of her watch. "Six o'clock?" Gad, the man kept *dreadful* hours. Groaning, she let her head drop back to the pillow. "I'm sleeping in this morning."

Aaron turned from the window and whacked her across the bottom as he walked to the washstand. "I don't know what you mean by 'sleeping in,' but if it means what I assume it to mean, I can assure you you aren't."

"Uh-huh," she countered.

His gaze ran lazily over the shapely outline of her backside beneath the blanket. "This 'uh-huh' word. It means yes?"

"Uh-huh."

"Time to get up, Mistress Wheeler."

"Huh-uh."

" 'Huh-uh' means no?"

"Uh-huh."

" 'Uh-huh,' yes?"

"Uh-huh."

"Huh-uh, no."

"Uh-huh."

Ashley grabbed for the cover as he quickly yanked it off her and tossed it on the floor. "Please"—she groaned— "just *ten* more minutes!"

"Up, woman, we have business to attend to."

Bolting up, she glared at him. "I'm exhausted. I didn't sleep five minutes last night," she accused.

His eyes centered on her disheveled hair. "Then who was snoring?"

"Snoring!" She drew back, offended. "I wasn't . . ." she denied lamely.

He absently smoothed the horrific rooster's tail that had formed at the crown of her head before he returned to the wash bowl. "Then mayhap we had a mouse in bed with us —a very worrisome little creature who wheezed and blew and—" He ducked as a pillow came sailing toward him.

Pouring fresh water into the bowl, he watched as Ashley settled back on the pillow, closing her eyes again.

Gradually she became aware of the mouth-watering aroma of meat and potatoes wafting lightly on the air. Cracking one eye open, she saw a large tray laden with eggs, meat, bread, potatoes, and large, red ripe strawberries set on a table beside the bed.

She sat up, reached for one of the strawberries, and popped it into her mouth.

"You have five minutes to dress and be ready to leave," Aaron warned.

"Where am I going?" she asked tauntingly. "To the *gallows*?"

"Mayhap."

"Mayhap, mayhap," she mimicked, wondering why, if she had to dream, it couldn't have been in 2075 instead of 1775. She dropped back onto the pillow and pulled the blanket over her head.

As Aaron washed and shaved, she dozed, wondering what he *really* planned to do with her this morning. The appointed hour of doom had arrived, and he didn't look like a man who was about to commit murder. If for one moment she thought he would actually harm her, she would be terrified, but she wasn't. Though Aaron's commitment to protecting his country was apparent, she didn't think that he would take any pleasure in harming a woman. And besides, she had seen the glint of interest in his eye when he'd looked at her, and she had to admit that she was beginning to like it.

"Are you going to get up?" he asked again.

Rolling to her side, she stretched lazily, deciding to aggravate him a little. "Huh-uh."

As he leaned closer to the looking glass, Aaron pretended to ignore her attempts to incite him. He'd never met a woman like Ashley Wheeler; he didn't know why he had to now.

Wiggling her toes, Ashley sank deeper into the straw ticking, relishing the feel of having the whole bed to herself. If he would just go off and do whatever American patriots did, she could sleep all day.

"Are you comfortable?" His eyes studied her reflection in the mirror as he dipped the razor back into the water.

"Verrry, verrry, very, very."

"Mayhap you wish me to rejoin you," he offered pleasantly.

"Mmm, mayhap I don't," she warned, recalling how, because of his roving hands, she'd spent another virtually sleepless night.

"Ah, but I must if you are not out of that bed in two minutes."

Yawning, Ashley wiggled to the edge of the bed to select something from the tray. As she brought the berry lazily to her mouth, her hand suddenly froze as she saw him calmly unbutton his breeches.

"What are you doing?"

"If you are intent on staying in bed, then I shall join you."

Her eyes widened as his pants dropped to the floor, revealing a set of strong, muscular legs coated with light-brown hair.

Hurriedly scooting back to the center of the bed, she watched him warily. "You wouldn't."

He smiled as his hands reached for the laces on his shirtfront. "Ah, but you do misunderstand me, Mistress Wheeler. Actually, I find the thought of spending the day in bed with a woman quite appealing." His eyes grew darker as they skimmed the pale-pink bra and the tempting swell beneath the transparent fabric. "Extremely appealing."

"Any woman, Dr. Kenneman, or just me?" she mocked, wondering why she would be crazy enough to play such a dangerous game with him. There was a hungry, predatory look in his eye, one that hadn't been there earlier.

"Ah, you wish to play games, Mistress Wheeler?" He pulled his shirt over his head and Ashley was stunned by the sight of this *superb* specimen of manhood. Her gaze lingered on the thick mat of hair that spread across his breastbone, then spiraled lower and lower.

"Or do you merely intend to test me?" he countered in a deceptively negligent tone. "If it is the latter, then 'twould be wise that you reconsider."

His hand moved to remove the last of his clothing as Ashley quickly scrambled out of bed. After fumbling for her discarded dress, she slid it over her head, crammed her feet into the buckled slippers, and was standing by the door, ready to leave, in exactly one minute and twenty-five seconds flat.

Calmly reaching for his breeches, Aaron commented, "I thought you might see it my way, Mistress Wheeler."

"You are the worst male *chauvinist pig* I've ever met, Dr. Kenneman!"

His brows lifted mildly. "I am to assume I have been insulted?"

"You can safely assume that you have."

He nodded graciously. "And never by one so lovely."

Ashley snatched up her bag and followed him down the stairway a few minutes later, wondering how she could find him so damned attractive.

Ashley clung to Aaron's waist with every breathtaking turn of the road, fearing that he was going to kill them both. He seemed to know only one way to ride a horse: fast.

"The name Willie Shoemaker doesn't ring a bell with you, does it?" she called.

"Who?"

"Never mind!"

When the horse left the shabby inn district and headed

for the open road, her fingers relaxed her hold on his waist. At least he hadn't chosen public humiliation and death as the choice of punishment, she thought with relief.

Some twenty minutes later, the horse turned up a cool shady lane where trees grew thick along the road. Straight ahead, Ashley could see the roof of a house nestled in a small clearing.

"Where are we?"

"This is where I live."

"Your house?" She was relieved at first, then, on second thought, her pulse double-timed. Her fingers dug into his waist fearfully. Had he brought her out here to do away with her discreetly? Out here where there wasn't a sign of another person, where her screams for mercy would never be heard?

"Damn! Will you stop gouging me?" Aaron squirmed, trying to break her painful hold on his waist.

Ashley murmured her apology, unaware that she had been squeezing him like a lemon. "Why are we here? I want to go back to the Black Goat," she demanded.

"No, you don't."

"Yes, I do!"

After riding up to the house, Aaron reined in the horse and climbed out of the saddle. He lifted Ashley down, hurriedly turning her in the direction of a small shed at the side of the house.

"Will you walk!" he demanded impatiently when her feet failed to respond.

"No." Her heart was beating like a jackhammer. "Please let me go," she whimpered.

But her plea fell on deaf ears. Her feet felt like two blocks of concrete as he began to drag her along the overgrown path. Her heels stubbornly dug into the dirt as her eyes fixed on the shed. How was he going to kill her? A single ball from a musket to the head? A clean slit across her throat? A brief moment with his strong hands around her neck?

Or would he be less merciful? What if he just decided to tie her up and leave her in the shed to die of starvation? No one would hear her screams; no one would come to rescue her. Or maybe he would club her senseless, then leave her to die, alone and bleeding. Oh, how could she have been so foolish to feel secure with him! She should have tried to escape again. Maybe she still could . . .

The shed loomed closer, and Ashley willed herself not to faint. She had to talk him out of it. Somehow she had to bargain with him, maybe offer to tell him the British plans even if that resulted in completely modifying history. She wracked her brain. What were the British getting ready to do one day before Paul Revere's ride?

As he hauled her up to the shed, Aaron quickly fumbled with the front of his breeches.

Oh, Lord! He was going to rape her first!

Grasping the door to the shed with one hand, he pointed at her sternly. "You stay right here. Do you understand?"

She nodded vacantly, fighting to keep from passing out. Did he have to prepare for her murder? Sharpen knives? Load guns?

He stepped inside the small building, and a moment later she collapsed against the side of the shed, nearly fainting with relief when she heard him relieving himself. An *outhouse*.

Leaning against the wall, she felt hysteria bubbling inside her. It wasn't a shed he was going to kill her in, it was an *outhouse!*

Aaron emerged a moment later and found her giggling almost hysterically.

"I hardly think a gentleman going to the jakes is an occasion for such merriment," he admonished.

"You would"—Ashley gasped, trying to catch her breath—"if you had thought you were about to be murdered!"

He frowned. "Murdered?"

"Yes . . . I thought that was what you had brought me out here to do!"

"If I were to murder you, it wouldn't be in the necessary," he said indignantly. Color stung his cheeks now.

With a grin, she reached out and pulled his nose affectionately. "I don't think you're going to do it anywhere."

He drew back, affronted. "Are *all* women in your century like you?"

"Only the good ones," she assured solemnly.

Turning, he walked back down the narrow path that led through a tall hedge.

Ashley meekly followed behind, still snickering.

"I thought you'd live in town."

"No. I'm an outliver."

"What's an 'outliver'?"

"Someone who lives near the outskirts of the town. I've loved this house since I was a small child. I finally was able to purchase it a few years ago."

Ashley had somehow pictured Aaron living in a small, quaint cottage in the middle of Boston, but this house was large and quite grand.

The tall, two-story building with a gambrel roof had a

wide front door framed by carved pilasters and capped by a graceful swan's-neck pediment with ornamental rosettes. Two windows were set on either side of the door with four above on the upper story. The house resembled the pictures of saltbox houses she had seen at the museum.

"But it's so large for one person!"

Aaron shrugged. "It will be filled with children someday."

"Yours and who else's?" she teased.

He ignored the comment as they climbed the steps together, and he opened the door.

Entering the house, Ashley was filled with curiosity. The inside was every bit as elegant as the outside. The spacious entry hall had a rich dark wainscoting that extended to a tasteful room to the right of the entry.

"Is that a drawing room?"

Aaron smiled as she stepped inside the room just off the hallway. There was a crystal lamp on a table in front of the window, flanked by two chairs. Two wing chairs and a sofa were setting on a blue rug situated near the fireplace, and several pieces that would be priceless antiques in her day were scattered throughout the room.

"It's lovely," she murmured, reaching out to touch one of the polished oak tables.

"I find it comfortable."

"Did you know the former owners?"

"Yes, they passed on several years ago."

Ashley followed Aaron to the next room and peeked inside. This room looked cozy. A spinning wheel had been shoved into a corner. A large desk, littered with papers and various accounting records tucked into its cubbyholes, was set near the fireplace. A poker resting against the stone face made Ashley think that this fireplace was the one most frequently used.

"I bet this is where you work," she guessed.

She moved to the silk sampler hanging on the wall over the desk and read the inscription aloud: *"Agatha Benchly born May 27, 1710, died 1770. Jonathan Benchly born August 12, 1705, died 1770."*

Turning, she looked at Aaron. "Why, they died the same year."

"The same day," Aaron said. "Agatha and Jonathan's sons inherited the farm upon the deaths of their parents. The boys were a greedy lot and they couldn't come to terms on how to disperse the land, so they decided to split it. Consequently, I was able to purchase the house and a few acres. I had the samplers made in Agatha and Jonathan's memory. Come, the kitchen is this way."

Clasping her hands behind her back, Ashley took a peek up the stairway as they walked past, wondering if he would choose to show her his bedroom.

As they entered the kitchen, she saw a wide, deep fireplace with a very long mantel. A variety of iron rods rested against the wall flanking the fireplace, along with a couple of large trivets upon which the pots were placed after they cooked over coals. A hook set into the stone held a variety of small skewers, and a blackened teakettle rested on a trivet on top of a cold fire. In the middle of one wall, there was a tall chest, and its open door revealed a collection of small crockery pieces. A pot with a lid was setting on the floor nearby as if the owner of the house had simply run out of room to store the crockery.

In the center of the room was a table with four ladder-back chairs. Centered on the table were two silver candlesticks, a small lamp, and a pewter pitcher.

Ashley picked up one of the candlesticks, marveling at its excellent craftsmanship.

"A gift from Paul," Aaron remarked.

"It's priceless," she murmured, carefully returning the candlestick to its resting place.

Aaron was busy now trying to coax a fire from some kindling taken from a small box beside the fireplace.

"You've been gone several days. What do your patients do when that happens?"

"It doesn't happen often." He rose, dusting off his hands. "But I have been remiss the past two days. I must see to a few this afternoon."

"Do I have to go with you?"

"If I permitted you to stay here in the house, could I trust you?" His gaze caught hers, and she made no attempt to look away.

"Yes . . . I would do as you say."

"You will do nothing to draw attention, either to me or to you?"

"No, I promise."

"Then I will allow you stay. I thought mayhap you'd like a bath."

"Oh." She wilted with relief. "I would *love* a bath."

His gaze grew softer. "I will bring in the tub and fill it. We will heat water to temper the cold."

"That would be heavenly. May I help?"

"No, 'tis man's work."

She smiled as he turned to leave. "I shouldn't be gone long. The middle door leads to a large pantry. While I'm away, you might heat some pottage. When I return, we could have some with bread and quiddany."

"Quiddany?" Ashley winced.

"Yes . . . a quince marmalade. Mrs. Bandy keeps me supplied with small foodstuff."

"Mrs. Bandy? A friendly neighbor?" Ashley bantered with lifted brow.

"An old widow lady." He winked. "She cleans occasionally and bakes. Makes a fine jumbal."

"Jumbal," Ashley repeated.

"A small sugar cake."

"Like a cookie!"

"Mayhap," he said patiently.

"I'll find everything, don't worry."

"The pantry is well stocked. Some liberty tea would be welcome and there may be a puffet or two, if you're too hungry to wait for my return."

"Right. A puffet."

He grinned. "Another small cake."

"Oh."

"Will you be safe while I'm gone?"

"I don't know. Maybe safer than I would be if you were here," she countered, recalling her earlier fright at the outhouse.

His features softened. "I will not hurt you."

"I know." She smiled as the invisible bond between them grew stronger.

"You could come with me," he suggested.

"No, I'll wait here, thank you."

While he was gone, she puttered around the kitchen, exploring the pantry and cooking utensils.

When he returned a few minutes later, he was carrying a huge copper tub, which he set in front of the fireplace.

Ashley smiled as she viewed the tub. Any antique dealer would give his eyeteeth to have it!

"I'll take the piggin and begin filling the tub, while the

pot of water heats." Aaron reached for the small wooden pail with an erect handle. "There's some soft soap that Mrs. Bandy provides. You'll find it easier to lather than the bar," he told her with a teasing glint in his eye.

"If I remember," Ashley returned saucily, "I didn't get much of an opportunity to try."

"No, and you would have had considerably less if Paul hadn't arrived." He gave a decidedly wicked chuckle when he saw her cheeks turn pink.

After filling a large pot, he set it on a trivet in the fireplace, then made the trip to the well several times to fill the tub.

Finally it was half full, and Aaron rolled his sleeves down. "I must see about my patients."

Clasping her hands behind her back, Ashley walked to the door with him. She suddenly felt very domestic, as if they were married and she was seeing him off to work. "Will you be gone long?"

"I hope to return by early afternoon."

After helping him into his coat, she brushed away an imaginary speck of lint. "I'll take a bath, then fix us something to eat. By then you should be back."

He turned, and their eyes met again. "You are to be alert. Do not open the door to anyone."

"I won't."

He started off the porch, but her softly spoken request stopped him. "Aaron."

Pausing, he said quietly, "Yes?"

"You be careful too."

While the water was heating, Ashley explored the downstairs of the house. She smiled as she viewed the carnage of bachelor living: dishes scattered randomly throughout the house, a pair of muddy boots in the drawing room, a discarded pair of blue socks with holes in both heels. What Aaron Kenneman needed was a wife, she decided.

She picked up one of the five shirts that was draped over a chair and hugged it close to her, drinking in his familiar scent. The dream was becoming painful now. She was falling deeply in love with this strange man, and she was powerless to stop it. Her feelings were much stronger than she had ever experienced before, yet she knew that he wasn't real. When she awoke, he would be gone. The thought was so frightening that Ashley quickly forced it aside.

A knock suddenly sounded at the door, startling her.

Swiping guiltily at the tears that had sprung to her eyes, she hurried to answer it. Her hand was on the latch when Aaron's earlier warning came back to her. *Do not open the door to anyone.*

"Aaron?" a woman's voice called. The knock sounded again.

Ashley waited, hoping whoever it was would go away.

"Aaron? Are you sleeping? Wake up, sleepyhead!"

Deciding that it was a friendly caller, Ashley unlatched the door and peeked out through the crack. "Dr. Kenneman isn't here," she murmured.

A pair of the most beautiful amethyst eyes looked back at her. "Oh? Where is he?"

"Making house calls."

The stunning young woman smiled. "And who might you be?"

"I'm . . . just visiting." She was not to call attention to herself or to Aaron.

"Oh? A niece, mayhap?"

"Yes . . . that's it. A niece."

"Well, tell Aaron that I called." The woman extended a basket that contained two loaves of bread and a jar of jam. "Tell him I'm sorry to have missed him, and I'll return again late tomorrow afternoon."

Ashley opened the door just wide enough to accept the basket, then closed it again quickly.

Remembering her manners, she called through the heavy wood. "Who should I say called?"

"Elizabeth Bandy" came the muffled reply.

"The *widow* Bandy?"

"Yes."

"I'll tell him."

The dirty rat.

9

Twenty minutes later Ashley settled deep into a tub of hot water. For several minutes she lay soaking away the weariness and grime of the past few hectic hours.

It was close to an hour before she could find enough energy to scrub her hair. Dipping cups of water from the water pail, she rinsed her hair clean, then forced herself out of the water that by now had grown cold.

After washing her clothes in the remaining hot water, she hung them to dry near the fireplace. Aaron had provided her with a thick robe, though it was big enough to wrap around her twice.

She was thinking about brewing the tea when another knock sounded at the door. Frowning, she set the teakettle aside. Aaron had said not to answer the door for anyone.

The knock came again, more urgent this time. "Doctor! Doctor?"

After sneaking to the window, Ashley pulled the curtain aside and saw a woman and a young girl standing on the porch.

Ashley dropped the curtain back into place and walked to the door. If it was another one of Aaron's friendly "widows," she was going to scream.

Opening the door, she smiled. "May I help you?"

"The Doctor . . . would he be in?" the woman asked.

"No, I'm afraid not. He should be back soon though."

The young girl accompanying the woman suddenly groaned and doubled over with pain. "Ohhh . . . do *something,* Momma!"

"Oh, dear," the woman fretted. She began to wring her hands as the gangly girl dropped to her knees, her moans becoming louder.

"What's . . . the trouble?" Ashley asked hesitantly. The girl seemed to be in a good deal of pain.

Glancing about nervously, the woman leaned closer, whispering. "It's her monthly miseries. 'Tis worse than usual."

"Oh." Ashley winced as she watched the girl writhing in pain at her feet.

"I thought the doctor might know what to do," the woman confided. "We've walked such a long ways."

"Well." Ashley bit her lower lip. Did she dare offer the girl one of the Midol tablets she had in her bag? No, she couldn't. Aaron would kill her. Literally. "Maybe a cup of tea would make her feel better."

The girl turned green at the thought, but the mother hurriedly pulled her to her feet and urged her through the doorway. "Thank you, missy. My daughter would appreciate it."

"Do you live nearby?" Ashley asked as she showed the women into the kitchen.

"Oh, just a few miles, but 'tis a brisk walk," the woman added. She nudged her daughter ahead of her. "I'm Amelia Briar, and this here is my Sarah."

"I'm Ashley Wheeler." She paused, glancing around

the unfamiliar kitchen helplessly. "About the tea," she said apologetically. "I'm not sure how to brew it."

"You don't know how to brew *tea?*" The woman looked at her strangely.

"No . . . not 'liberty' tea. I can make Lipton okay," she added quickly, in case the woman thought she was completely deficient.

The woman edged toward the kettle. "I can make liberty tea."

"Great!" Ashley hurried to get the hot water. "Exactly what is liberty tea?"

The woman looked at her oddly again. "Why . . . it's the stalks and leaves of the four-leafed loosestrife."

Ashley paused, glancing back at her vacantly. "Oh, sure . . . I knew that."

"We brew it so that we don't have to buy imported tea."

"Yes, I'd just forgotten."

The woman bustled about the kitchen and in just a few minutes had three cups of hot tea on the table. The young girl pushed hers away and lay her head down on the table, moaning.

"Say, this isn't bad," Ashley commented as she took a sip of the hot brew.

"You related to the doctor?" Mrs. Briar asked, eyeing the large robe Ashley was wearing.

"No—"

Sarah's moans grew more assertive.

"Oh dear, oh dear. Will the doctor be long?" the woman fretted.

"I'm not sure." Ashley stood up. "Excuse me a moment." She left the room and returned in a few minutes lugging her canvas bag. After setting it down on the table, she began to rummage through the contents until she found the bottle she wanted. She removed the cap, then spilled two of the tablets into the palm of Sarah's hand. "These will make you feel better in no time at all. Just swallow them with a little water."

The woman peered anxiously over Sarah's shoulders. "Are you a doctor?"

"No, but this will help. I promise."

After dumping four more tablets out on the table, Ashley put the cap back on the bottle. "In another four hours, take two more, then take the last two in another four hours. By then you should be feeling much better."

Sarah glanced at her mother, mutely seeking permission to take the pills.

"There's nothing in it that will hurt her," Ashley assured Mrs. Briar.

The woman nodded hesitantly, though Ashley could see she wasn't convinced that she was doing the right thing.

As the three women waited for the pills to take effect, Mrs. Briar talked about this neighbor or that one and about the lack of tea and sugar since the colonies had refused to accept English imports. Thirty minutes and three cups of tea later, Mrs. Briar finally pushed her cup aside. The color was coming back into Sarah's cheeks, and she seemed to be feeling better now. "Well, this has been pleasant, but I have a washing that won't get done without me, and the mister will be wanting his supper."

"Are you feeling better now, Sarah?" Ashley asked as she walked the two women to the door.

The girl seemed surprised that someone would think to address her directly. She nodded shyly. "All me hurtin's almost gone."

"Why, that's a wonder if I ever saw one!" Mrs. Briar exclaimed. " 'Tis a miracle, for sure!"

"I'm glad I could help," Ashley said warmly as she saw the women out the doorway. She watched them as they struck off down the road toward home, still exclaiming over the miracle.

For the next half hour Ashley busied herself emptying the tub and dragging it back outside where it was stored.

Afterward, she inspected the contents of the pantry, lifting lids and unwrapping various items until she ran across a container that faintly resembled soup. It must be the pottage Aaron had mentioned, she decided, and poured it into a pot that she hung over the fire to warm.

She went back for the small cake, a tin of butter, and a loaf of bread wrapped tightly in cloth.

She'd just rinsed out the teacups when there was another knock at the door.

"Good grief!" Ashley murmured as she hurried to answer it.

An old lady stood on the porch this time.

"Yes?"

"Mistress Wheeler?"

Ashley froze. She wasn't being careful enough. Here she'd opened the door again against Aaron's warning. "May I help you?"

"Are you Mistress Wheeler?"

Ashley nodded hesitantly.

"Mrs. Briar said you might have something to help me."

"What's wrong with you?"

The woman's hand cupped her jaw. "Got me a *teeerible* pain."

"Well . . . the doctor isn't here . . ." Ashley began.

"The pain's been *teeerible* for days now. I'm not able to eat or sleep, and what with the doctor being gone. . . . Mrs. Briar said you'd helped Saree with her miseries, so I thought . . ."

"Oh, jeez." Ashley bit her lower lip, realizing that she shouldn't be swayed by compassion, but the woman did look terrible. "Well . . . come in."

Ashley reluctantly ushered the woman into the kitchen. If Aaron heard about her dispensing medicine, he would have a fit.

"I hopes you can help," the woman said, still holding her jaw with one hand. "Don't think I can stand the misery much longer."

Once again, Ashley rummaged inside her bag until she found the bottle of aspirin. "Here, take a couple of these. Have you seen a dentist lately?"

"Dentist?"

"You know, a man who cares for your teeth?"

The old woman shook her head. "No. No man cares what happens to me teeth. I hears of such a man, but never met one," she admitted.

Ashley poured the woman a cup of tea, then hung the pot over the fire again.

"Mrs. Briar said you was a kindly soul," the woman said as she settled herself at the table. "Me name's Constance Connors, and I've known the good doctor since he was just a wee babe. Wiped his butt many a time, I has."

Ashley grinned, wondering what Aaron would say about the colorful recollection.

"Never would have imagined him a doctor," Constance mused. "He was always such a rapscallion."

For a half hour and two cups of tea, Mrs. Connors entertained Ashley with tales of Aaron's boyhood escapades.

The afternoon wore on, and Ashley thought the woman would never leave, but finally she rose, declaring that the pain in her jaw was cured.

"Mrs. Briar surely was right. You are a 'miracle worker,'" she praised lavishly as Ashley walked with her to the door. "Praise be to the Maker!"

"It was nothing," Ashley said modestly. "But, please, Mrs. Connors, don't mention a word of this to anyone," she urged. She didn't want rumor spreading that Aaron had some sort of a miracle worker at his house.

"Oh, I won't," Constance promised, looking perkier now.

But not fifteen minutes after Mrs. Connors had scurried down the road, there was another knock at the door. This time it was a woman with a child in her arms.

"Mistress Wheeler? I'm Della Morton, and this here's my little Henry. Henry's feelin' real poorly."

"I'm sorry, the doctor isn't here," Ashley said firmly. By now she was just a little put out with Constance for telling, when she'd agreed that she wouldn't.

"Amelia Briar said that you had things in that bag of yours that were purely miracles," Della countered.

"No, Mrs. Briar's wrong. I just gave her a—" Ashley glanced at the little boy the woman was holding and frowned. "What's wrong with little Henry?"

Mrs. Morton quickly drew the blanket away from the flush-faced child. "My boy's got the fever."

Ashley drew back. *"Putrid fever!"*

The mother's eyes widened. "No, just the regular fever, methinks!"

Kneeling in front of the little boy, Ashley touched his cheek. It was very hot. "How old are you, Henry?" she asked softly.

When he didn't answer, Ashley glanced up at Della.

"He's five. Had a runny nose earlier in the week and jest draggy until today. I know it be askin' a lot, but since Dr. Kenneman hasn't been home for a few days, I was hopin' you might help me."

"Dr. Kenneman has been very busy," Ashley apologized.

"Can you do something for my Henry? He's so hot. And today he's got a rattly cough that won't let him rest none."

"Oh, dear." Ashley viewed the child worriedly.

"I know it's askin' a whole lot, but you can see how sick he be," Della coaxed.

"I don't know if I can do anything for him."

"If you'd jest try. Amelia said you'd helped Sarah, and I passed Constance Connors on the road a while ago."

"Their problems weren't nearly as serious as little Henry's," Ashley explained. "He could have pneumonia or a bronchial infection. He might need antibiotics that only a doctor can prescribe."

The woman looked back at her blankly, and Ashley realized no one in this century had even *heard* of antibiotics, nor could they know anything about bronchitis or related problems.

"Please. Can't you do something?" Della pleaded when Henry dissolved into a fit of dry hacking.

Ashley hesitated, biting her lip again. "Jeez . . . I really shouldn't."

Henry's mother moved Henry inside the house before Ashley could stop her. Once again she rummaged through her bag and fished out the bottle of cough medicine she'd been taking before she'd fallen into eighteenth-century

Boston. She read the directions on the bottle, then poured a small amount into a spoon.

"Henry, you must swallow this. It doesn't taste too bad."

The little boy eyed the green syrup warily.

"It's just an elixir, Henry," Della urged. "Take it, lovey."

Finally the boy's lips parted, and Ashley gently poured the medicine into his mouth, wiping away a drop that escaped onto his chin.

"That may make him a little sleepy, but it will help the cough. And if you'll crush half of this"—she broke an aspirin in two—"and give it to him every four hours, it should help his fever."

Demonstrating her directions for Della, Ashley crushed half the aspirin and mixed it with water in a spoon, then coaxed Henry to open his mouth again. "This won't taste quite as good," she admitted. She made a face with him. "I should have given this to you first, shouldn't I?" she said gently when Henry shuddered involuntarily at the bitter taste.

Della cuddled her little son and murmured to him soothingly.

Ashley smiled at Della. "Take him home, bathe him in lukewarm water, and bring him back later this evening when Dr. Kenneman is here. I'd feel more comfortable if he would look at Henry."

"I will, and bless you for helping, missy." Della bundled Henry back into his blanket, then stored the bottle of cough medicine and two aspirin in a small bag that hung from a ribbon around her wrist.

"And Della, please, don't mention this to anyone," Ashley pleaded.

"Oh, I won't. You can be sure of that, missy."

Ashley reached back into her bag and found the roll of Life Savers. She peeled away the wrapper and handed Henry a lemon one. "Here, Henry, this is for being such a good patient."

Henry looked at the funny thing she held in her palm. "Go ahead," Ashley coaxed. "It's a Life Saver."

"Eat it, Henry!" his mother demanded. "It's a *life saver!*"

Henry popped the thing into his mouth as Ashley led Della to the door and closed it after her. She leaned against it with a sigh of relief.

The frantic screams of a small child sent Ashley rushing to the door thirty minutes later.

"Please," the young woman pleaded when Ashley swung open the door. "My Jeanine burned herself!"

"Bring her in," Ashley said without any hesitation this time.

There was an ugly red burn running down the child's arm. The wound was already starting to blister.

Ashley raced to her bag and seized the sample of first aid spray she'd gotten in the mail.

"This will make it feel better, darling," she crooned to the frightened little girl. "Here. Hold tight to my hand."

Ashley quickly sprayed the burned area. The child screamed, scrambling toward her mother with fright. When the cool spray had penetrated the scalded skin, the child ceased her wailing, staring at her arm.

"How does that feel?" Ashley asked.

"Not hurt . . . no more," the child murmured.

The mother's eyes were wide with wonder. "Why, 'tis another miracle!"

"No, it's just first aid spray—"

"No, no! Whatever you did, it's a *miracle!*" She gathered her daughter close, openly sobbing now. "Thank you, thank you!"

After giving Jeanine a cherry Life Saver, Ashley hurried the two to the door, but before she could bid them good-bye, another couple came up the path.

Oh, Lord, Ashley breathed. What had she done?

By the time she'd brewed more tea—something she was learning to do well by now—and dispensed more aspirin for the aches and pains of arthritis and dog bite—it was a good thing she always carried a large bottle—there were three more people waiting to see the "miracle worker."

"Aaron, where are you?" Ashley muttered as she refreshed old Mr. Feinstein, who had an earache, with a cup of tea. The situation was clearly getting out of hand.

When Ashley heard the front door open again, she raced through the house to ward off the newcomer. By now the drawing room was chock-full of people, and at least ten more patients were sitting on the porch, waiting for Ashley to see them and dispense one of her miraculous "life savers."

Skidding around the corner, she came face to face with Aaron, who was peering into the drawing room with disbelief.

"Oh, hi there," she said lamely.

White-faced, he turned to look at her. "*What* is going on?"

Sighing, she leaned against the door frame wearily. There was no way on earth she was going to talk her way out of this one.

10

Stunned, Aaron walked to the window to peer out at the mass of humanity congregated on his front lawn. There were people there that he hadn't seen in years! Voices rang out as the old, the young, the sick, the lame, and the destitute chanted Ashley's name.

Mistress Wheeler, Mistress Wheeler, Mistress Wheeler!

Aaron turned back to stare at her dumbfounded.

Shrugging lamely, she grinned. "It's been like this all day; they think I'm some sort of a miracle worker."

"Miracle worker!"

"Yeah, it's the strangest thing—"

"What have you been giving them?"

"Just over-the-counter medicine that I carry with me most of the time," she said in her own defense. "Midol, aspirin, cough syrup . . ."

Aaron walked to the door and flung it open. "Please, return to your homes!" he pleaded with the frenzied crowd. "There is no miracle worker here!"

Ashley began shooing people out of the drawing room, trying to quell their loud protests.

"But me foot hurts!" one called.

"And I got this pain in me side!" another argued.

Aaron was forced aside as the disgruntled patients

made their way down the steps and immediately formed a long line in front of the house. It was clear that they weren't giving up.

"Please, there's been a mistake. You must all return to your homes," Aaron beseeched. "Mistress Wheeler is not a doctor!"

"No, she's a *miracle* worker!" someone in the crowd called.

"No, you must go home!"

Screams of protests went up as the crowd surged forward, hands straining to touch the miracle worker.

After pushing Ashley back, Aaron slammed the door. He threw the heavy bolt, strode to the windows, and jerked the curtains closed.

"You see—" Ashley began, hoping to explain the peculiar circumstance he had found there. But his angry words stopped her.

"No, I *don't* see!" he roared. "What in the *hell* have you done?"

"Well, if you'd just calm down, I could explain. There were these two or three people who came looking for you, and you weren't here, so since one of them had a headache, and one had . . . pain that plagues women only, and another had a toothache, I just gave them some aspirin."

"You *burned* my patients' asses?" he accused incredulously.

"No! I gave them *aspirin!*"

"What is this 'ass burn'?"

"It's medicine. Oh, aspirin didn't come into existence until the late 1800s." She groaned. It was *impossible* to explain all that had happened in the medical field in the past two hundred years!

A knock sounded at the door, and Aaron swore under his breath. " 'Tis a fine kettle of snakes you have us in now," he accused. "I strive to be inconspicuous, and what do you do? Entice half of Boston—"

The knock came at the door again, more insistent this time. Aaron slid the bolt back and cracked the door open a slit. He was relieved to find Paul Revere standing on the porch viewing the milling crowd with astonishment.

After pulling Paul inside, Aaron quickly closed the door behind him.

"Pray tell, Kenneman. Has there been a *death* in the family?" Paul asked.

"No, only a slight misunderstanding. 'Tis nothing to be alarmed about."

"Then *why* are all those people on your lawn?"

Shooting Ashley a disenchanted look, Aaron said curtly, "Mistress Wheeler has been 'healing' the afflicted."

"Healing the afflicted? I say, isn't that a bit odd?"

Realizing that Paul wouldn't be there at such a late hour unless something important was happening, Aaron set aside the immediate crisis. "Have you news?"

Revere walked to the window and pulled the curtain aside to view the thinning crowd. "Trouble grows near."

Aaron scowled. "Is it imminent?"

Revere nodded, his gaze going back to Ashley.

"God's eyes!" Aaron breathed softly. "Gage is a crazed man."

"Much my same thoughts," Revere admitted.

"We must find a way to stop the bastard!"

"You can't."

The two men turned, staring at Ashley.

"You can't," she repeated calmly. "The British are already on their way."

"Aaron, why is she still with you?" Paul asked quietly. "I assumed that by now you would have carried out your mission."

Aaron turned, refusing to meet Paul's gaze. "I think we should listen to her, Paul."

Paul shook his head. "The woman knows not of what she speaks," he scoffed. "How could she have acquired such information? Has she not been with you all day?"

Moving to stand by the fire, Aaron thought about what Ashley had told him the night before. Was she from a time two hundred and seventeen years in the future? "Mayhap she speaks the truth, Paul."

"The truth! God's teeth, Kenneman. How could she have gained such information? Our patrols only learned of events a few hours ago!"

Ashley listened to the conversation, sympathizing with their anguish. General Gage, who had been kept informed of the colonists' efforts by his spies, had found himself in a difficult position in mid-April 1775. England was urging him to take control of the colony by force, and, while he was hesitant, it seemed he was left with little choice. Having made the decision, he had sent an advance patrol tonight to locate John Hancock and Samuel Adams. With these two powerful men out of the way, he assumed his chances of overpowering the colonists would be greatly improved.

But Hancock and Adams, having attended meetings at the Provincial Congress, were entrenched in Lexington, six miles from Concord. Gage had thought trouble could be avoided by sending men in the dark of night, but Revere's appearance here tonight proved that the colonists had a spy system equal to Gage's own.

After turning from the window, Aaron started to pace.

"I don't know, Paul. But the things she speaks of, though curious, have a ring of truth to them."

"What could she know that we don't?"

"She claims to know the future."

" 'Tis sheer folly! No one can know the future."

"I do."

The men turned to look at Ashley again.

"Please, listen to me." Ashley forced Paul to meet her eyes. "Joseph Warren summoned you to his house earlier tonight with the intention of sending you to Lexington to warn Hancock and Adams that Gage is about to send an advance force of seven hundred and fifty men to seize and destroy the stores at Concord," she said quietly. "But when you reached Warren's house, Warren had already sent another messenger earlier. Willie Dawes is at this moment on his way to warn Hancock and Adams of the impending assault."

Paul glanced at Aaron, speechless.

"Is this true?" Aaron asked.

"Yes, but, pray tell . . . how?"

"Time grows short. We must listen to her," Aaron returned gravely.

The men's eyes now focused on Ashley. She could see by the somber expressions on their faces that they were willing to try to make sense of what she said.

"According to your history books, what do we do now?" Aaron felt the question was absurd, yet if she spoke the truth, her knowledge could give the colonists an edge they would not otherwise have.

"Paul must ride through the towns and villages warning the citizens to arm themselves," she said. "He will do this as he rides to Lexington to make sure that Hancock and Adams have been properly notified."

"And I?"

"I don't know about you," she admitted. "For the life of me, I can't remember anything about you—although the history books don't name all of Revere's friends and associates."

She winced as she saw the crestfallen look on his face. "*Nothing* about me?"

She shook her head. "Nothing . . . that I can remember."

"Well, hell."

Ashley could see that she had severely wounded his male ego.

"If she speaks the truth, I should be on my way," Revere said. "Gage's troops grow near?"

Ashley nodded. "But don't worry: you'll complete the mission in time."

Paul glanced at Aaron solemnly. "I hope she knows what she's talking about."

"The hour grows late," Aaron returned. "We have little choice but to believe her."

"How will the British attack? By land or by water?" Paul asked. "If we must divide our forces . . ."

Aaron glanced at Ashley.

"Water, but I can't tell you anymore," she told Paul, "or history will be altered."

"By water?" Paul asked again.

She nodded.

"Then we must have a messenger," he decided. "Someone to watch the movements of the troops."

"Activity on the road this late at night will cause suspicion." Aaron began to pace again.

"Yes." Paul fell into step with him. "And if we ring the church bells, the British will know something is amiss."

The men glanced at Ashley, but she only shrugged. "I'd really like to help, but I'm afraid you have to figure it out on your own."

Aaron's brow lifted imperiously. "You are not willing to help us?"

"I saw *Back to the Future*. If I say anything, then . . ."

Ignoring her prattle, he added wearily, "History will be changed." The two men cupped their chins thoughtfully.

Aaron suddenly paused, turning to her again. "But will you inform us if we make the wrong decision?"

"I think I could do that." She felt she was pretty safe there. They had made the right decisions. History affirmed that.

Satisfied she would do what she could, Aaron resumed pacing. "Paul, you'll get a boat and row across the Charles to where the *Somerset* lays," he directed.

"I know we have spoken of this before, Aaron, but I was in Lexington last Sunday, at the Reverend Mr. Clark's house? On my return I passed through Charlestown, where I had opportunity to speak with Colonel Conant and others. They were apprehensive that should this very event occur, it would be difficult for a messenger to cross the Charles River. They suggested that we devise a signal in case of trouble."

"Of course, a signal." Aaron's pace quickened. "If the British come by water—which Ashley says they will—"

"I didn't mean to let that slip," Ashley defended quickly.

"But you did. We will show three lanterns in the North Church steeple—"

Ashley cleared her throat.

"If they come by land, then we'll show two lanterns."

Ashley cleared her throat again, a little louder this time.

Aaron's footsteps slowed as he turned to look at her.

She shook her head.

"That's wrong?"

She nodded.

"What is it?"

She shook her head again.

"You can't say?"

She nodded.

"Damn!" He resumed his pacing, then whirled to face her again. "Am I close?"

She nodded.

"Three lanterns by land, two by sea?"

She shook her head.

"One by land, three by sea?"

She shook her head, smiling lamely.

"*One* by sea, *two* by land!"

She shook her head harder.

"*Three* by sea, *two* by land?" Paul supplied, but again she shook her head.

"*Two by water, one by land!*" the men parroted in exasperated unison.

She grinned, nodding enthusiastically.

"What the *hell* difference does it make?" Aaron exploded.

"A lot of difference!" Ashley defended. "History will be changed."

"We can delay no longer," Paul warned. He moved to leave, and Aaron followed him.

Ashley was suddenly seized with panic. What if Aaron never came back? What if he was killed as he tried to assist Paul? She had struggled all day to remember every shred of history she'd ever read about Paul Revere's famous ride. Try as she might, she couldn't recall ever reading a single thing about Dr. Aaron Kenneman.

Fear coiled itself around her heart as she tried to convince herself that history books didn't record everything. But history books did record that 247 Englishmen and 88 colonists lost their lives in the first shots fired in the Revolutionary War.

Tears stung her eyes as she watched Aaron preparing to leave. *Oh, please,* she prayed. *Don't let him be one of the eighty-eight who died.*

"I'm sorry, Ashley." Aaron's voice broke into her troubled thoughts. "You will have to come with us."

"Where?" Ashley said, automatically reaching for her bag.

"I can't leave you here," Aaron said quietly. "You will be at risk when news of the attack spreads."

Ashley numbly slipped her arms into the coat that he was holding for her. Now she was going to become a *participant* in the Revolutionary War?

Aaron extinguished the lantern, and the three slipped out the front door a few minutes later. Bright moonlight lit the now-empty pathway as they mounted the horses.

"I will go to North Church and see that the lanterns are lit. You can go by the house and let Rachel know where you're going," Aaron called.

Picking up the reins of his horse, Paul sighed. "I won't be long. I want to change my boots, and Joshua seems feverish tonight. Rachel's concerned that he is developing a raw throat again."

"Would you like for me to examine him?"

"I don't think it's necessary. You know how Rachel frets. Mayhap tomorrow, if the boy isn't feeling better by morning." Turning the horse, Paul's gaze met Aaron's in the moonlight. "Mistress Wheeler could keep Rachel company while we're gone."

"I want her in my protection," Aaron returned gravely.

Ashley tightened her hold on his waist gratefully. "Thank you," she whispered.

If anything was going to happen to him, she wanted to be there. She knew CPR and other life-saving procedures from a first aid course she'd taken a few months earlier. In an emergency, she might be able to save his life.

Turning the horse, Paul muttered, " 'Twould be easier if we knew Gage's plans."

"I told you, he's after the supply depot in Concord," Ashley blurted without thinking again.

"The damn fool," Paul muttered.

"And he wants Adams and Hancock," she added, though she felt guilty for helping them. But she couldn't stand by and let Aaron be hurt.

Turning slightly in the saddle, Aaron winked at her. "But, alas, Gage will find nothing but a bum full of musket balls."

Ashley grinned.

"Am I right?"

She just grinned again.

The three rode hard under the cover of darkness.

"*Three* if by sea, *two* if by land," Revere would call occasionally over his shoulder.

"No, *one* if by land, *two* if by sea," Ashley would call back, wishing like blue blazes he could remember the proper signal!

At the crossroads, the horses turned and galloped off in different directions.

Revere detoured toward his house while Ashley and Aaron continued to the Old North Church.

A light was burning in the window as Paul rode into his yard.

The door flew open, and Rachel, in her nightgown, bounded down the steps. "Paul, I've been worried about you!"

"I'm sorry, love." After dismounting, Paul kissed her absently. Arm in arm they started toward the house. Paul failed to see Elizabeth's wagon, and he caught himself as he nearly stumbled over the toy.

As he righted himself, his boot came down on the wooden cow he'd made for Joshua, and he went to his knees. His ankle twisted painfully, and he muttered a sharp obscenity under his breath.

Rachel sent him a reprimanding look as they hurried toward the house. "Your language, Paul!"

"I have told those children a *hundred* times not to string toys around the yard! If they must play with *everything* they own, make them keep them in the backyard!"

"Yes, dear." Noting the urgency in his steps, Rachel become worried. "Has something happened?"

"Come inside," Paul murmured. "Time is of the essence."

A knot began to form in the pit of Rachel's stomach as she followed her husband into the house.

A moment later Paul rushed out the door again, pulling his coat on.

"How long will you be gone?" Rachel called as she tried to keep stride with him. By now most of the children were awake, some pressing their noses against the windows, others trailing after their father, babbling incessantly.

"I'm not sure, dear—watch the dog! Mortimer—" Before Paul could finish the dog had bounded out of the house and struck off down the road.

"Oh, dear, Paul! Mortimer is out again," Rachel called to Paul Jr.

"Mortimer!" Paul snapped his fingers. "Get back in there, boy!"

Mortimer paused only momentarily, then turned and bounded off in the opposite direction again.

A grumpy Paul Jr. appeared in the doorway, trying to rub the sleep from his eyes.

"Get Mortimer back in the house," Paul called.

Paul Jr. yawned. "I'll fetch him, Papa."

Patting little Joshua's head, Paul sidestepped him only to stumble over Elizabeth as she headed back to her wagon. "You children be good," he called. "Mind your mother!"

The confusion had awakened all the children by now, and they poured out of the house to tell their father goodbye. It was several minutes before Paul could kiss them all and get on his way again.

"You be careful," Rachel fretted as she helped to push him back up into the saddle.

"I'll be fine," he promised. He leaned down and kissed her, then gave her braid an affectionate tug. "Keep my side of the bed warm, Momma."

After turning his horse, he galloped out of the yard, clapping his hand to his hat, coattails flying.

Aaron and Ashley were just returning from the church when the three met up on the road again.

Dust fogged the air as they pulled the horses to a halt.

"How is John?" Ashley asked.

Paul looked completely blank for a moment. "I forgot to ask."

"Time is passing swiftly," Aaron cautioned. "We must be on our way."

"I have a boat hidden near Charlestown ferry," Paul supplied, "but I will need someone to row me across."

"I can row you across." Aaron lifted the reins and was about to be off again when Ashley called to him.

"No, you can't."

The two men glanced at Ashley.

"History doesn't record it that way," she said meekly.

"*Hell.*" Aaron thought for a moment. "Why can't I row him across?"

"Because . . ." She prompted their response with her fingers.

"Because . . . I'm not mentioned in the history books?" Aaron guessed.

She shook her head no.

He thought for another moment. "Because . . . someone else did?"

She smiled.

"*Who,* dammit!"

She held up her finger. "Temper, temper."

"We don't have time to play games!"

Paul shook his head, marveling at how the two could cross swords so often.

"Please, friend, let me try." Paul cleared his throat, accustomed to dealing with a woman. "Aaron can't row me across, but someone else can?"

Ashley nodded.

"David and Henry live not far from here. I can have them row me across," Paul said simply.

The two men glanced back to Ashley, and, to their relief, she nodded.

A short time later, four horses and five riders galloped toward the dock near Charlestown ferry where Paul's small boat was kept hidden in the shadows. The small craft bobbed in the water as the riders came to a stop.

A bright moon was hanging overhead as the four men and one woman viewed the large English transport lying in the harbor.

"It's the *Somerset*," Ashley whispered reverently.

Aaron's grave gaze fixed on the English man-of-war. "That it is."

"Is it armed?"

"You tell me."

She sighed. "It is. Sixty-four guns."

Aaron glanced at the moon, disturbed to find it so bright. Paul would have to row right by the British ship to reach the other side.

"God's eyes," Paul muttered. "I meant to bring a cloth to wrap around the oars to muffle the sound. I left the house in such a hurry, I forgot to get one."

"I'll be damned!" he muttered again a few moments later. "I've run off without my spurs too!"

Henry nudged Aaron, winking knowingly. "Doesn't Abigail Watson live just down the road?"

Ashley glanced up and frowned when she saw Henry and Aaron grinning at each other. "Who's Abigail Watson?"

Aaron's face sobered immediately. "No one."

"No one?"

"Just a woman I know," he said easily.

"Another 'widow' woman?"

The four men chuckled uneasily.

"Aaron, why don't you see if Abigail has something we can wrap around the oars?" Paul said with just a hint of a grin still lingering at the corners of his mouth.

As Aaron returned to his horse, Ashley followed him. After swinging into the saddle, he glanced down to find her standing there looking at him. "I'll be back momentarily."

She smiled nicely. "I'll go with you."

"It isn't necessary." He paused as guilt flooded his face. "Do the history books mention Abigail?"

"Not by name."

"Oh." He finally offered his hand and lifted her onto the horse behind him. Moments later they galloped off down the road.

"Who is this Abigail Watson?" she asked, trying to make herself heard above the thunder of hooves.

"Just a friend."

"How good a 'friend'?"

A smile curved the corners of his mouth. "Does it matter?"

Ashley was surprised to realize that it did. She had known Aaron Kenneman only days, but she was beginning to think of him as hers.

"How much are you going to tell her?" Ashley whispered as they crept around the corner of Abigail Watson's house a little later.

"As much as I need to."

"How do you know she won't run to the British?"

"She won't."

"You seem to know your 'friend' well."

She could see his wry grin in the moonlight. She reached out and punched him soundly.

Stooping down, Aaron selected several small stones, straightened, and tossed them at a second-story window that glowed with a faint light.

"Is this Abigail's bedroom?" she mocked.

"Has anyone ever told you that you talk too much?"

He picked up another handful of stones and tossed them at the window again. A moment later, the window was thrown open and a pretty young woman poked her head out.

"Aaron! You goose! Why are you standing out there? Come in, darlin'."

Aaron started forward, but Ashley latched on to the back of his coat. "Hold it, 'goose,'" she threatened. "You're here on business. Remember?"

"I can't stay, Abby," he called back with more regret in his voice than Ashley thought necessary. Stepping from the shadows, Ashley eased closer to him so that Abigail would be sure to see her.

"Then why be bothering me so late, darlin'?" Abigail's pretty features grew petulant as she spotted the young woman standing with Aaron.

"I need a favor," Aaron called.

"Of course. Anything . . . you know that."

"Just anything, you silly ol' goose. You know that." Ashley smirked under her breath.

"Jealous?" he returned under his before he lifted his head to Abigail. "A friend and I must cross the river, but we need something to muffle the oars. Some kind of cloth?"

"A cloth?"

Ashley punched him in his side.

"I'm in a bit of a hurry," he added.

Abigail hurriedly stepped out of her petticoat and pitched it out the window. "Will this do?"

Catching the garment in his hand, Aaron grinned. "Thank you—"

His words were caught in his throat as Ashley jerked his arm and turned him firmly back in the direction of his horse.

When they arrived back at the boat, Paul was still muttering to himself about leaving his spurs behind.

" 'Twould make the ride easier if I had the blasted things," he complained.

"I could ride back and get them for you," David offered.

"No, we haven't the time."

Mortimer suddenly came into view, loping down the road, his tongue hanging out in a heavy pant.

"Mortimer!" Paul stood up in the small boat, a smile breaking across his face. "Quick, a pen and paper."

"For what?" David asked.

"I need to send Rachel a note."

Ashley fumbled in her canvas bag and came up with bank deposit slip and a ballpoint pen, which she quickly handed to Paul.

Paul gazed at the strange implement, then hurriedly scribbled a note and tied it around the dog's neck. "Go home, Mortimer. Home, boy!"

The dog whirled and was off again, racing back down the road with seeming purpose now.

"Will he mind?"

"On rare occasions." Paul only hoped this was one of them.

Handing the pen back to Ashley, Paul viewed the blobs of black ink staining his fingers.

"Sorry," Ashley murmured when she saw his blank dismay. "I forgot the darn thing leaks."

Aaron and Paul busied themselves tearing Abigail's flannel petticoat into strips, then tying the pieces around the oars.

Ashley watched for Mortimer's return, praying the dog understood the importance of his mission.

Twenty minutes passed, and the dog failed to return.

"I can linger no longer," Paul whispered. Reaching out, he took Aaron's hand. "Wish me luck, friend."

The two men shook hands. "Godspeed, Paul."

"Thank you, good friend. I'll need it."

Aaron pushed the small boat out into the water with Paul, Henry, and David aboard.

"I surely do wish I had my spurs," Paul muttered as Henry and Paul began rowing away from the bank.

Ashley suddenly spotted Mortimer coming back down the road, running like the wind.

"Wait!" Ashley whispered. "Here comes Mortimer!"

"Mortimer! Good dog!" Revere whispered jubilantly.

Two minutes later Mortimer bounded up to the group with Paul's spurs tied to the strap around his neck.

"Bless you, Mortimer!" Paul cried out softly.

Aaron knelt and removed the spurs and hurriedly tossed them to Revere.

Paul caught them, smiling. "Mistress Wheeler?"

"Yes?"

"Do the history books mention my dog?"

Ashley grinned. "Yes!"

"That's nice," she heard Aaron grumble. "I'm risking my skin for a cause, and history's never heard of Aaron Kenneman, just Mortimer, Revere's *dog*."

11

The sound of the oars softly cutting through the water gradually began to fade.

Ashley and Aaron stood arm and arm, watching the small boat holding the three men skim soundlessly across the moonlit water.

When a few minutes had passed and Aaron had not spoken, Ashley squeezed his arm reassuringly. "You want to be with them, don't you?"

Disappointment tinged his voice now. "I have planned for a very long time to be a part of this night."

Laying her head on his shoulder, Ashley focused her eyes on the English vessel winding in the young flood. "You know, if we could find another boat we could follow them," she said softly.

He turned, hope springing to his eyes. "It would not alter history?"

"Not if we keep a safe distance. We can stay slightly behind Paul, and if he should run into any trouble, you can be there to run interference."

"This 'run interference'? What does this mean?"

"It's sort of a football term—do you know anything about football?"

"I have heard of the game."

"As long as you don't directly interfere with Paul's ride—"

"I would not interfere," he interrupted shortly. "I have helped shape the events of this night."

"I know." She patted him reassuringly again. "Do you know someone who can lend us a boat?"

"Yes."

"Someone nearby?"

"Yes."

"Then let's go, Kenneman. We have a very important ride to make."

"I might have known," Ashley complained as they climbed into the small boat a short time later.

The nearby "friend" had turned out to be yet another one of Aaron's female acquaintances. Molly Rahaus had proved only too eager to be of assistance to the handsome young doctor.

"Petticoats and boats—what a woman won't do for a man," Ashley groused.

Aaron caught her waist as her foot slipped, nearly dumping her into the water.

Ashley seated herself on the board seat directly behind him as he picked up the oars then pushed the boat away from the bank. "How many women 'friends' can one man have?"

"I can only answer for myself."

"And that is?"

"Not nearly enough." He winked and grinned at her.

Ashley watched the tight ridge of muscles in his forearms as he began to cut the oars through the water noiselessly.

A hoot owl called and Ashley scooted forward anxiously. Wrapping her arms around his waist, she closed her eyes, holding on to him tightly.

" 'Tis only an owl," he consoled.

" 'Tis a loud one!" she whispered back. Resting her head on his back, she sighed. "I know this is going to sound crazy, but at times I almost wish I wasn't dreaming." Her arms settled more possessively around his waist.

"At what times are those?" he asked.

"Times like now."

"What is tempting about this hour? We are in a small boat, praying to get by an English man-of-war before we are blown out of the water. 'Tis an unlikely event to relish."

Snuggling closer, she hugged him tighter. "I know, but even though we are in danger, I enjoy being with you, and I suspect that even if you are troubled about who I say I am, you have enjoyed me."

She had seen the way he listened with rapt interest when she talked about some event or amazing medical occurrence in the twentieth century.

Noting the way he stiffened at her remark, she whispered, "What's wrong?"

"What you said . . . it is improper."

"What?" Ashley tried to think what she might have said to offend him.

"That you . . . enjoy me," he murmured. " 'Tis not true."

"But, I *do.*"

" 'Tis not true," he snapped. "I have acted as a gentleman—no matter what the circumstance!"

"I didn't say you hadn't."

"You did. You said that I have enjoyed you, and you me —and . . . we haven't."

"You don't like me?"

"Like you? Yes. Enjoy you? I have not—although I do not find the thought disagreeable," he admitted.

She frowned. "You don't find the thought of enjoying me disagreeable?"

" 'Tis not the thing a man speaks of with a lady," he bristled.

"Wait a minute." It suddenly dawned on Ashley that they'd hit another communication gap. "Exactly what does 'enjoy' mean—to an eighteenth-century man?"

Aaron continued to row, his jaw set tightly. "It means . . . *What* does it mean to a twentieth-century woman?"

"It means to have a good time or to take pleasure in. What does it mean to you?"

"It means—well, to a man it means that he . . . *enjoys* his wife."

"He should."

"Physically."

"Oh." She grinned. "Well, he *should.*" Wriggling closer to him, she rather liked the thought that he wouldn't find "enjoying" her all that bad.

"Stop wiggling, wench. You'll dump us both in the river," he reprimanded gently.

"I was just thinking"—she deliberately made her breath warm against his ear now—"that being out here with you is really quite romantic."

"We are on a grave mission. There is no time for . . . this." He squirmed as she hugged him closer.

"But this doesn't take much time, and it's so . . . tempting, wouldn't you say? The river, the moonlight . . ."

"The British waiting to level us with their cannon," he returned dryly.

"Being here with you," she continued. "Moonlight always makes me . . . feel romantic, doesn't it you?" She smiled when she felt him tense again. "Am I making you nervous?"

"I am not accustomed to having a woman be so—"

"Forward?"

"Yes."

Sighing, Ashley shifted back to her seat as Aaron resumed rowing. If circumstances were different, she'd show him how daring a twentieth-century woman could really be.

"Stay well to the right of the ship," she whispered.

" 'Twould be easier to go to the left."

"No, to the *right*. I can see men standing on the left side of the ship," she murmured.

A man's voice carried occasionally on the air, and the smell of pipe tobacco came to her.

Silence filled the small boat as the English man-of-war loomed closer. Since there was nothing in the history books about either her or Aaron, she wasn't at all sure how this spontaneous little outing would turn out.

After lifting the oars from the water, Aaron rested them on the sides of the boat, allowing it to drift silently beneath the bow of the *Somerset*.

Holding her breath, Ashley shut her eyes and prayed that fate was as committed to keeping history as intact as she was.

She was practically certain that history hadn't mentioned the man-of-war firing on anybody . . . or almost certain.

The small boat bobbed along, skimming lightly across the water as it sailed past the English ship.

When they were safely on the other side, Ashley wilted with relief. "Bingo!" she whispered.

"Bingo?"

"Never mind."

Grinning, they exchanged a brief victory kiss.

"Good job, Kenneman!"

"The credit goes to you, Mistress Wheeler. You're an excellent navigator!"

Their gazes suddenly locked in the moonlight.

"Like you, Mistress Wheeler, I suddenly find myself wishing that we were sharing more than what you claim is only a dream," he said softly.

"Ditto, Dr. Kenneman, a big ditto."

Paul and two other men were just pulling their small craft onto shore when they heard Aaron and Ashley approaching.

They called softly to Paul, who was just starting to climb the steep ravine. Turning, he quickly made his way back to the shoreline.

"What are you doing here?" Paul asked.

Aaron helped Ashley out of the boat, then turned to Paul. "I will stay close behind you, for I cannot let you make this ride without my protection."

Paul glanced at Ashley. "Can he do this?"

Ashley nodded. "We'll be nearby if you need us."

"Then we must be off," Paul whispered.

Aaron stepped forward, his features grave as the two men's eyes met.

"If anything should happen . . ."

"Rachel and the children will be cared for," Aaron returned quietly. "Ride well."

"This night we begin our fight for freedom."

"And fight we will."

The men shook hands again, then bidding the others good-bye, Paul, Aaron, and Ashley scaled the ravine, then struck off down the road on foot. When they'd gone about a mile, Ashley and Aaron dropped back, leaving Paul to proceed to Charleston alone.

Within a few minutes, lanterns came into view. Paul quickly proceeded to a white clapboard house where a man was waiting in the shadows with a horse saddled and ready to travel.

"I have seen the signal in the church." Colonel Conant stepped out of the shadows and handed Paul the reins of the horse. "The redcoats come by sea?"

Paul nodded.

"God's teeth, 'tis what we have feared," he breathed.

"The British are on their way to Concord to destroy supplies and take Adams and Hancock. I must rouse the countryside," Paul returned gravely.

"Of course. God's speed, my good man."

"I will need two more swift horses," Revere requested as he mounted.

Colonel Conant hurried away and returned awhile later leading the horses.

Pointing to Ashley and Aaron, Paul tipped his hat, then whirled and was off in a fast gallop.

Five minutes later Ashley was warily eyeing the black gelding she was to ride. The animal looked hostile to her, and she wasn't crazy about the thought of keeping company with him for the next few hours.

"I can't ride this thing," she declared.

"There is little choice unless you ride with me," Aaron whispered as he swung into his saddle.

Ashley thought about the harrowing rides she'd taken with him lately and suddenly the horse didn't look so menacing.

"I've never ridden alone before," she warned as she tried unsuccessfully to hook her foot into the stirrup.

"Then 'tis a good time to begin, wouldn't you say?" He looked at her and grinned as she danced around, struggling to hoist herself aboard the beast.

Grunting, she finally heaved herself into the saddle. Glancing at Aaron, her face flushed with victory. "I guess it 'tis, pilgrim."

"Pilgrim?"

"That's my John Wayne impersonation." He was about to open his mouth when she stopped him. "John Wayne was one of the best dern cowboys that ever rode the big screen, pilgrim."

This time he didn't even bother to ask.

Ashley managed to find the reins, which Conant had thoughtfully tied over the horse's neck.

"How do I make him turn?" She studied the bridle as if it were a long, repulsive black snake dangling across the saddle.

"If you want him to go right, pull the reins to the right. If left, pull to the left. Kick his sides to go, and pull back evenly on the reins to stop."

"Oh, sure thing." Ashley lifted the reins gingerly. *Right, right. Left, left. Brakes, pull back.*

"Ready?"

"No." Ashley moaned quietly as they started off at a bone-jarring trot. But by that time, it didn't matter. They were off.

* * *

For the first mile, Ashley's horse contentedly loped along behind Aaron's. Managing to sit up straighter in the saddle, Ashley decided that this wasn't going to be so bad. It wasn't going to take her long to get the hang of it.

But five minutes later, she was forced to amend her optimistic view. She was in trouble. Big trouble. The stirrups were too long, and she had difficulty staying in the saddle. With each bounce, she slid sideways, which seemed to annoy the horse. In retaliation, he tossed his head and made strange whinnying noises that in turn annoyed her.

Just when she was convinced that she would be able to keep up, Aaron would kick his mount into a faster canter. There was nothing she could do but follow, her teeth jarring with every hoofbeat.

By the time they'd ridden a half hour, it was all she could do to hang on to the saddle, keep hold of the reins, and attempt to keep her feet in the stirrups. By this time, her thighs were raw, her ankles bruised and bleeding from being beaten by the wooden stirrups, and her feet and calves locked in one long painful cramp from the unnatural strain.

Turning to glance over his shoulder at her, Aaron grinned. "Are you okay?"

"Fine," Ashley muttered, losing all hope now that she would ever bear children. "Just *peachy.*"

"Well, bear up, *'pilgrim,'*" he called. "We have a long ride ahead of us!"

The horses continued their rapid pace. The night was pleasant with the moon climbing high above them in a diamond-studded sky.

Just outside Charleston Neck, Aaron suddenly reined his horse to the side of the road. Straight ahead of Paul, he could faintly detect two men on horseback sitting under a tree. He watched, wondering if Paul had spotted the two riders.

Trotting up beside him, Ashley pulled back on the reins, trying to halt her mount. "Whoa . . . whoa . . . whoa, dammit!"

Aaron turned to look at her, scowling. "Mistress Wheeler, your language is distressing."

"You want to talk distressing? Ride this nag for ten minutes, then we'll talk distressing."

Aaron turned back to watch as Paul galloped closer to the horsemen hidden in the shadows.

Suddenly one of the riders sprang out ahead of Revere, while the other attempted to overtake him from behind.

Swinging around, Paul raced back toward Charlestown Neck with the two men in hot pursuit on his tail.

Aaron caught the flash of a red coat as he spurred his mount into action. Groaning, Ashley held on for her life as her horse broke into a gallop to follow.

The two English officers rode hard, but Revere managed deftly to outmaneuver them as they sped along the moonlit countryside.

"Slow down," Ashley shouted as her horse rounded a bend at breakneck speed. Her fingers dug into his mane as she hung on, reciting prayers.

"Keep up!" Aaron shouted over his shoulder. After lifting his pistol, he fired at the officers who were in a close race with Revere now. The shot rang out in the darkness, then another.

Oh, Lord! Ashley closed her eyes tightly and hung on.

Yea, though I walk through the valley of death I shall fear no evil. . . . forget that! Yes, I do! Help me!

A pond sprang into view directly in Paul's path, but his horse never broke stride. Paul nimbly reined his mount around the perimeter of the muddy water and raced on.

Pulling their horses to a standstill, Ashley and Aaron broke out laughing as they watched the two English officers plow straight into the water.

Swearing and flinging hot accusations at one another, the officers fumed as they found themselves sitting waist deep in mud.

As Aaron and Ashley rode past them a moment later, the two men were still trying to pry each other free of the muck.

12

By the time the riders approached the next town, Ashley was ready to shoot the horse she was riding. Each time Aaron glanced back to make sure she was following, she smiled gamely and pretended she was just fine, but she had gained a new respect for those oldtime western stars Roy Rogers and Dale Evans.

If those two could stay in a saddle for eight hours a day and still sing "Happy Trails to You," they had her undying admiration.

As they rode through the night, Paul dashed down the narrow lanes, calling out the alarm to each farmhouse he came to until a light appeared in a window.

Ashley sighed with relief when she saw the small wooden sign into which the name MEDFORD had been crudely carved. The men would surely stop here to catch their breath for a moment, she thought.

Her horse slowed, and she closed her eyes for the briefest of moments.

A second later she was jolted in her saddle, aware that someone had called her name. "Yes?"

She could see Aaron sitting quietly on his horse in the shadows, watching for Paul's return.

"Did you say something?" she called softly.

He shook his head, motioning for her to fall silent.

Funny, she thought, *I know that someone called my name.*

Paul galloped past again, and Aaron spurred his horse. Ashley gritted her teeth and did the same.

As they approached Medford, the houses seemed closer together. Proceeding immediately to the house of the captain of the minutemen, Paul awakened him, then rode on.

"Awake! Awake!" Paul called out. "To arms, the British are coming!"

The sash on a downstairs window flew up, and a man poked his head outside.

"What say you?" he demanded.

"The British are coming! Arm yourself!"

"Who might *you* be?"

"Paul Revere of Boston! Rouse your friends and neighbors! Time is fleeting!"

Paul dashed back to the road and rode on with Aaron and Ashley following close behind. At the next house, Paul's voice rang out. "To arms, to arms!" he called. When the house remained dark, he called out again.

When Paul seemed to be having difficulty rousing the household, Aaron stirred his horse. "Mayhap they sleep soundly," he whispered.

"To arms, to arms!" Paul called again, but still he received no reply.

Following close behind Aaron, Ashley irritably pulled on the horse's reins. "I said *whoa,* you stupid ninny!"

Paul and Aaron shot her a harsh look, and she quickly lowered her voice and stared back at them sullenly. It wasn't her idea to be in this dream. "I hate this animal."

After sliding down off the horse, she tried to stomp feeling back into her legs.

Turning back to the window, Paul cupped his hands to his mouth and called loudly, *"To arms! To arms!* The British are coming!" But again he was met by silence.

Ashley bent down, picked up several small stones, and tossed them at an upstairs window. When the first stones didn't bring a light, she tossed a second handful.

She gasped in horror when the window shattered, the shards of glass sprinkling down upon Paul and Aaron.

"I'm sorry," she murmured. She grinned lamely. "Bet that got their attention."

The owner of the house awakened and was now leaning out the hole in the window, staring sleepily down at the trio standing beneath him.

"What is the meaning of this?" he bellowed.

"The British are coming!" Paul called out.

"Did ye have to break me blasted window to tell me!"

"Rouse your family and friends," Paul shouted. "And prepare to fight for your freedom!" With that, Paul wheeled his mount and was on his way again.

After that, Ashley lost track of the homes where Paul paused to rouse the sleeping occupants. She found it heartwarming that no householder questioned what was happening but readily roused his family and prepared to fight for freedom.

Hour after hour she hung on to the horse's mane, trying to keep up with Paul and Aaron as they darted through yards, flower beds, and rows of prickly hedge.

Paul had just emerged from a lone farmhouse and rode on ahead when Ashley's horse stumbled in a deep rut, flinging her to the side.

Grasping for a hold on the saddle, Ashley felt her foot slip free from the stirrup. She'd given up on wearing her glasses so at least she wouldn't *see* her own death.

"Aaron!" she screamed, praying she could hold on to the saddle long enough for him to hear her above the sound of thundering hooves.

The horse, startled by her screams, surged back on its hind feet, flinging Ashley aside like a rag doll.

Aaron turned to look over his shoulder just as the steed was rearing. He watched in horror as Ashley's body flew through the air and landed with a dull thud and a cloud of dust.

Though the force of her momentum rolled her from beneath the horse's flashing hooves, the hard landing completely knocked the breath out of her.

After spinning his mount around, Aaron raced back to her. He flung the reins over the gelding's head and jumped off, certain he'd find her unconscious from the fall.

He knelt beside her and began to feel for broken bones. "Lie still," he demanded, and Ashley was surprised to hear the fear in his voice.

"I've broken every bone in my body." She moaned. It was several long, painful moments before she could force air back into her lungs.

"No, you haven't broken every bone in your body." His hands moved along her rib cage, probing for injury.

"I have!"

"You haven't."

Assured she hadn't broken a single bone, he gently helped her to her feet.

"I'm all right," Ashley managed to whisper. "Just let me catch my breath."

"From now on, stay closer!"

"Closer! It's all I can do to keep you in sight!"

He brushed off her dress. "You scared the life out of me," he said gruffly.

She managed a weak smile. "That's better than what was scared out of me."

Her pulse quickened as he drew her to him for a moment, holding her close. "I was a fool to insist that you make this ride," he admitted. " 'Tis much too dangerous for a woman. I will tell Paul that we are returning to—"

"No!" Ashley straightened, suppressing a moan. She would not permit him to relinquish his part in shaping history because of her. "I'm fine, really."

"Ashley—"

Pressing her fingers over his mouth, she protested softly. "Aaron. I insist. We must go on."

"I cannot go on. Not at your expense."

"But you must." Their eyes met, and for the first time in Ashley's life, she saw the honest expression of love in a man's eyes. Her pulse raced and she felt lightheaded as she realized how very much she loved him, too. "And I will be right beside you, all the way."

Drawing her back to him, he held her tightly. "When this is over, I will take you somewhere where you will be safe," he promised. His arms tightened more possessively around her. "I give you my word. No one will hurt you."

Oh, Aaron, you still refuse to believe that neither of us is real. We're both caught in a fantasy over which we have no control.

Bringing her mouth to his, he tenderly brushed her lips. "You taste as I thought you would," he murmured.

"You have thought about how I'd taste?" she bantered lightly.

He nodded gravely. " 'Tis been the cause of my restless nights."

"That's nice to know." Pressing closer, she opened her mouth beneath his as he took full possession of her.

Rockets exploded, bells rang, and firecrackers burst in a glorious spray of color in Ashley's head at the sound of his masculine groan of pleasure.

She wasn't sure what would have happened next if Paul had not come thundering back down the road, looking for them.

"Are you hurt?"

Moving away from Aaron, she smiled. "I'm fine, really."

Aaron steadied her horse and helped her into the saddle. "Are you *sure* you're all right?"

"I . . ." She was tempted to tell him how badly her muscles ached, but she couldn't. Paul Revere, with Aaron Kenneman in the background, was charting the course of American history. She couldn't delay them any longer. "I'll be fine, really."

Aaron remounted and, giving her a warm smile, wheeled and rode off.

Ashley wearily kicked her mount, setting off in another uncomfortable trot down the road.

All along the road from Medford to Lexington, Paul roused the occupants of farmhouses, urging them to bear arms against the advancing British.

As they rode into Lexington, Paul proceeded directly to a large, redbrick house.

After jumping off his horse, he raced up the steps and pounded on the door. It took several tries to raise the occupant, but eventually the door flew open, and a tousle-haired man haphazardly dressed loomed threateningly in the doorway.

John Hancock stared at Paul Revere grumpily. "I trust you have a purpose for disturbing me at this hour?"

Paul grinned. "Hope I didn't interrupt anything worthwhile, John."

"I should be so fortunate."

"Have you spoken with Dawes?"

"Yes, I'm preparing to leave momentarily."

Ashley and Aaron waited as Revere and Hancock conversed in hurried tones. With a departing wave, Paul left Hancock standing on the porch and sprang to his horse. A moment later he galloped off down the road.

Turning their horses, Ashley and Aaron followed.

Farther down the road, Paul stopped at a small brownstone house. He sprang from his horse again, raced up the steps, and pounded on Samuel Adams's door.

The men conversed briefly, then Paul turned and strode toward Aaron.

Nudging his horse from the shadows, Aaron met him halfway.

"How fares Mistress Wheeler?" Paul asked.

"She grows weary." Aaron glanced over his shoulder, then lowered his voice. "Mayhap we might spare a moment for her to rest. 'Twould only be a short interruption."

"There is an inn not far down the road. We will spare a few moments," Paul acknowledged.

The three riders set off again. As they galloped down the road, a rider approached from the opposite direction, traveling hard.

The riders stopped short, their horses prancing. Paul recognized the traveler and called to him cordially. "Dawes! Good to see you!"

Willie Dawes tipped his hat to Revere. "I assume we make the same journey?"

"Yes, I too have spoken with Hancock and Adams."

Dawes nodded. "I will ride with you if you desire."

Paul nodded. "Your presence is welcome. But first we spare a few brief moments for the lady to rest."

Dawes glanced questioningly at Ashley, then back to Paul. "As you say."

The inn was small, virtually deserted at that hour. After lifting Ashley out of the saddle, Aaron helped her up the wooden steps.

"You're walking rather oddly," he teased.

She gave him a dour look that discouraged him from elaborating further.

Revere and Dawes were deep in conversation as Ashley gingerly took the seat Aaron provided for her.

A yawning serving girl set a mug of ale in front of the men, then turned to Ashley.

"What'll it be, mistress?"

"Oh . . . a Miller Lite, I guess." Ashley didn't care for beer as a rule, but she hoped the alcohol might dull the ache in her thighs.

Revere and Dawes interrupted their conversation to look at her.

"A glass of cider," she amended, too weary to try to explain. She lay her head down on the table, exhausted.

At Aaron's signal, the buxom girl brought meat pies for the four of them. The men conversed in low tones as they ate, ignoring her.

The meal was hurried, and long before Ashley was ready to ride again Paul consulted his pocket-watch, frowning. "I must be on my way to warn Concord."

After flipping a coin to the innkeeper, Aaron took Ashley's arm and helped her outside.

He escorted her to the horse, where he stole another

brief kiss. Lifting her hands to his face, she framed it as she returned the embrace, thinking that history be damned. She would do anything within her power to protect this man.

They were on the road only a short while when a rider suddenly appeared as a black silhouette against the moonlit sky.

Easing his horse closer to hers, Aaron said quietly, "If there is trouble, I want you to turn and ride back to Lexington. There is a small grove of trees on the outskirts of town. Wait there until I return. We will draw fire away from you to ensure that you won't be harmed."

"Don't worry. I have a can of Mace with me." Ashley's heart thumped erratically as the riders reined to a halt. Her hand moved to her canvas bag cautiously.

As the dust settled, a handsome young man hailed Aaron and Revere amiably.

"Revere! Kenneman! You near scared the waddin' out of me!"

"Prescott! God's eyes!" Revere exclaimed. "What are you doing out at this hour?"

Ashley's heartbeat slowed. Dr. Samuel Prescott was a patriot, and one whom she knew would eventually join the ride.

"In Lexington, visiting my sweetheart," Prescott exclaimed. "What is the purpose of your midnight jaunt?"

"The British have made their move," Paul said, "and we're riding to warn the colonists to gather arms."

Prescott's features darkened. "God's teeth . . . then I shall join the cause."

"You are welcome," Paul invited.

The five started out again, riding at a fast clip. When

they drew close to a house, Ashley and Aaron would drop back to remain within hailing distance but far enough away to allow the three men to go about their mission.

Toward dawn, the weary group looked up to see a group of redcoats riding toward them.

Ashley's heart rose to her throat as the men reined their mounts, watching the approaching riders warily.

"What do we do now?" Prescott asked.

"We ride like Satan himself was chasing us," Paul returned gravely.

Aaron and Ashley hurriedly cut their horses off the road and disappeared behind a thick row of undergrowth.

The redcoats drew closer, slowing to a walk now. "Halt! Who goes there?"

Dawes and Prescott suddenly kicked their horses and shot past the small patrol as Revere wheeled and took off in the opposite direction.

Shouts went up as the patrol broke into two groups, one riding after Revere, the other giving hot chase to Willie Dawes and Samuel Prescott.

Aaron tensed, about to leap to his friends' rescue, when Ashley reached over and grabbed his horse's bridle. Lifting her fingers to her lips, she shook her head.

"Why not?" Aaron whispered hotly. "They need my help!"

"They'll be all right," she assured him. "Watch."

In the ensuing melee, Dawes and Prescott rode to escape the patrol, but Revere's horse was not as fresh as the other men's and he was about to be overtaken.

"Damn you! Stop!" one of the officers shouted. "If you go an inch farther, you're a dead man!"

Realizing that he would be of no use to anyone dead, Paul slowed to a standstill.

A moment later the second patrol returned, ushering Dawes and Prescott ahead of them.

Aaron and Ashley watched as Paul, Willie, and Samuel were ordered into a pasture at the side of the road.

The patrol assembled again, and for the first time Aaron noticed they had three other prisoners under armed guard.

"Who are those men?" Aaron whispered.

"I don't remember the men's names, but history says that they spotted the patrol as it passed through Lexington. They attempted to follow it and keep it under surveillance, but the British discovered them and they were captured," Ashley whispered back.

"Move along quickly," the British soldier commanded to the four captives, "unless, mayhap, you want your brains blown out?"

Aaron slid quietly off his horse, dropping the reins. Moments later Ashley did the same. Keeping low to the ground, they crept through the tall grass toward the gathering in an attempt to hear the conversation.

A second soldier grabbed the bridle of Paul's horse. "From whence come you?"

Paul's voice rang out. "Boston."

"What time did you leave there? And why are you traveling at this hour?"

Aaron and Ashley crept closer. By now Ashley was almost afraid to breathe for fear of being detected. The moonlight made the night as bright as day, but the shadows created by the grove of trees and the tall grass provided adequate cover.

Her foot suddenly encountered a twig, and it snapped loudly. Ashley froze, reaching out to grasp Aaron's hand.

The soldier whirled, his eyes searching the bushes. "Who goes there!" he called out.

When he was met by silence, he turned back to Paul, smiling lazily. "Mayhap it is a friend of yours?" he prompted.

"We travel alone," Paul returned stoically.

"The man's a liar," one of the other soldiers snapped.

After turning his horse, he urged it into the undergrowth.

Whirling, Ashley and Aaron tried to run, but the British soldier fired a shot over their heads.

"Halt!"

Stumbling, Ashley tried to catch herself, but she lost her footing and pitched forward.

Aaron turned back to help her, but the soldier sprang from his horse and knocked him to his knees with the butt of his rifle.

Ashley and Aaron were both jerked to their feet and marched in double-step time to where Paul and the other three were held prisoner.

The officer looked surprised when his men emerged from the thicket leading a woman. "What say this! A fair maid you bring me?"

When Ashley failed to answer, the soldier holding her jerked her arm to prompt her response.

"Gently, man. Gently," the officer chided. " 'Tis a comely wench we have discovered."

Ashley sensed rather than saw Aaron's move toward the soldier. She quietly reached out to restrain him.

"Would that we had more time . . . and less company," the officer commented in a low voice that seemed meant only for Ashley's ears. His eyes traveled over her hungrily. " 'Tis been a long time since I have feasted on such beauty."

His hand reached out and selected a strand of her hair between his fingers, admiring the silky texture.

Aaron's muscles flexed beneath her hand, and Ashley tightened her hold on him.

The officer's eyes reluctantly left Ashley to return to Aaron. "You are here to help your friend?"

"We were . . . having a tryst," Ashley answered before Aaron could.

"Ah," the soldier murmured. "A tryst." His eyes met Aaron's enviously. "You are a lucky man."

Ashley could see the muscle in Aaron's jaw working tightly, and she prayed he would remain quiet.

"And you, sir," the soldier turned to Paul. "Who are you?"

The soldier prodded Revere with his gun. "State your name!"

"Revere."

"First name!"

"Paul."

The soldier stepped back. "Paul Revere? The silversmith and patriot?"

"The same," Paul stated.

"Then we have done well this day," the red-coated officer said with satisfaction. He glanced at his patrol. "Let us continue with our growing band of prisoners." He turned again to Ashley. "Mayhap you would do me the honor of riding with me, lovely maid?" His smile broadened. "We can spend the hours becoming . . . better acquainted?"

Aaron swore, taking a step forward, but Ashley firmly restrained him.

"I would be happy to ride with you, Captain." She smiled. "If you would be so kind as to bring my horse?"

The captain signaled for their mounts to be brought around.

"Are you comfortable?" the captain inquired graciously when Ashley was safely aboard the horse again.

"Quite comfortable, Captain. Thank you."

Lifting his hand, the captain moved the patrol out.

Two men rode in front, two behind. Two rode in the middle of the group so that Aaron had no opportunity to exchange words with Paul. Ashley could tell by Aaron's expression that he was worried about what had happened, but there was nothing she could do or say to him.

As they approached Lexington, the loud volley of gunfire reached them.

Slowing the patrol, the captain listened as the shots grew louder.

One of the three men captured earlier burst out laughing. "Ha! The bells are ringing! The town has been alarmed. You're all dead men!"

"What does he speak of?" the captain snapped.

"I don't know, sir . . . unless the town has been warned."

The patrol was halted, and, with their guns trained on the prisoners, the officers hurriedly conferred among themselves.

Paul worked his horse closer to Ashley and Aaron.

"What happens now?" He whispered.

"I don't remember," Ashley whispered back.

Paul glared at her irritably. Wonderful! *Now* her memory failed her.

13

Ashley watched as one of the officers separated from his companions and rode back to Elijah Sanderson, one of the first three prisoners.

"I must do you an injury," the redcoat said as he quickly dismounted.

Elijah drew back protectively, and Ashley tensed as she watched the officer draw out his knife. Was he going to kill the man right in front of them? Would she and Aaron be next?

Edging forward in the saddle anxiously, she watched as the officer stepped closer.

"Dismount," the redcoat ordered.

Elijah got off his horse slowly. He stood beside his mount, visibly quaking now. "Make it merciful, gov'nor. I have no wish to die a lingerin' death."

Stepping forward, the officer firmly gripped the horse's bridle. The knife flashed in the moonlight. With a surgical slash the officer cut the bridle, then the girth. The saddle and bridle hit the ground simultaneously.

The officer then turned to Jonathan Loring and Solomon Brown. "Dismount!"

The two men obeyed, their eyes fixed on the young Tory. Again the knife flashed. Moments later three horses stood free of their saddles and bridles, and three men were standing in the road, waiting to meet their fate.

Ashley glanced apprehensively at Aaron and Paul, wondering if one or the other would attempt to intervene.

"On your way," the officer ordered with an absent sweep of his hand.

Sanderson, Brown, and Loring stood rooted to the spot, their eyes still fixed upon the young British soldier.

Loring regained his bearings first. Clearing his throat, he stepped forward. "Uh . . . begging your pardon, gov'nor . . . did you say for me to be on me way?"

"Yes, you fool. On your way," the redcoat snapped. "We've no time to be bothered with prisoners."

The three men suddenly broke into a run, disappearing into the thicket seconds later. Twigs snapped, branches popped, and bushes rustled as the men beat a hurried retreat.

Remounting, the officer lifted his hand and the patrol moved forward with Aaron, Ashley, and Paul Revere still under guard.

They hadn't ridden far when the sound of gunfire reached them. Ashley glanced reassuringly at Aaron as the patrol reined in.

The soldiers sat for a moment, listening to the shot echoing over the countryside. By the frowns on their faces, they were clearly puzzled by the loud volley.

The British began to confer in low, anxious tones as a second volley sounded.

Ashley edged her horse closer to Aaron's. "Why have they stopped?"

"The militiamen have assembled," Aaron returned quietly.

The officer in charge suddenly turned to call over his shoulder to Revere. "How far is it to Cambridge?"

"Some distance," Revere returned vaguely.

The officers resumed their conversation in hushed whispers.

"What do you think they're discussing?" Ashley murmured.

Aaron shifted in the saddle, his eyes riveted on the two officers. "I would say that they're trying to decide what to do. It would be ill fortune for a small troop to be caught without reinforcements, under the circumstances. By the looks on their faces, I believe they realize that."

One of the officers suddenly turned and threaded his way back through the pack. When he reached Paul, he reined the horse to a halt.

Viewing the soldier who sat guarding Aaron, the officer asked, "Does your horse grow weary?"

"Stumbling, sir."

The officer's eyes motioned toward Paul. "Then take his."

"Yes, sir."

Turning to the guard sitting on the left of Ashley, the officer asked, "And your mounts?"

"The same, sir. Extremely weary."

The officer's gaze fixed on Ashley coldly now. "I pray that you will excuse our deplorable manners, lovely one, but our horses grow weary. If you and your . . . gentleman friend would be so kind as to offer yours?"

Aaron and Ashley quietly dismounted. Handing the guard her reins, Ashley murmured softly, "Good luck. With this horse, you'll need it."

The guard raised an imperious brow at her.

"Believe me, you'll understand completely a mile down the road."

The assigned guards dismounted, then turned to strip the saddles and bridles. Slapping their horses' rumps, they sent them off into the night.

As they mounted the confiscated animals, they listened as the sounds of gunfire grew closer.

"You're a lucky man, Revere!" the officer called.

"As you say, Captain."

The officer wheeled his horse, and the patrol rode off.

Ashley, Aaron, and Paul stood in the middle of the road, choking on the British dust.

"Well, *how* do you like that?" Ashley complained.

"I can't say that I do." Aaron watched as the patrol grew smaller.

"Now what?" Ashley sighed, sitting down for a moment on a large rock.

"We go on." Paul straightened his waistcoat irritably.

"I was afraid you'd say that," Ashley murmured, getting up again.

"The moon is too bright to follow the road. I know a less traveled way. Follow me."

Ashley fell into step with the two men as they started off through a pasture.

"Damn, damn, damn!" Paul cursed as they hurried along. "*History's* being made and me without a horse!"

It seemed to Ashley that she had been in love with Aaron Kenneman all of her life. As they walked along the moonlit road, she thought about the men she'd dated over the past few years. There wasn't a one—with the exception of Joel—whom she felt so close to or trusted as much. She would trust Aaron with her life—she *was* trusting him with her life—and somehow, though they had barely come to know each other, she knew he'd changed her life forever.

Dropping back a few steps, Aaron urged Paul to proceed ahead of them.

"We're in the *midst* of crisis," Paul complained as he obediently took the lead. "And all you two can think about is . . . each other."

Drawing Ashley close, Aaron grinned then pressed his lips to her temples. "Does he speak the truth? Are your thoughts consumed with me?" he teased.

She blushed, realizing that somehow her earlier reflection had been transmitted to him—which really didn't surprise her. It seemed everything about him was designed to make her think.

Becoming serious, Aaron said softly, "If this was a different time . . . if we weren't embroiled in this battle . . ." He paused, finding it difficult to go on. "I would hold you close and make you promises," he finished gently.

Taking his hand, she smiled. "And I would nurture your promises."

He paused, caressing the outline of her face with the tips of his fingers. "This Joel that you speak of. Is he good to you?"

"Yes . . . he is. In so many ways he reminds me of you."

"Then when this is over, you must go to him."

"I can't. I was so selfish. I thought that if he loved me he had to spend every minute with me."

"I'm sure he wanted to." He tenderly brushed a wisp of hair from her cheek.

"But he couldn't. Being with you has shown me

that . . . and so much more." Her fingers rested against his cheek. "Now I understand that a doctor's life is different from a baker's or a shopkeeper's. People don't need you just between the hours of dawn and dusk."

His smile was warm. "Would that sickness were so considerate."

"You see, I thought Joel could just tell his patients to take an aspirin and call him in the morning. Now I understand why he couldn't. And I appreciate him all the more because he wouldn't."

."Then you must tell him so."

"If I ever have the chance. He probably will never forgive me, but I feel better."

"He'll forgive you."

"No, I was too thoughtless. You just don't know . . ."

"I do know. If he's the kind of man you could love, he'll forgive you anything. When this is over you'll tell him how you feel, and he'll understand. And one day, after you've been married for a very long time, you'll look back and laugh at how afraid you were that he'd stopped loving you." His gaze searched hers in the moonlight. "And when you do, I hope you'll remember me fondly."

"I'll never forget you," she promised. "Oh, Aaron, I'm so scared."

His eyes grew infinitely more tender. "I cannot believe the Ashley Wheeler that I know is scared of anything."

Ashley sighed. "But I am, Aaron. I'm such a mess."

"You are reluctant to allow a man to love you?"

"No, I'm afraid that I'll never be able to commit to one man. I'm terrified that if I marry, one day we'll both wake up and not be able to stand each other. Can you understand . . . does that make sense?"

"Mayhap it would be easier to understand if I, too, were not the man who was in love with you."

"Oh, Aaron . . ." She pressed toward him, engaging him in a long, urgent kiss.

As their lips parted, his eyes searched hers again.

"Have many men asked to marry you?"

She nodded, ashamed to confess just how many chances she'd been given to make a lasting commitment.

She frowned when she saw his look of disappointment at her candor.

He draped his arm around her waist, and they began walking. "Mayhap there is a bond between us that will remain long after we're parted," he said. "I would like to believe this is true."

"A bond?" She didn't want to think about losing him. She couldn't bear to think about losing him. "No, if this is a dream, I don't want to wake up. Maybe it is a time warp and I won't ever have to go back."

His mouth lowered to hers again, stilling her protests. Savoring the moment, she closed her eyes, trying to capture and hold him in her memory forever.

Distant sounds of gunfire eventually drew them back to the present. Aaron sighed regretfully. "Paul is outdistancing us greatly. We must keep up."

"Come, come!" Paul called, urging them to stop their nonsense and get on with business.

Ashley clasped Aaron's hand, and together they began running across the field after Revere.

They raced through the night. At first, Ashley was able to keep pace with the men effortlessly, but after fifteen minutes or so, she began to lag behind.

When they had gone a mile or more, her breath was

beginning to come in gasps. She had no idea where they were or where they were going; she just kept running.

On they ran, scrambling through brush and thicket. Ashley gasped as a branch came back to whack her in the face. The force of the blow nearly knocked her off her feet, and Aaron's hasty apology did little to dull the sting.

They jumped a ditch, and her ankle twisted as she landed, but on she limped, clinging tightly to Aaron's hand.

Stumbling over clumps of grass, she was certain she had just stepped into a fresh cow pile, but she was afraid to stop long enough to investigate.

The pungent aroma a few minutes later told her she had been right. She winced, skidding into another wet pile. This time she pitched forward, her eyes widening as she slid past the squashy patty.

Struggling back to her feet, she called to Aaron, who paused only long enough to see that she was all right before he ran on.

Up ahead she could see Paul's silhouette as he set an even faster pace toward Lexington.

As they neared a small farmhouse, a stone wall loomed before them.

She groaned aloud as she watched Aaron leap the wall behind Revere, then reach out to drag her over after him.

Tumbling over the top, she lost her balance and fell, landing on top of Aaron.

Collapsed beneath her weight, Aaron tried to struggle out from beneath her, but she suddenly broke out laughing. This was so *absurd!*

"Dammit, Ashley, we have to hurry," Aaron scolded, struggling back to his feet.

Rolling her head to one side, Ashley's merriment

quickly dissolved when she saw a granite headstone not more than six inches away.

"Oh!" She scrambled to her feet, anxiously backing away from the gravesite.

"Come now, 'tis only a family graveyard," Aaron whispered.

"*Only* a graveyard?" Now she was running around a *graveyard* in the dead of night. She forced herself to swallow the lump of panic in her throat. She *refused* to attend funerals, and it would take a team of pack mules to drag her into a cemetery!

Muttering a quick apology to the occupant of the grave she was trampling, she ran on.

"Paul is almost out of sight," Aaron called. "Run faster!"

"Oh, Lord." She groaned, trying to ignore a painful cramp forming in her left side.

By the time Lexington was in sight, Ashley was gasping for breath.

Collapsing on the steps of John Hancock's house, she listened as Paul rapped on the door insistently.

Hancock opened the door a moment later, still pulling on his coat.

"John! God's teeth, am I glad to see you. I thought you might have left," Paul said, leaning against the door frame to catch his breath.

"Paul?" Hancock was surprised to see Revere standing on his porch again. "What's wrong now? Adams and I are just leaving."

Paul quickly explained the circumstances, and John summoned his clerk, John Lowell.

"John, fetch my carriage," he ordered. "Revere, Kenneman, and Mistress Wheeler will be riding with us."

John bowed, hurrying off a second later.

In a matter of minutes, the carriage was brought around. Aaron quickly helped Ashley aboard, then Hancock, Adams, Lowell, and Paul joined them.

Inside the coach, Ashley sat squeezed tightly into a corner next to Aaron, who held her protectively as the carriage lurched forward.

The coach careened wildly through town as the driver whipped the team into top speed and sped back along the moonlit road. Ashley clung to Aaron tightly, wondering if they would live through the night.

Aware of her anguish, Aaron pressed his lips to her temple, holding her reassuringly.

Hancock and Revere were deep in conversation when suddenly Hancock jerked to attention.

"God's eyes! I've left my trunk of papers in Lexington!"

"Damn, John!" For the first time Aaron lost his patience.

"We have to go back. If the British find them, we're lost!" John leaned out the window of the carriage, shouting "Stop!"

"What is going on?" The driver fought the horses, trying to bring the carriage to a complete halt.

Hancock laid a restraining hand on Paul's arm. "It is risky to return by carriage, Paul. The British draw closer."

"Then I will walk back," Paul said firmly. "You cannot risk being caught, and we can't leave those papers behind, John. If the English find them, our cause will be irreparably harmed."

Paul opened the door and stepped out of the carriage. "Continue on. I shall secure the papers and then meet up with you later."

Releasing Ashley reluctantly, Aaron prepared to go with Paul.

John Lowell reached out to block his efforts. The older man's eyes radiated deep concern. "I will accompany Paul."

Aaron glanced at Ashley, who by now was staring at him, near tears.

"John, I can't allow you do that. 'Tis too dangerous," Aaron protested.

"Please." John's smile was gentle. "I have only myself to look after." His eyes returned to Ashley tenderly. "Grant me the honor of going, instead of you."

Ashley gripped Aaron's arm tightly. "Please, Aaron, let him go." Her heart was in her eyes as she gazed back at him. She had an inexplicable feeling that if he went with Paul, she would never see him again.

After giving John's shoulder a firm squeeze, Aaron moved around him to exit the carriage. "You are welcome to come along, John, but I must go with Paul."

Ashley sat forward as John exited the coach behind Aaron. As Aaron closed the carriage door, his eyes met Ashley's. "I will be safe. You are not to be concerned."

"I'm coming with you." Pushing the door open, Ashley tried to scramble out of the coach.

"No!" Aaron caught the door and held it. "You are to continue on with Hancock and Adams."

"No!" Ashley argued. "I'm going with you."

"Ashley," Aaron began patiently, "you cannot go with me. You are near exhaustion as it is. Paul, Lowell, and I will return to Lexington, and you will—"

"I'm going." Again Ashley tried to force the door open, but Aaron stubbornly refused to permit it.

"*No*, you're not."

"*Yes*, I am.

"You will *do* what I say."

"I *won't*," Ashley stated emphatically. "I'm afraid you'll be hurt."

"Kenneman," Hancock said wearily, "are you going or not? We could all be old men by the time you settle this dispute."

"I'm going." Aaron pointed at Ashley sternly. "You're staying."

Leaning inside the carriage window, he captured her face between his hands and looked deeply into her eyes. "Ashley, please listen to reason. Anything could happen. I cannot take the chance that you will be harmed," he whispered.

"I know that anything can happen. That's why I want to be with you." Her voice caught in a sob. "Please, Aaron, I'm so frightened for you."

Her eyes filled with tears, and he kissed them away tenderly. His lips trailed down her face, clinging briefly to hers before he drew away.

"Please don't leave me," she whispered.

"I don't want to leave you, but you'll be safer in Hancock's care." He kissed her one last time, then turned and started after Paul and John, who were already walking back toward Lexington.

"Paul!" Ashley leaned out the carriage window anxiously. "Don't let him get hurt!"

Aaron glanced at Paul and rolled his eyes.

"I'll hold his hand at every corner," Paul returned, winking at Aaron. "You can be sure of that!"

Hancock leaned forward, patting her hand reassuringly. "The battle for freedom claims many casualties, my dear."

Ashley's eyes refused to leave Aaron until his tall figure disappeared over a small rise. "Although I was born in America, and I've enjoyed all the liberty and indepen-

dence that men like you and Aaron and Paul have sacri-
ficed their very lives for, I'm only now realizing how precious freedom is . . . and how precious truly loving one
man can be," she confessed.

John understood (as Paul had confided to him) and said,
"Ah, child, I wish I knew the America of which you
speak." He leaned back, smiling now as his eyes clouded
with a prescient vision. "But someday, and very soon I
pray, we shall declare ourselves separate from the state of
Great Britain, declaring that *all* men possess the God-
given rights to life, liberty, and the pursuit of happiness.
Only then will we be free." He sighed. "Only then."

Samuel Adams, who had been quiet until now, spoke
up. " 'Tis a dream we shall see, John. We cannot despair."

The carriage lurched forward, and Ashley rested her
head on the back of the seat, wondering if she would ever
see Aaron again.

As the coach rolled along, Hancock and Adams relaxed
against the wall and dozed, weary from their hectic night.

They hadn't gone more than a mile when Ashley suddenly leaned out the window and called for the driver to
stop the carriage.

Ashley heard the driver shouting an assortment of colorful epithets as he fought to bring the coach to a stop.

Hancock stirred sleepily, cocking one eye open. "What
is it now?"

"I need to . . . take a walk," she said.

"A walk?" Hancock's brows raised with suspicion. "At
this hour?"

"I . . . um, need to take a walk," Ashley said again,
hoping that he wouldn't press for details.

"Oh, yes . . . certainly," he muttered as the source of

her distress finally dawned on him. He opened the carriage door for her.

Ashley climbed down and picked her way carefully through the brush at the side of the road.

As she parted the bushes, Ashley saw that Hancock and Adams had gone back to dozing and the driver had seized his opportunity to do the same. Lifting her skirts, she turned and tiptoed away.

There wasn't much time; she had to put as much distance between her and the carriage as she possibly could before Hancock discovered that she was gone.

She ran faster, her breath coming in short spurts now. She had to find Aaron before he left the tavern. If anything happened to him, she couldn't bear it.

Holding her side with one hand, she darted out on the road, running faster as she glanced over her shoulder to see if her plan had been discovered.

She was relieved when she saw that it hadn't. As she disappeared over the rise, the coach was still sitting in the middle of the road, the three male occupants dozing peacefully.

14

"**M**istress Wheeler, why do I have the impression you're not listening to me?" Aaron stood before Ashley thirty minutes later, arms crossed, staring at her crossly.

"I know you're upset, but I had to come. I couldn't just sit there and let anything happen to you!"

"Ashley, 'tis too dangerous—"

"Aaron." Ashley laid her hand over his mouth to still his protests. "Please, I'm here, and there's nothing you can do about it. We'll only be wasting time if we stand around arguing, and it won't do any good to *take* me back—I'll just run away again."

"Where is Hancock?"

"He was sleeping last time I saw him."

"Sleeping!"

Paul sighed. "She speaks the truth, Aaron. If we return her to Hancock, we lose yet more valuable time."

"Paul, I don't like it."

Turning Aaron and Paul toward the tavern, Ashley hooked her arms through theirs and set them to walking. "Look at it this way, guys. There's a lot of things *I* don't like." She smiled up at the two men brightly. "We'll just all have to learn to be more flexible."

* * *

The morning sun was a fiery red ball in the eastern sky by the time Ashley, Aaron, Paul, and John Lowell approached Lexington. The morning air had a chill to it, causing Ashley to huddle deeper into the coat Aaron had lent her.

She drew closer to Aaron's side as she noticed that the men were keeping a close eye out for British soldiers.

As they neared town, they had taken to the ditches and underbrush each time they heard someone approaching, only to see a farmer striding determinedly down the road with his muzzle loader over his shoulder.

" 'Tis obvious the town has been alarmed," Paul whispered as they crouched in a ditch waiting for the latest traveler to pass. "We must proceed to the green where the militia meets. There we can observe what is transpiring."

The four continued on, creeping between houses and down alleyways until Lexington Green was in sight.

Crouching behind a thorny bush, they watched as a young boy slung the strap of a drum over his shoulder and beat a roll. Fifty to sixty militiamen gathered in formation, wearing a variety of ragtag uniforms. Each man's face was stamped with firm determination. Ashley shook her head sadly as she watched the preparations for battle, knowing that many of them would never see the end of this day.

After brief instructions, the commander of the group dismissed the militia.

"Dismissed," he called out. "But stay within call of the drum and at the ready!"

The air was thick with anxiety. Ashley's heart beat like a trip-hammer as she watched young farmers becoming soldiers to fight for a conviction they felt was precious enough for which to risk their lives—freedom.

The group broke up slowly, many walking across the green to a tavern adjoining the common to await further orders.

" 'Tis a stroke of good luck that Captain Parker leads them," Paul murmured.

After slipping from the bushes, Paul hurried to the captain. The two men shook hands, then began to converse in quiet undertones.

Suddenly a man ran up to Captain Parker, gesturing excitedly down the road. Captain Parker listened, his features tightening as he tried to follow the man's rapid, anxious discourse.

"How far, Thaddeus?"

"Within a mile, sir. I saw them with mine own eyes!"

A moment later Paul hurried back to Aaron, Ashley, and John. "Bowman has been out on the road. He says the British troops are within a mile."

Aaron's jaw grew firm. "I want Ashley at the tavern, where she'll be protected."

"Be quick about it." Paul crawled off, looking for a better vantage point to observe the British when they entered town.

"No." Ashley's hand gripped Aaron's arm tightly, "I want to stay with you."

"This time there'll be no argument," Aaron said shortly. "The British are within minutes of here. There will be a battle, and I will not allow you to remain in danger."

Ashley couldn't deny that she was concerned. She was about to be caught up in a war, a very bloody, brutal war between men who had once been countrymen but who now were at odds on an issue that they felt could be resolved in no other way. Blood would be spilled today. Men would die—*please God, not Aaron.* She wanted to cry out and stop the madness, but she knew her efforts would be useless. She was powerless to prevent the battle about to take place.

The bushes parted, and Paul returned. He extended his hand to Aaron. "I take my leave now. The British are nearly upon us."

"Be careful, Paul," Aaron responded solemnly.

"And you too, my good friend. His hand upon us this day." The two men shook hands, aware that it might be for the last time.

Revere turned to Ashley. "And you, young lady. You've been an education." A faint smile curved his lips. "In many ways, you're like my Rachel. She would never have stayed behind—had it not been for the children."

"Oh, Paul." Ashley went into his arms, giving him a warm hug. "I've never appreciated you enough."

"Nonsense. If what you say is true, then you know that our efforts will not be in vain." Squeezing her hand, he smiled. "Take care, little one." Turning to John, he said quietly, "It is time we retrieved Hancock's papers and were on our way." Giving Ashley's hand another quick squeeze, he nodded gravely to Aaron, and then he was gone.

Aaron's features were grim as he watched Paul and John make their way across the green. "Ah, would that I could see the future," he said softly.

"Paul will be fine," Ashley murmured. "He will return to his family and finish out his days in his silversmith shop, raise his children, and enjoy his many grandchildren."

Aaron turned, a ray of hope lighting his eyes. "This is certain?"

Ashley smiled. "It is certain."

Reaching for her hand, he said, "Come. We must get you safely away from the common."

This time Ashley didn't argue with him. Until now she'd been fairly certain of what was happening or what was about to happen. But now she wasn't so confident. Nothing was certain, she realized, and that frightened her.

Within minutes, Aaron had escorted Ashley into the tavern and secured a room.

They mounted the stairs quietly, each absorbed in thought. As they entered the room, Ashley went immediately to the window that directly overlooked the green. If she could endure it, she planned to watch the battle. She didn't want to be a witness to the upheaval, for she suspected that Aaron would be in the thick of it, but she would have to know that he was safe.

Ashley turned from the window as she heard the door close and the bolt slip into the lock. Aaron stood in the middle of the room, gazing at her.

A sob caught in her throat as she realized how easily she could lose him now. "Oh, Aaron, I'm so frightened," she whispered.

"I know."

"If this is a dream, I want it to be over and for you to be safe."

"But it isn't a dream. What's about to happen is very real."

"If I could wish you away—"

"I would not go. I have a commitment to this cause."

"But what if I never see you again?" She swallowed back tears.

His eyes met hers, and Ashley died a thousand deaths. She had callously cast so many men aside in her life. How could this man—this handsome, magnificent figment of her imagination—have captured her heart so effortlessly?

"Then you must remember that I have loved you dearly."

The terrible, lonely ache in her heart told her that her time with him was growing very short.

After crossing the room, he drew her into his arms and rested his chin on top of her head. Ashley sighed and closed her eyes, wondering how she would live without him. "I'm so afraid."

"There is no need for fear. You will not be harmed."

"I wish—"

"Shhhh," he cautioned. "We have only this moment. Let us not spoil it with tears and regrets."

"I can't help it. I wish I knew what was happening to me. . . . I don't want to lose you." She sobbed. "For the first time in my life, I'm in love, and I'm going to lose you."

He smiled, holding her closer. "Are you saying, Ashley Wheeler, that if it were possible, you would be my wife?"

"Oh, Aaron, yes—yes!" Though this dream could end at any moment, sending her careening back to her real life, knowing he wanted to marry her meant everything.

"And you would be willing to set aside a day that we would marry?" he whispered, his breath fanning her hair softly.

Tears slipped down her cheeks as her arms crept about his waist tighter. "Yes, I would marry you any day, anywhere, anytime you'd want."

His mouth inched lower, his breath barely a whisper against hers. "And if it were possible, we would not delay a moment, my love."

Her breath came quickly now as his mouth lowered to

taste her lips. Longing seared through her as their mouths
slowly came together. Ashley pressed closer, aware of the
flash of blinding heat his touch aroused in her. For the
first time in her life, she wanted to give rather than take.
But, as fate would have it, the man whom she would capture with her love was already a prisoner of time.

Passion flared to the surface as the kiss deepened. His
hands became bolder, weaving them both in a web of
white-hot desire. Time was so short, and Ashley had so
much she longed to share with him.

She gently caught his tongue between her teeth and
relished his groan of male pleasure as sounds of impending battle drifted through the window to them.

"I must go. The British will be here in minutes, and my
services will be needed," he murmured.

Ashley suddenly realized that Aaron wouldn't be carrying a gun in the battle; he would be a field surgeon in the
thick of the battle without protection. Another sob escaped her, and once it had, others followed until she buried her face in his chest and wept openly.

"Please, 'tis impossible for me to leave you this way.
Send me off with your kiss, not your tears."

Ashley clasped his face between her hands and pulled
it back down to hers, pressing her lips against his. The
sweetness of good-bye in their kiss made her want to cling
to him all the more.

"I don't want to live without you, Aaron Kenneman,"
she whispered.

"You will forever be in my heart, my love."

After tilting her face up to his for one last kiss, Aaron
turned and walked to the door. Over his shoulder, he sent
her a smile that melted her heart. A moment later, the
door closed, and she was alone.

Dropping onto the bed, she listened to the scrape of his boots descending the stairway.

A moment later she rose and crossed to the window to watch the scurry of activity in the common below. Her hands clasped together in an unconscious posture of prayer as her eyes searched for Aaron.

From her vantage point, she could hear Captain Parker ordering the drummer to beat to arms. Militiamen began pouring out of the tavern and assembled on the green, forming lines that reached from the meetinghouse toward the south.

Ashley counted approximately seventy men by this time, all hurrying to take up arms.

Suddenly the sound of the drumbeat quickened. The men in the common turned to see a line of British regulars marching toward them in brisk formation.

When the regulars were within sound of the militiamen they halted, charged their guns, and doubled ranks. Ashley held her breath as she watched. Knowing that the ultimate victory would belong to the colonists failed to diminish her fear.

The British began to march in a quick-step toward the green as Captain Parker sang out his order.

"Stand your ground! Don't molest the regulars unless they meddle with us!"

Ashley's hands came to her mouth as the drama began to unfold. Her eyes searched desperately for Aaron, but she failed to locate him anywhere.

The British troops marched straight toward the colonists. A shout went up, and the regulars paused. The commanding officer advanced a few yards out front, yelling *"Disperse, you damned rebels! You dogs! Run!"* Raising his pistol, he shouted, *"Rush on, my boys!"* A shot rang out, reverberating throughout the countryside.

The Americans stood at attention, waiting. Silence hung thick in the air as the British troops started forward again.

"We be hopelessly outnumbered," militiaman Ebenezer Munroe murmured to the man standing to his left.

"Aye, this day we die for our country," Corporal John Munroe returned gravely. Both men took aim at the main body of the troops and opened fire.

As a spirited volley of fire was exchanged, Ashley saw Paul and John dart from the main floor of the tavern carrying the trunk of papers Hancock had left behind. Smoke was heavy now as the two men slackened their pace to saunter casually through the American lines with the trunk.

Once clear of the militiamen, they broke into a run as a volley of gunfire echoed across the green.

"Who's firing?" John shouted.

"I don't know, and I don't plan to take the time to ask!" Paul exclaimed. Ducking low to the ground, the two ran on.

Ashley closed her eyes, praying for their safety as she listened to the rapid succession of guns firing back and forth.

"They're firing nothing but powder!" John Munroe shouted.

"Are you sure?" Ebenezer shouted back.

"No—they're firing more than *powder!*" John amended sourly as he lifted his arm to survey the blood on it a moment later. "I'll give them the guts of my gun!"

Ashley watched as the colonists attempted to hold their ground although they were taking British fire and falling.

Some retreated up the north road and were pursued by a British officer on horseback. As he rode after them, Ashley could hear him yelling over the sound of musketfire, "Damn you, *stop*, or you will die!"

One colonist sprang over a pair of bars and made a stand, firing his gun. The British officer wheeled his horse and returned to the main group to rejoin the fray.

By now the smoke of battle was so thick that Ashley could see only the heads of the British horses. Her eyes searched in vain for any sign of Aaron, but she failed to find one. *Oh, please,* she prayed. *Don't let him be lying wounded somewhere.*

The volley of fire continued from the regulars, and Ashley recoiled. Some of the colonists fell back a few feet to reload. She saw one at the edge of the battle reload and fire, and then a shot from the British regulars hit his gun barrel and broke it in two.

Ashley leaned out of the window and shouted a warning to a militiaman sitting on the ground trying to reload his gun. Just as the man glanced up at her, a British soldier ran his bayonet through him. Ashley covered her eyes and moaned as the man slumped to the ground.

The British were firing so furiously and there was so much confusion that Ashley felt faint. It was impossible to know the number of colonists who fell at each volley, but the firing continued in all directions.

Then as suddenly as it had started, the colonists began to drop back into formation. Ashley saw a British soldier fire one last volley at Solomon Brown, who was stationed behind a wall. She gasped as the wall smoked after it was hit.

Brown rose and fired into the solid column of regulars, then beat a hasty retreat, using the wall as a shield.

Suddenly the battle quieted.

A moment later Ashley heard the sound of a drummer, beating the call to retreat.

The British ceased fire and began moving into columns. Once formed, they fired a last volley for victory and gave three rousing cheers.

Ashley watched as the red-coated men moved forward to the tune of fife and drum, marching in the direction of Concord.

The smoke began to clear and the cadence of drums dimmed as Ashley slumped weakly against the window-sill.

The British would march on to Concord. The colonists would regather their forces and meet the redcoats again, but none of these men would realize the repercussions of what had happened here on this green today.

The first battle of the Revolutionary War had been fired, the first blood spilled in the fight for the colonies' right to separate from Britain. The upstart youngster, as the British termed the colonies, had begun to stretch and grow, and America would never again be the same.

Ashley felt strange standing at the window staring down upon a site where a battle had just been fought. It had lasted such a short time, already it seemed unreal. Ever since she'd fallen through the roof of the Green Dragon Tavern, time had meant nothing to her, just one inconceivable event strung upon another.

"Ashley."

"Yes?" She whirled from the window, trying to locate the whispered voice. For one crazy moment, she thought Aaron had called her name, but that was impossible: He couldn't be here.

Was she going completely mad? She closed her eyes

and her fingers came to her temples to still the sudden pounding. The abrupt pain was like a hammer upon an anvil, beating relentlessly against her skull.

"Ashley."

At the sound of her name, she opened her eyes slowly, squinting against the building pressure in her cranium. Once again she found the room empty.

"I *am* losing my mind," she murmured.

Suddenly the door burst open. She cried out when she saw Aaron standing in the doorway, grinning at her. With tears in her eyes, she threw herself into his arms.

"You're all right!"

"A little singed, but unharmed." Aaron gave a whoop of victory as he swept her up into his arms, hugging her. "I may not be in your history books, Ashley Wheeler, but I was there today!"

"I was so afraid—" His mouth closed over hers, muffling her words. "I couldn't find you anywhere!" she murmured against his lips.

"I was damned busy! We had eight dead and ten wounded at last count. Once I had to grab a pistol and fire when a Tory rode in upon me and refused to recognize my medical box."

Throwing back his head, he began to laugh. The laughter rolled out of him so long that Ashley thought he might be hysterical.

"We won! We won against those lobsterbacks!"

Ashley didn't have the heart to tell him that the colonists hadn't actually "won," though they had survived to fight again.

His mouth came back to hers, savoring the victory they shared.

"I have to get you out of here to safety," he murmured when their lips finally parted. "The British may return."

"They won't. They're on their way to Concord."

He smiled at her indulgently as he hurried her toward the door. "Mayhap, but I'm taking no chances."

The townsfolk were beginning to recover from their shock. They bustled around, trying to aid the wounded and comfort those whose loved ones had paid the ultimate price for freedom.

Aaron and Ashley made their way down the street, trying to reach the edge of town unnoticed. Aaron paused occasionally to kneel beside a wounded man, quickly administering help before he moved on.

It took over forty minutes for them to reach the edge of Lexington.

"We will take to the woods," Aaron called as he took her hand and they ran across the road. " 'Twill be dark soon, and we can't risk running into a British patrol."

"Where are we going?" Ashley called back.

He glanced back at her, smiling. "We are going to find a place where we can be alone."

Ashley frowned, feeling a sudden pang in her heart. *Where they could be alone—or where they could say good-bye?*

15

The barn had not been used for some time, but the hay was dry and pleasantly fragrant. The late-afternoon light filtered weakly through the cracks, and motes of dust floated through the air as Ashley and Aaron entered the building's cool interior.

"It's not the Green Dragon," Aaron apologized. "But it will afford us a measure of privacy."

After picking up a stick, Ashley poked at the mound of straw gingerly, hoping there weren't any mice and snakes hiding in it. The sound of tiny feet scurrying into dark corners drew her back rapidly to Aaron's side. "It's okay, I don't mind."

"We'll spend the night here, then be on our way back to Boston at early light."

"Then what?"

Aaron sighed. "I know not what."

Her eyes roamed about the interior of the barn, and she sighed. Everything seemed surrealistic to her now. They were in danger of capture by British soldiers; she had just witnessed the opening battle of the Revolutionary War; and now she was willing to spend the night with a special man in a mice-infested barn. She would never complain of being bored again.

"The hay looks soft," she said, sinking down upon it. She lay back and closed her eyes, letting the scent of the hay wash over her. "I'm hungry again." The meat pies they had eaten earlier had barely satisfied her.

She opened her eyes slowly to find Aaron smiling down at her.

"My hunger is of a different nature," he confessed.

Offering him her hand, she pulled him down on the sweet-smelling hay beside her.

"You're wearing your glasses again."

"I'm trying too." His mouth met hers, and they kissed, a long, intimate kiss that said more than words ever could. Murmuring each other's name, they rolled over in the hay as the kiss grew deeper.

"Ah, but you are sweet," Aaron whispered many long minutes later.

Ashley smiled as she held him closer. "You didn't think so once."

"Ahh, but I only portrayed indifference," he confessed. "You are a most winsome morsel, Ashley Wheeler."

His hand caressed her breast, and she permitted it. As his mouth lowered to take hers again, she knew she would freely offer more than he would ever ask. "You are so beautiful," he whispered.

Later she laughed, wondering why he could make it sound so believable. "When I think back to the day that I fell through the roof of the Green Dragon I'm tempted to laugh—though it was not so amusing at the time. The looks on your faces . . ."

"It must have been quite amusing," he agreed dryly.

"If you remember, you wanted to choke me," she reminded.

"Only because I thought you were a spy."

Her hand drifted across the front of his shirt, teasing the tuft of hair that peaked over the coarse linen. She loved the feel of him against her . . . she loved the anticipation of his dark energy, a force that only now was she beginning to know.

"Are you aware of how much I want you?" he whispered.

She was. Over the past few hours, she had grown to believe that their lives were indelibly bound. How or why, she couldn't explain. Nor did she want to try; being there in his arms was enough.

"I know in my heart that you are not real, Aaron, yet I have never loved a man as I love you."

Catching her hand to his mouth, he kissed it.

"I want you to make love to me," she whispered.

"Even though you remain convinced that I am a figment of your imagination?"

"Oh, Aaron, I don't know *what* you are. I only know I have never loved anyone as much as I love you."

"Even Joel?"

The mention of Joel's name jolted her.

"Aaron, I'm so confused," she admitted softly. "I'm not sure of anything anymore."

His eyes darkened as her hand explored the contours of his chest, and she smiled as his breathing grew more ragged. "Ah, my love, as sorely as I am tempted, 'twould be improper for me to make love to you, and yet, I too sense that time is fleeting—"

Placing her hand across his mouth, she stopped him. He didn't have to explain his feelings; hers were just as confused. She knew only one thing: She wanted to spend what time was left in his arms.

Their mouths met again, and Ashley drifted down

through a soft, melting tunnel. Her hands slid up the broad expanse of his back, pressing closer as she rhythmically stroked his shoulders. She wanted to lie with him naked, to know every inch of his magnificent body.

He lifted his head, watching her hands unhurriedly work open the front of her gown and release the hook on her bra. His eyes darkened as she slowly slid his shirt aside, then pressed the warmth of her breasts against the hair coiled on his chest.

"Do I scare you?" she murmured. She realized that few women in his time behaved so boldly. Her hands were now conducting a shameless exploration of his body, yet the heat of his passion penetrated her gown, driving her on.

He buried one hand in her tangled hair, then let the fingers of his other drift down her cheek to follow the line of her jaw. The pad of his thumb caressed her bottom lip as his gaze captured and held hers. "I think you are outrageously brazen, Mistress Wheeler, and I am indeed going to make love to you."

"Perhaps it will be the other way round," she breathed before her tongue joined masterfully with his.

"Mayhap, but I consider it doubtful."

"Don't argue . . . just make love to me."

With a wry smile, he removed her glasses and laid them aside. Then his mouth returned to hers hungrily, and for too brief of a time, the world belonged only to them.

Much later, Ashley stirred, snuggling closer to the warm body nestled tightly against her side.

Suddenly a light appeared—a very bright light, and Joel's voice came to her as clearly as if he were standing in the barn. Startled, she tried to lift herself up to go to him, but her body refused to move.

His face wavered slightly out of focus, yet she could see that concern and . . . love . . . yes, love darkened his eyes. He spoke, but his words were garbled, and she couldn't understand what he was saying.

She tried to reach out to him and call his name, but her arms were so heavy that she was powerless to lift them. She tried to speak, but the words refused to form. *Joel . . . Joel . . .*

Ashley . . . Ashley . . .

Joel!

Come on, sweetheart . . . Ash . . .

Ashley awoke with a start. Aaron was holding her, his hand brushing her hair back from her face.

"Are you all right?"

Ashley struggled to clear her mind. "I think so."

"You were calling out a name."

"Joel?"

Aaron nodded gravely.

"I saw him . . . in a dream. It was so strange." She closed her eyes, helplessly trying to recapture his image. "He was here, and yet he wasn't. I tried to reach out to him, but I couldn't."

Sighing, Aaron drew her closer.

"It seemed so real," she whispered.

"It will all be over very soon," he promised softly.

"*What* will be over soon? Aaron, do you *know* what has been happening to me?"

"I only know that I love you, Ashley." Gathering her close in his arms, he held her tightly as the shadows in the old barn deepened. She clung to him with a silent desper-

ation that matched his own. Turning onto her side, she
burrowed her face against his chest.

"What will I do without you?" she whispered.

"Shhh, there is no time for such thoughts. Let us spend
our time sharing our love."

When Ashley woke again it was morning. Opening her
eyes, she gazed at the loft and the high ceiling of the barn
overhead. For a moment she couldn't remember where
she was or why she was there, then a delicious feeling of
happiness washed over her. *Aaron*.

She turned her head in the hay and gazed at him. He
lay sleeping, his lashes two dark crescents against his lean
cheeks. After rolling onto her side, she rested her head in
her hand and reached out to touch him, then hesitated.
Like her, he was exhausted. She couldn't bear to wake
him. Yet she longed to touch him, to assure herself that he
was real. So few things seemed real to her right now.

He was sleeping so soundly that when her fingertips
traced his strong jaw and the outline of his lips, he never
moved. Suddenly, touching him wasn't enough. She
scooted closer and leaned over him, pressing her lips to
his, tasting him, remembering the exquisite moments in
his arms just a few hours earlier.

"You are courting danger," Aaron murmured.

"Maybe I like danger," she teased.

His eyes opened and he studied her seriously for a long
moment. "I love you, Ashley."

"I love you, Aaron."

Sighing, she nestled back into his arms, listening to the
early-morning sounds filtering through the cracks of the
barn. "I wish we could stay here forever," she confessed.

"We are in constant danger. This barn won't provide us protection for very long."

"I know." She rolled onto her back, her gaze meeting his. "What's going to happen to us?"

"You do not know?" he teased.

"I only have this horrible feeling that I'm about to lose you."

With a gentle smile, he smoothed his hand over her hair absently. "You will never lose me, love. Though we may be apart, I will forever hold you in my heart."

"Oh, Aaron . . . I wish it could be different. I wish I could stay here with you. We could get married, and once a week Paul and Rachel could come over to have dinner with us."

"And our children, all six of them, would have red hair and blue eyes exactly like yours," he predicted.

"*Six* children?"

"Mayhap six is too small a family. Ten might be more appropriate. Five boys and five girls."

Grinning, she thought about the chaos and happiness such a large household would bring. "If I could stay, there would be so many things I could help you accomplish. So many strides in medicine have been made."

"I wish I could have access to a great quantity of your miracles," he confessed. "Many lives would be saved."

"I wish I could provide them for you. I'd like to tell you about all the modern wonders that have been invented in my time. Did you know that ninety percent of all the scientists who have ever lived are alive in my time?"

He smiled at her lovingly. "I did not know. 'Tis difficult to comprehend."

"Yes . . . though I may never get back there." A tinge of sadness entered her voice now, an unspoken longing.

Aaron gathered her closer. "Do you wish to go back?"

Ashley was silent for a very long time, then she said softly, "I have mixed feelings. I know that I don't belong here. Part of me knows I won't ever belong here, yet another very important part of me can't bear to think of leaving you."

For the first time in her life she understood that love wasn't taking, or even accepting; it was giving.

Aaron understood that kind of love. He'd put himself in a precarious position with the patriots by not killing her as he had been ordered to do. He'd taken a wild gamble in choosing to protect her, even when he had found it difficult to believe that she came from a different century. During their time together, he'd protected her and taught her much about dedication to a cause bigger than himself. And last night he'd taught her about tenderness and love. He'd shown her that if a man and woman could share that, nothing else mattered. Whatever the future held, she would never forget these hours in an old barn with Aaron Kenneman on an April morning when the whole world was changing.

Tears misted her eyes as she clung to him, trying to free herself of the ominous sense of impending doom.

"We must go now," Aaron said softly.

"No." Her arms tightened more securely around him.

"We must, Ashley."

"Why? The British—"

"We must return to Boston. There will be more opportunity for escape there, should it become necessary."

She knew he was right. Boston would have strengthened its fortification against the British troops. They would both be safer there, but she wondered how they would make it back without being taken prisoner. British troops would dominate the road for the next several days. How could they hope to avoid discovery while traveling the fifteen or so miles back to Boston?

They held each other tightly, trying to hold back the reality that awaited them outside the barn. It suddenly occurred to her that the same qualities she admired in Aaron, she'd complained about in Joel. Every time a patient had taken him from her, she'd whined like a spoiled child. She realized now that at least Joel had always returned to her. There had never been anything between them nearly so large and threatening as a war.

Moving toward the door, Aaron suddenly held out his arm warningly.

"What's wrong?" she whispered.

Cocking his head, Aaron listened to the jangle of bridles as horsemen approached.

Ashley grasped his hand tightly. "Is it the British?"

"Get back," Aaron whispered, moving her into the shadows.

After returning to the door alone, Aaron peered out through the crack.

"Is it the British?" Ashley asked again.

The muscle in Aaron's jaw worked tightly as he viewed the company of redcoats riding toward the barn.

He glanced around to see if there was another exit from the barn. He quickly located a matching set of weathered doors on the opposite end, but he frowned when he saw that the bottom edges were firmly implanted in the dirt and debris that the wind had swept in.

"Quickly," he whispered. "Into the loft."

Aaron tested the ladder, then motioned Ashley to proceed ahead of him. They scrambled up the ladder and disappeared into the shadows as the riders grew nearer.

Crouching against the far wall, they held their breath as the soldiers entered the barn a minute later.

"Looks decent enough for a few hours' rest," one of the soldiers commented.

"I say we ride on. The horses can last for several more hours," the man with him said.

"The horses may, but I can't." The first man's eyes surveyed the barn's dark interior. "We'll bed down here for the day."

"As you say. Anything is better than the open country where those rebel dogs can creep upon us."

Ashley and Aaron could hear the jingle of bridles and saddles being removed from mounts and tossed aside. By the sounds, Aaron could tell that it was a small patrol, not more than six or seven men.

Ashley glanced anxiously at Aaron as the soldiers tied their horses inside the barn, then closed the door. They couldn't crouch this way all day without being discovered.

Aaron shook his head, lifting his finger to his lips to silence her.

They listened as the soldiers made preparations for their morning meal. When the meager fare had been eaten, they rolled up in blankets, and far sooner than Ashley expected, deep, resonant snores began to fill the air.

Aaron nudged her, moving her farther back into the shadows.

"What do we do now?" she whispered.

Pressing his mouth to her ear, he whispered, "We do nothing. They will only sleep a few hours. They will sleep too light for us to attempt an escape. We must wait until they leave."

Ashley nodded mutely.

Taking her hand, they lay down again.

The morning wore on. Ashley lay with her head on Aaron's chest, counting the swallows that flew in and out of the old loft.

By noon heat was building inside the loft, making it uncomfortably warm. By midafternoon, Ashley was about to despair of the soldiers ever waking up when suddenly something spooked the horses.

Three of the soldiers sprang to their feet, trying to orient themselves. When the horses shied again, the other men bolted to their feet.

Taking advantage of the momentary confusion, Ashley and Aaron inched silently across the floor of the loft.

Peering down between the cracks, they saw the British trying to quiet their horses.

"Must have been a mouse," one man grunted in a voice still deep from sleep.

"How long have we slept?"

"Long enough. It is past noon, 'twould be my guess."

The men knelt and began to roll up their blankets.

Something suddenly ran up inside Ashley's skirt, and she froze. Clutching Aaron's hand, she mouthed a silent scream as the mouse darted back out.

The furry little rodent halted, trying to decide if it should run on its way or investigate this strange thing in its loft.

Ashley stiffened as Aaron's hand shot to cover her mouth.

The mouse decided to investigate the hem of her dress. Ashley watched in horror as it nosed the material, then she glanced at Aaron, who was equally engrossed in the creature's movements.

Squirming, Ashley tried to move away, but Aaron held her still.

He leaned down and with his thumb and forefinger flicked the mouse over the edge of the loft.

The mouse squeaked with protest as it landed with a soft thud on the floor of the barn.

Ashley closed her eyes, certain the soldiers would have heard it and come investigating.

Glancing toward the noise, one of the soldiers grinned. "Perhaps we could have a little meat with our beans," he joked.

One of the others choked with disgust. "This may be a backward country, but I'm not reduced to eating mice yet. I much prefer patriot roasted on a spit."

The group laughed heartily at the joke, but Ashley could see that Aaron didn't find the comment particularly amusing.

"How far is it to Boston?" one of the soldiers asked.

"According to the map, between fifteen and twenty miles."

"Then we should reach there by morning. Just in time to teach those minutemen a lesson and be home for dinner."

Ashley glanced at Aaron again and saw his face tighten with anger. The British were arrogant in their assumption that they could whip the colonists so easily.

"This hay will make a nice meal for the horses."

"That it will. I wonder if there is more in the loft."

Ashley and Aaron froze as they heard one of the men approaching the ladder.

"I will see."

Scooting back into the shadows, Ashley and Aaron listened as the soldier began to climb the ladder.

A moment later the top of his head appeared above the

edge of the loft, but instead of looking up, he was looking down.

"When I was a small lad, I remember jumping out of the loft of our barn at home into a stack of straw." He laughed. "I missed once and plunged myself into a pile of manure. Me mum wasn't happy with me that day."

The soldier leaned forward, peering more intently into the loft. All of a sudden he spotted the two figures crouching in the shadows. Stiffening, he called out, "I say! What have we here? Visitors?"

Ashley heard the scramble of soldiers coming to their feet.

"Visitors, you say!"

"Or mayhap lovers. Come, come, young lovers. Favor us with your names." A pistol appeared in the soldier's hand now, pointed directly at Aaron.

Ashley and Aaron slowly got to their feet. Holding hands, they stepped out of the shadows, trying to look like two guilty lovers who had been caught in a compromising situation.

"Down there," the soldier commanded, gesturing with his pistol.

After descending the ladder, Ashley stood behind Aaron as he turned to face the soldiers. Flashing a boyish grin, he said heartily, "Well, well, gentlemen. It looks as if you've caught us in a bit of a bind."

"State your name."

"Smith," Aaron returned in a friendly fashion, "George Smith."

"What are you doing in this barn, Smith?"

"Sir . . ." Aaron glanced at Ashley, his grin widening, " 'Twould be most improper for me to say."

The soldier laughed. "You seem a bit old to be sneaking into barn lofts for a dalliance."

Aaron shrugged. "The lady has a husband."

All of the men laughed this time, Aaron included.

"Step into the light," the soldier commanded Ashley.

Ashley quietly stepped forward. The soldier studied her for a moment, before his gaze returned to Aaron.

"A tryst, huh?"

"Yes, sir."

Turning to the officer behind him, he said quietly, "Is this not the pair Church spoke about?"

"The woman matches the description. Red hair and she wears those curious spectacles."

Aaron glanced at Ashley.

"By the way, I've been meaning to tell you: Benjamin Church is a spy," she said softly. "He's been working with the British all along."

"Dammit!" Aaron snapped.

"Ah, then this must be Kenneman." The soldier's smile didn't quite reach his lips now. "How nice of you to honor us with your presence. I'm sure Gage will want to visit with you at length." The officer turned to his men. "We'll take them both back to Boston."

16

$\approx \times \times \times$

$\mathbf{C}$rouching, Aaron shoved the British officer aside, then grabbed Ashley by the hand and dragged her toward the door as bedlam broke loose.

"Halt!" The officer lifted his pistol and took aim.

"Aaron!" Ashley shouted as they burst through the barn doors and started running across the field.

"Run, Ashley, *run!*" Aaron shouted back.

They raced across the field of clover as a volley of musket balls whizzed over their heads.

"*Aaaaarrronn!*" Ashley's breath was coming in gasps as they ran on.

As she screamed, they dove for the ground as another volley of gunfire shattered the stillness.

Aaron grabbed her hand to pull her back to her feet as they dodged another volley of bullets. He glanced over his shoulder and saw that the soldiers were gaining on them. "Faster, Ashley, faster!"

Ashley's head pounded as she tried to match his long-legged stride. Her breath was coming in labored gasps as another volley of fire rang out. Aaron pitched forward, and she screamed as a vivid splash of crimson appeared on the back of his shirt.

She watched in horrified silence as a second ball hit

him and his body jerked in reflex and slumped to the ground.

"Aaron . . . oh, my God . . . *Aaron!*" Falling to her knees, she began sobbing. Cradling him to her breasts, she gently rocked him back and forth. "Oh, please, don't let him die . . . don't let him die."

She brought her hand to his lips. He kissed her fingertips, his eyes filled with pain as he gazed at her. "Don't be afraid, little one."

"No . . . don't leave me, Aaron," she pleaded raggedly. He was gravely wounded, and she didn't have the slightest idea of how to help him. "Don't leave me." Tears streamed down her cheeks, dotting the front of his blood-stained shirt.

He gazed up at her, his strength ebbing slowly away as she gathered the hem of her skirt over his chest, trying to staunch the flow of his blood.

"It is all according to plan, you are not to be concerned," he soothed. "I know now that everything you said was true." He swallowed with effort. "You'll go back . . . to your time, and I'll . . . go on to mine."

After drawing her head down to his chest, he held her as his tears ran down his cheeks to mingle with hers. "I will always be with you, my love, forever, Ashley—you will never be alone."

Ashley could hear the soldiers running toward them now, but she no longer cared. Her hands were covered with his blood as she moaned and continued to rock him. "Hold on, darling . . . hold on."

"I love you, Ashley Wheeler . . . woman of the twentieth century."

Sobbing, Ashley cradled his head. "And I love you so very, very much, Aaron Kenneman."

Gazing up at her, he smiled weakly. "Mayhap we know now why I am not in your history books."

She buried her face in his chest and wept as his breathing grew more ragged.

She knew the moment he left her. It was as if he had reached for her hand, and they had walked, hand and hand, the last few achingly sweet miles together. Peace suddenly came over her, and she was no longer afraid.

For the briefest of moments, his hand had squeezed hers. Then with a smile that would remain in her heart forever, he had drawn a long breath and his hand relaxed in hers.

Lying her head on his chest, she continued to hold him as the birds in the meadow darted in and out of the clover.

"The dog is dead."

Ashley lifted her head, her pain-glazed eyes meeting the British soldier's. His words slowly sank in, and she began trembling. "No! *No!*"

With trembling fingers, she touched Aaron's face, trying to memorize his features. He was so pale, so still now.

"You must come with me, Mistress Wheeler." The soldier reached for her arm, compassion filling his voice now.

"No! *Aaron.*" Ashley turned back to look at Aaron's body, lying so motionless on the ground.

"Please, Mistress Wheeler. . . ." The soldier's manner was more kindhearted than threatening as he helped her to her feet.

With an anguished sob, Ashley dropped back to her knees and gathered Aaron's lifeless body to her again. "No." She moaned, her anguished sobs shattering the quiet countryside. *"Noooooooo!"*

Ashley suddenly jerked upright and her eyes flew open.

With a groan, she moved her hand up to shield her eyes against the agonizingly bright light bearing down upon her. Sinking back to the pillow, she closed her eyes against the excruciating pain.

"Thank God, she's coming out of it."

It was Joel's voice again, only much clearer than it had been in the past.

"Ash, sweetheart . . . can you hear me?" A pair of strong hands gripped her shoulders, shaking her gently.

"Joel?"

"Yes, sweetheart . . . oh, God, Ash." Ashley felt herself being lifted gently into an incredibly strong pair of arms and held tightly for a moment. "You scared the hell out of me."

Her arms closed around his neck, her pulse jumping. *Aaron. It was Aaron's voice. He wasn't dead, he was right here holding her!*

"We've got a fluctuating pressure, Doctor."

"Ashley, open your eyes for me." Joel's voice was firmer now.

"No," she murmured. "Light hurts . . ."

"Cut the light for a minute."

The light faded. The smell of antiseptic washed over her, and she could hear the bustle of activity around her.

"The light's out now. Open your eyes for me, Ashley."

"No, Joel."

"Come on, sweetheart, you can do it."

Ashley slowly opened her eyes and looked directly into Aaron's eyes. His face was filled with such love that it made her heart ache.

"Oh, darling." She smiled, lifting her hand to touch his cheek. "I thought . . . I thought I had lost you."

Joel's body went limp with relief as he gathered her into his arms to hold her close for a moment. "Oh, honey, don't ever do that to me again."

Wincing against the pain in her head, she clung to him, aware that something still wasn't right. After pulling back from him slightly, she gazed at him. "Joel?"

"Yes, darling, take it easy. You had a blow to the head, but you're doing fine."

"You nearly scared the peawaddin' out of us." Sue's shaky voice came to her.

Turning her head, she saw Sue staring down at her. "Sue?"

"Jeez, Ash. You nearly killed yourself. You should have taken those shoes off before you ran outside in the rain." Sue stepped closer, and Ashley could see that her face was pale.

Confused, Ashley turned back to Joel. "What happened?"

"You had a nasty fall, Ashley."

"I fell?" She glanced down and saw that she was lying on a hospital gurney.

"Did you ever!" Sue exhaled a breath of relief. "You nearly killed yourself, kiddo."

"Joel?" Ashley's gaze returned to Joel, her heart pounding. It was Joel, but his eyes were . . . Aaron's.

"You're going to be fine, sweetheart."

She suddenly threw her arms around his neck, and their mouths met hungrily. As the kiss grew more heated, Sue cleared her throat and glanced at the nurses and orderlies in attendance in the hospital emergency room. "They . . . have a thing for each other." She shrugged and grinned sheepishly.

When their lips finally parted, Ashley gazed at Joel lovingly. "Oh, Joel, I *love* you." It was all coming back to her now. The rain, the fall, the dream . . .

"Well, it's about time you said that with conviction." He smiled and lowered his mouth to take hers again. Then she knew. She *knew* that Aaron had not died in her arms in that lonely field outside of Boston this morning. He was right here with her; he had been with her from the moment she had met Joel Harrison.

"I've been unconscious?" she whispered when their mouths finally parted.

"Have you ever!" Sue exclaimed. "You've been out going on seven hours now."

"Seven hours!" Hysteria bubbled in Ashley's throat. *Seven hours,* and during that time she had been thrown into an eighteenth-century prison, accompanied Paul Revere on his ride, fallen in love with Aaron Kenneman, witnessed the first shots of the Revolutionary War, and watched the only man she would ever love die in her arms.

Sue glanced at Joel worriedly, but he just grinned. "Relax, Suzy, Neal says Ashley has a slight concussion, a few bruises, a couple of cracked ribs, and one hell of a headache, but she's going to be fine."

"Oh, Joel, I'm sorry to have kept you from your patients," she whispered. Never, *ever* again would she complain about his job.

Joel's features sobered as he looked down on her. "Ashley, you are more important to me than anything or anyone. Maybe I haven't told you that enough . . ."

She reached for his hand and held it tightly. "Maybe we've both been a little neglectful . . . but not anymore, Joel. Not anymore."

Should she tell him what had happened? Would she?

Maybe, someday. But for now all she wanted was to share just a few private moments alone with the man she loved.

A nurse stepped into the emergency room and called softly to Joel, "I'm sorry, Dr. Harrison, you're wanted in ICU."

Joel leaned down and kissed her briefly again. "I'll be back shortly. I love you, sweetheart, and don't worry. Neal says you're going to be fine." He turned to leave as she reached out, grasping his hand. "Joel."

"Yes?"

"I want to get married."

He looked at her, surprised. "Are you serious?"

Drawing him back to her, she kissed him, muffling his stunned response. She knew that he found the request odd since he had been pleading with her for months to set a wedding date.

"Are you serious?" he murmured when the kiss finally ended. "You're actually ready to set a date?"

"Never more serious. How about tonight?"

"Tonight?" He grinned. "Maybe Neal should order another set of X rays for your head—"

"No, Joel." Her features sobered as she gazed up at him. "There is not one single doubt in my mind. I want to marry you, have your children, and spend the rest of our lives running through fields of clover."

"Clover?"

She nodded, grinning.

"But what about your parents and mine? I thought a church wedding—"

"Would be fine," she finished, "and once I'm recovered, we'll have one. But right now"—she touched his cheek, so grateful that she had been given a second chance at love —"I just want to know that you're mine."

"I'll always be yours," he said quietly, and it was Aaron speaking to her all over again.

"Yeah, but I want to make absolutely sure," she whispered.

"Won't be much of a honeymoon," he teased softly. "You have two broken ribs and a concussion."

"Ah, who needs all that moon and spoon and June stuff?" she said lightly. Sobering, she brushed her fingers through his hair, knowing that she loved him with all her heart. "We don't need it. As long as we have each other, that's enough for me."

He gazed back at her with such overwhelming love that she knew. She *knew*.

"I'll arrange for the chaplain to marry us before the night is over," he said quietly.

He stood, and she caught his hand again. "Could you see if you could get me a bouquet of clover?"

"Clover? At this time of the year?"

She smiled. "If you can't, roses will do."

As he disappeared out the door a moment later, Ashley reached for her friend's hand expectantly. "Sue!"

With a sigh, Sue reached into the jacket of her pocket. A second later she pressed Ashley's engagement ring into her hand firmly. "Listen, kiddo, don't ask me *how* I knew you'd change your mind, something just told me to get the ring back."

Weak with relief, Ashley brought the ring to her chest and held it. Somewhere there was someone watching over her. "Joel doesn't know?"

"Joel doesn't even *suspect*, kiddo."

"How did you manage to get inside his office?"

"Easy." Sue flipped her hair, which was tinted a strange shade of lavender this week. "Once I'd notified

Joel that you were in the emergency room I slipped into the storage room, put on a pair of scrubs, told this cute orderly with a tush you'd die for that Dr. Harrison had sent me up to get a file from his office, and voilà, I got the ring *and* the note and then got the devil out of there."

"Oh, Sue," Ashley closed her eyes weakly, "how can I ever thank you?" Sue and someone up above had just kept her from making the biggest mistake of her life.

Sue flashed her an engaging grin as she winked. "Who knows, kiddo, but I'm sure I'll think of something!"

Epilogue

A soft chime sounded throughout the hall. Daniel stood up quickly, taking one final glance through the well-worn folder he carried.

The palatial doors swung open, and an older man, clad in a long, butterscotch-colored robe, appeared. "Daniel?"

"Yes, sir?"

"Gerrbria will see you now."

"Thank you." Taking a deep breath, Daniel entered the Great Hall.

Daniel hurried across the floor of glowing pearl, moving swiftly toward Gerrbria, who rose to meet him.

"Daniel, so good to see you. I understand our plan worked perfectly."

"Perfectly, sir, but then I'm not surprised. You're the best!"

"Fratmore?"

"No, thank you," Daniel refused. "I'm attending a wedding in a moment."

"Ah, yes. That would be Ashley and Joel's."

Daniel smiled. "That it is, sir."

After walking back to his desk, Gerrbria settled his considerable girth into his chair. "Then all is well with our Miss Wheeler?"

"I have never seen her happier."

"Then our choice was a wise one."

"Yes, sir."

Grinning, the two men rose, exchanged an energetic series of high fives, then Daniel left and Gerrbria returned to work.

After all, Ashley Wheeler wasn't the only woman in the world looking for a good man.